RUTH AXTELL MORREN

Hearts in the Highlands

D0556490

Steeple
Hill®

Published by Steeple Hill Books™

STEEPLE HILL BOOKS

Steeple
Hill®

ISBN-13: 978-0-373-82786-2
ISBN-10:   0-373-82786-5

HEARTS IN THE HIGHLANDS

Copyright © 2008 by Ruth Axtell

www.SteepleHill.com

Printed in U.S.A.

Books by Ruth Axtell Morren

Love Inspired Historical

Hearts in the Highlands #6

Steeple Hill Single Title

Winter Is Past
Wild Rose
Lilac Spring
Dawn In My Heart
The Healing Season
The Rogue's Redemption

RUTH AXTELL MORREN

Ruth Axtell Morren wrote her first story when she was twelve—a spy thriller—and knew she wanted to be a writer. There were many detours along the way. She studied comparative literature at Smith College, spent her junior year in Paris, taught English in the Canary Islands and worked in international development in Miami, Florida, where she met her future husband, who took her to the Netherlands to live for six years.

She first gained recognition as a writer when her second manuscript finaled in the Romance Writers of America Golden Heart contest in 1994. Ruth's first two Steeple Hill novels, *Winter Is Past* (2003) and *Wild Rose* (2004) both won awards in contests sponsored by Romance Writers of America. *Wild Rose* was selected as a *Booklist* Top 10 Christian Novel in 2005.

After living several years on the down east coast of Maine, Ruth and her family moved back to the Netherlands, to the polderland of Flevoland, where she still lives by the sea. Ruth loves hearing from readers. You can contact her through her Web site: www.ruthaxtellmorren.com.

"Tomorrow I'll show you some of the highlands' landmarks."

Mr. Gallagher pointed to the west, where the sun was beginning its slow descent behind the mountains beyond the loch. "The highest peak is Ben Lawers. I've always wanted to climb it."

Maddie looked at him curiously. "Why?"

"Why not?" He smiled, a smile that began in his blue eyes and slowly reached his lips. "Think of the view from the summit. On the other side of the range lies Glen Lyon, one of the loveliest glens in all the highlands."

"It sounds spectacular." She was no longer looking at the mountain, but at Mr. Gallagher. He was a man of action, like her brothers. While she was… What *did* she have to show for her life?

"Would you like to climb it, too?" His eyes met hers once more.

"Yes," she found herself saying. "Has any woman ever climbed it?"

There was a challenge in his blue eyes. "What does that matter? You could be the first."

And let us not be weary in well doing, for in due season we shall reap, if we faint not.

—*Galatians* 6:9

For Susan,
Remember, it's never too late.

Wherever I wander, wherever I rove,
The hills of the Highlands for ever I love.

—Robert Burns,
"Farewell to the Highlands"

Chapter One

London, 1890

"Imagine waking up, a knife at your throat—"

Since Reid Gallagher stepped into his great-aunt's parlor, Maddie had been transported to another time and place.

He leaned forward in the velvet upholstered armchair, rumpling the lace covers on each arm with his strong hands.

"It was touch and go for a while there." Humor underscored the quiet rumble of his words. "They stormed us on horseback, surrounding our camp in the dead of night, brandishing their knives and cudgels. All we could do was fumble for our weapons in the dark—"

Maddie sat riveted, listening to the rugged man with the lean, deeply tanned face, sun-bleached sandy hair and thick mustache a shade darker. His words evoked a kaleidoscope of images—a British surveying party in the midst of the lonely desert, the night air cool, the stillness broken by a band of rebels, the neigh of horses and bray of camels….

"Oh, dear heavens!" Lady Haversham left off stroking her Yorkshire terrier. "Was anyone killed?"

He looked down, his tone grim. "Two, including Colonel Parker, the head of our expedition. Our men rallied immediately, of course. We sleep with our weapons near at hand, so we were able to rout the group in no time—"

"My smelling salts!" Lady Haversham fanned her face. "I feel about to faint. Madeleine!" The terrier, Lilah, jumped up with a sharp bark.

Maddie hurried to her employer's side. "Hush, Lilah!"

"Do please hurry." Lady Haversham sat with her head against the antimacassar, her eyes closed, her breathing shallow.

Maddie reached for the tapestry bag that kept a host of things Lady Haversham might need at any given moment. In a second, she located the small vial and waved it under the elderly lady's nostrils.

She started at the whiff. "Oh!"

Maddie immediately withdrew the vial and fetched a small cross-stitched cushion to place behind her. At the terrier's continued barking, she took the tiny dog in her arms. "See, your mistress is perfectly fine," she crooned, petting Lilah's long, silky hair until the dog was quiet.

"That's better," Lady Haversham said. "I felt so light-headed for a moment." She reached for her pet. "Come, my darling, Mama's right here."

The russet-colored terrier settled back down on her mistress's lap. Mr. Gallagher stood beside his great-aunt's chair, anxiety etching his brow. Lady Haversham reached out a hand, which trembled slightly. His sun-browned one grasped her pale, age-spotted one like a great bird enfolding a baby bird under its wing.

"You see, my boy, how I am. I'm so glad you've come home at last." Her voice quavered while her watery blue eyes gazed up into his with relief.

Mr. Gallagher's glance shifted to M lie, and she was struck by their light hue against his dark, weathered features, like finding a bright blue marble amidst rough burlap. She gave a hesitant smile, wishing to reassure him. If only she could tell him a week didn't go by that Lady Haversham wouldn't come near to dying in one form or another.

But Mr. Gallagher had turned his attention back to his great-aunt. "Maybe I should call your physician?"

"No, don't trouble yourself. I'll be well if I just sit quietly." She closed her eyes again, but kept her hold on her nephew's hand, her gnarled fingers clutching it as if to a lifeline.

"I worry about you, living so far away in a heathen land. I don't know what I'd do if anything happened to you. You and Vera are my only relations."

Something flickered in the tall man's eyes, as if he weren't used to having any emotional ties. "You needn't have worried. You see me here fit as always. Don't upset yourself anymore thinking of it."

Lady Haversham reopened her eyes. "I can't help it. Thank God you're back on British soil. At least this incident caused your return, for which I am grateful. I hope you are home in England for good."

"I'm back for a few weeks, at any rate." His tone betrayed no joy at the fact. "Until the two governments satisfy themselves that it's safe to continue our work."

When it appeared his aunt had recovered, Mr. Gallagher slowly disengaged his hand from hers. "The situation as it stands now is that two bands of Bedouin presently think they own the Sinai. There are continual skirmishes between the two tribes. Our British party happened to be caught in the middle of this one. The Tuara who attacked our camp wanted to make sure we were hiding no Tiyaha among us."

Lady Haversham waved away his description. "Oh, it's too

confusing for me. All I know is my heart can't take the thought of you among those savages."

"Well, you needn't fear for now. The attack on our camp stopped all work while both the Egyptian and British authorities investigate things." He moved back a pace and ran a hand through his hair, leaving the thick blond strands disheveled. Maddie could hear the frustration underlying the words, and she sensed he was a man who wouldn't willingly endure enforced idleness.

Lady Haversham continued to stroke Lilah's long hair. "Well, I am thankful for that at least. Please ring for some tea, Madeleine. I'm sure we could all use some. This news has been most upsetting…." The old lady brought her lace-edged handkerchief up to her mouth and shook her head.

"Of course." Maddie headed for the bellpull.

With a last look at his aunt, Mr. Gallagher returned to his chair. "I'm sorry, Aunt Millicent. I shouldn't have been so blunt."

"It's not your fault. You haven't been back in a few years. It's understandable you didn't realize my frail condition. The least thing upsets me. It's my heart, you see. Dr. Aldwin says I mustn't have anything upset me."

"I didn't realize how…delicate you'd become since I last saw you." He gave an awkward laugh. "I've been so far from British society during that time, in the company of men, I've forgotten how to put things more gently for a lady's ears."

"Good heavens, you mustn't let yourself become uncivilized." Lady Haversham sat straighter, letting the cushion fall to the floor and causing Lilah to let out a bark. "We shall have to remedy that now you're back in London. Of course, I no longer entertain. My nerves can't take crowds. But your sister and her husband can organize things."

He leaned forward, alarm in his blue eyes. "Aunt Millicent, you know I'm not interested in attending parties—"

"Nonsense. Your friends and acquaintances want to know you're back in town. It would be a disservice to deprive them of your company."

He scrubbed a large hand across his jaw, as if wanting to argue the point but afraid of upsetting his aunt further.

Maddie resumed her own seat and took up her needlepoint.

His aunt settled Lilah back down. "As I was saying, Vera will hold a few teas for you, perhaps a musicale one evening."

"I'm here only to cool my heels until the ambassador finds out what kind of trick the sultan is playing—"

"I know you don't like to socialize. But your friends will be hurt if you come stealing into town like a thief in the night, no one the wiser."

"I only came back because I was forced to…."

Maddie wrenched her attention away from this interesting exchange when a black-clad maid with frilly white apron entered the room. Knowing exactly how Lady Haversham preferred her tea, Maddie set about pouring the older lady's cup first. But her heart couldn't help being moved by the man who so clearly felt out of his element in London. She remembered her own difficulty readjusting to England when she and her family had first returned from the Middle East.

Maddie placed the cup and saucer beside Lady Haversham and took Lilah from her. "Give her a little platter of cake."

"Yes, my lady." Maddie set the miniature dog on the carpet, knowing she'd probably have to clean up after her within the hour. As she approached Mr. Gallagher's chair, the dog following at her heels, Maddie felt a tremor of nervousness at addressing him directly. "How do you take your tea?" she inquired above Lilah's barking.

"Just one lump and a wedge of lemon, thank you." He

spared Maddie only a glance then sat back, an elbow against the chair's arm, his fingers idly smoothing his mustache, his thoughts clearly elsewhere.

"Very good," she said, stifling the desire to be noticed by this man. By now she should be used to being overlooked by Lady Haversham's visitors like another piece of furniture in the room. Taking herself to task, she walked back to the tea cart. The terrier jumped onto the settee and leaned eagerly toward the loaded cart, barking her interest in its delicacies. With a grim sigh, Maddie cut her a sliver of cake and placed it on the flower-edged Limoges dessert plate. Lilah was ahead of her, already back on the ground and barking her impatience. Maddie set the treat down on the floor, where Lilah immediately began to devour it, her little body twitching in eagerness.

Maddie proceeded to pour Mr. Gallagher his cup, hoping Lilah would hold down the cake at least until their guest had departed. When she returned to him, he reached for the cup before she had a chance to set it down.

"Thank you. Perfect," he added with a smile of approval at the wedge of lemon she had set beside the cup on its saucer.

The sudden smile relieved the harshness of his features. Maddie felt a warmth steal over her. Dismayed by her own reaction, she stepped away from him. "Would you care for a slice of cake?"

"That would be fine." Again he gave her a smile, which affected her more than it should for such a brief, superficial exchange. A part of her yearned to prolong the conversation. Instead, she bowed her head and hurried back to the tea table.

She scolded herself for the pleasure it gave her to fill his request. Knowing how good her employer's appetite was, Maddie cut Lady Haversham a large slice.

"I've brought back some pieces collected last year at a dig in Hawara," Mr. Gallagher said to his aunt. "The British Museum was quite pleased with them. I'll be doing a series of lectures while I'm here."

"Your Uncle George had quite a collection of artifacts himself from all his travels in the Orient."

He smiled, looking more relaxed than he had since he'd entered the overstuffed room. "Yes, I recall. He used to show me things every time I visited."

"He had countless items. I've kept everything carefully stored in boxes over the years." She sighed. "If anything should happen to me, what is to become of all of it?"

He cleared his throat, as if uncomfortable with the drift of the conversation.

"There was a pyramid at the site of our dig."

She brightened. "How fascinating."

When Maddie had poured her own cup, she set it down to cool and took up her needlepoint. Under the guise of re-threading her needle, she observed Mr. Gallagher, unconcerned that he would notice. His focus was on his great-aunt, as he described the project. Thankfully, Lilah had settled at Maddie's feet for another nap.

Although he wore a well-tailored sack coat, vest and trousers, the light khaki material of the trousers and the light-weight tweed of his jacket gave Mr. Gallagher a much less formal look than the average man about London. The few gentlemen to visit Lady Haversham—her solicitor, physician and old Reverend Steele—all wore long dark frock coats with matching vests and trousers, their somber colors seeming to underscore their lofty positions.

This man's lighter-colored garments, like the desert sand, brought a foreign element into the parlor, making the room with its heavy dark furniture and surfaces covered with brica-brac suddenly appear more confined and overcrowded than usual.

Maddie drank in Mr. Gallagher's words as he described the relatively new study of how long-ago civilizations had lived their daily lives. Maddie could picture it all so clearly because she'd spent a good portion of her girlhood in the Holy Land with her missionary parents. Egypt was very close to Palestine, and Mr. Gallagher's narrative brought back memories of desert sands, swarthy people riding their camels or donkeys and bleached huts at the foothills of scrubby mountains.

As he described the harsh conditions of the dig, Maddie pictured him in wrinkled khakis and tall scuffed boots, a battered hat shading his piercing blue eyes from the sun. She'd noticed their color as soon as she'd been introduced to him, the moment he'd taken her hand in his in a strong, though brief, handshake. She judged him to be in his late thirties or early forties.

Mr. Gallagher would probably be startled at how much she already knew about him. When Lady Haversham wasn't discussing her various ailments, she boasted of her great-nephew, who had followed in his great-uncle's footsteps to become an Egyptologist and surveyor to the Crown in the lands between Africa and India.

Maddie's attention quickened when she heard Mr. Gallagher tell his great-aunt, "The Royal Egypt Fund is sponsoring the lectures. It's in their interest to promote Egyptology with the general public."

"Yes, your uncle was on the forefront of getting the government interested in the artifacts over there. You must tell me when you're to lecture, although I hardly get out anymore, you know. It was a dreadful winter. I didn't think I'd survive that attack of pleurisy. Then with my usual neuralgia, I don't know how I manage."

"My first lecture is at the end of the week."

"Oh, goodness. Well, this April weather is still much too changeable for me to venture forth."

"Of course. I wouldn't expect you to take any risks with your health."

Maddie hoped he'd say more about when and where the lecture would be.

There was a lull in the conversation, then Mr. Gallagher said, "I've brought back a mummified head."

"You haven't!" His aunt's eyes widened. "How ever did you find one?"

His fingers stroked his chin as he mused, "Sometimes it's when you stop searching for something that you find it." His glance crossed Maddie's at that moment, and she realized she'd been staring at him.

To cover her embarrassment, she blurted out, "Would you like some more tea?"

"Oh, my yes, how remiss of us," his aunt said immediately.

He looked down at his cup as if he'd forgotten he'd been holding it. "Yes, that would be just the thing."

Before Maddie could rise, Mr. Gallagher stood and ambled over to the tea cart. Lilah stirred, but she only twitched her nose at the toes of his boots and didn't bark.

Maddie felt dwarfed by the man's above-average height as he paused in front of the cart. He continued his line of conversation as he held out his cup and saucer to Maddie with a smile.

"We discovered several mummy portraits dating to the Roman period. The site around the pyramid appears to be a royal burial ground."

"Your Uncle George always wanted to find some proof of this procedure, but alas, was unsuccessful."

Maddie poured the tea, hoping her hand didn't shake. Then

she lifted one lump of sugar with the silver tongs and set it into the cup with a small plop, fearful the tea would splatter. All the while, she was aware of his hand holding the saucer. Strong looking, tanned, like his face, to a deep hue. Then she noticed the gold wedding band on his ring finger. Lady Haversham had told her he was a widower of many years. Maddie's heart went out to him in sympathy, thinking how he must continue to mourn his late wife, if he still wore the ring.

She discarded the used lemon slice and took a fresh one with another pair of tongs, then placed it on the edge of the saucer. There it slipped off, and as her hand flinched, trying to retrieve the lemon, he covered it for an instant with his free one.

"Steady there." A trace of humor laced his husky voice.

She met his blue gaze and whispered a thank-you. "Anytime," he murmured, before moving away from her.

She sat for the rest of his visit remembering the feel of his warm palm against her skin. Warm like the Egyptian sun.

Her mother used to say, "Your hands are always like ice." Her father would immediately reply, "Cold hands, warm heart."

Was it true? Did she have a warm heart? Sometimes, lately, she felt it squeezed dry by her employer. She shook aside the thought, reminding herself of her Christian duty to serve.

Mr. Gallagher sat back down. "I'll be featuring the mummy's head at my first lecture. It should draw a crowd."

His aunt cut into her piece of cake. "When is the lecture precisely?"

Maddie's hand stilled on her cup as she listened to his answer.

"The first one will be Thursday morning at ten. Another

will be held on Friday afternoon. We'll judge which times draw the most attendance before scheduling the others."

Thursday at ten. That would be perfect. Lady Haversham generally didn't stir until noon. Maddie would have plenty of time to get to the museum and back before she was even missed.

Thursday at ten. She committed the time to memory and determined to read everything she could lay her hands on about Egyptology in the meantime.

A new fear cropped up. Would Mr. Gallagher see her at the lecture? If so, what would he think? She didn't want to appear forward in any way. After all she was only his great-aunt's paid companion.

Paid companion. The ugly words reminded her who and what she had been for the last decade of her life.

From a young woman who'd dreamed of serving the Lord on the mission field, to a poorly paid employee at the beck and call of a spoiled society lady, the only difference between Maddie's position and that of the other servants was the dubious distinction of sitting at her employer's table. In everything else, she was repeatedly demeaned by word and gesture countless times a day.

Maddie sat back with a sigh, telling herself, as she'd been telling herself each day since she'd begun her job under Lady Haversham, that she should take joy in her service. She'd almost convinced herself until this afternoon, when Reid Gallagher had entered this airless parlor and reminded her of that other world out there that once had been her world, too.

Chapter Two

"These gilded mummy masks are particularly nice specimens." Reid held up a pair of shiny gold heads for the audience to view. His eyes scanned the packed hall of the British Museum. The Egyptian Fund would be pleased with the sold-out crowd. There were even people standing in the back.

"We also have coverings for the upper parts of the body and the feet." As he spoke, he set down the masks and took up the carved forms, the former showing crossed arms, and the latter, bare feet molded in gold.

"These were discovered in what we presume is a burial ground in Hawara, a few miles west of the Nile. The pyramid in the midst of this area was the burial tomb of King Amenemhat III.

"We were fortunate to uncover so many undisturbed items. Because they were buried so well, looters hadn't yet discovered them."

Reid kept looking from the objects he described to the people in the audience, trying to gauge if they were following what he was saying. He knew from previous presentations that his audience was composed of people from all walks of life. Few would have any in-depth archaeological knowledge.

His eyes swung back from the rear of the hall toward the front. Suddenly, his gaze backtracked, thinking he'd recognized a face. He had to peer behind a lady's wide straw hat, flanked on either side by two large bird's wings. A young woman sat behind and to one side of it. She appeared to be listening intently to his talk. A pity that from where she sat, there was little detail she'd be able to discern of the artifacts.

"This king lived in what is known as the Middle Kingdom." He held up a large sculpted head of the pharaoh, all the while trying to place the face of the young woman. Reid had few acquaintances in London anymore, much less female ones.

Then it came to him. Aunt Millie's latest companion. Reid glanced once again at the woman in the back as he explained how excavations were carried out. "We use a system called stratification, where a series of layers are carefully dug."

He walked over to the tables covered with dozens of pots and numerous pottery fragments. "These pieces of sculpture and glazed faience were obtained in this manner. Although it's more dramatic to come across a large monument like a pyramid, as my acclaimed colleague William Petrie says, to uncover the secrets of the past, it's much more significant to study the everyday utensils of these buried sites. Hence, our emphasis on pottery shards."

Although the young woman sat at the very rear of the large hall, Reid was almost sure she was the young lady he'd met in his great-aunt's parlor the other day. She'd participated little in their conversation, but he'd been impressed with her quiet, competent manner toward Aunt Millie. What a contrast to her previous companions, women of indeterminate age with their nervous titters who fluttered around Aunt Millie every time she had an attack of the vapors.

Reid himself hardly knew how to deal with Aunt Millicent's nerves. As a boy he'd always been slightly afraid of her exacting ways. He'd been relieved the other afternoon, when he'd thought Aunt Millie about to faint, and the steady Miss Norton had given him a reassuring look. Her light brown eyes had been sympathetic, as if telling him not to worry, she'd been through enough of these spells to manage.

Reid wrapped up the lecture with a brief description of the ancient Egyptian symbols called hieroglyphics that covered several wall painting fragments on display.

As the audience poured out of the lecture hall, Reid was immediately besieged by people asking him questions. He listened patiently and replied as briefly as possible knowing from experience that he could be kept hours after a lecture if he wasn't careful.

The hall had cleared of most people when he spotted Miss Norton again, this time making her way to the front tables. He was in midsentence with a gentleman.

"Excuse me a moment, would you?"

"Oh—what? Certainly, Mr. Gallagher, certainly."

Reid headed toward Miss Norton, glad he'd have a chance to repay the woman's kindness to his aunt. He stood in front of her with a smile. "Miss Norton?"

"Yes?" she said, her eyes widening in surprise. They were the same shade as her hair, a light tawny brown.

"Did Aunt Millicent decide to brave the weather and come to the lecture?"

"Oh, no—that is, she would have liked to but she didn't feel quite up to it—"

Of course his aunt wouldn't have come to this crowded lecture hall. Too great a chance of catching some infectious disease. "I understand completely. I hadn't expected her to show. You came on your own, then?"

Her cheeks deepened with color, creating an attractive effect. "Yes…"

"You're interested in Egyptology?"

"Yes. It's a fascinating subject. I—I heard you mention the lecture to Lady Haversham. I thought it would be educational. I used to live in Palestine, you see," she said quickly, her voice sounding breathless.

He raised an eyebrow, his interest deepening. "Really? When was that?"

She looked away as if embarrassed. "It was years ago, when I was a girl. My parents were missionaries there for some years."

He sensed more to the story. When she remained silent, he cleared his throat. "I hope you enjoyed the lecture." Too late he realized it sounded as if he was hunting for a compliment.

"Oh, yes, very much so!"

Her enthusiasm encouraged him. "I'm glad. With a general audience, it's hard to know whether one is hitting the right note. I don't like to simplify things too much, but neither do I want to make things so technical I lose people's understanding."

"Oh, you adopted just the right tone, I believe. When I looked around me, everyone seemed most attentive to everything you were saying."

His lips curled up. "No one dozing off or fidgeting?"

She returned the smile. Her mouth was wide and generous, creating the impression that when she enjoyed something, she wouldn't stint with her feelings. He was struck once again by the color of her eyes, a warm caramel hue. His mother, a painter, had instilled in him a sense of color, line and dimension, especially for the human face.

"I don't believe so, though the hall was so crowded, I wasn't able to observe everyone."

"I usually make eye contact with my audience. That's how I saw you, although I'm surprised I spotted you, you were so far back."

She laughed. "I was behind someone with quite a prominent hat."

He chuckled. "Yes, I noticed the bird hat. It's a wonder you were able to see any of the artifacts at all. I wished I'd known you were here this morning. I would have had you seated up front."

"That's quite all right. I was fine where I was…although it *was* difficult seeing any of the detail of the objects."

"Would you like to see them now?"

She moistened her lips, her glance straying to the artifacts. "That's actually where I was headed when you saw me. I didn't mean to interrupt you." She indicated the group of people waiting to speak to him.

"If you're worried about them, don't be. Come along." Giving her no time for further consideration, nor to ask himself why he was taking the trouble with her, he took her gently by the elbow and directed her toward the front.

"Oh, Mr. Gallagher—" Reid turned to see the museum's assistant curator approaching him. The slim young man cleared his throat and lowered his voice. "There are some gentlemen, museum patrons, you understand, who wish to have a word—"

"Yes, in a moment." Before he knew what he was doing, he lowered his own voice, and indicated Miss Norton at his side. "A donor." He mouthed the words, "Major donor."

The man's lips rounded in a silent O. Then he quickly backed away, bowing and smiling to Miss Norton.

Reid led her to the nearest table. When they reached the

artifacts, Miss Norton turned to him. "You needn't stay with me. I don't want to take you away from those waiting to speak with you—"

For some reason, her very reluctance to keep him at her side strengthened his own resolve to remain there. "I told them you were a possible donor."

She stared at him. "A what?"

He grinned, and suddenly he felt like a mischievousness boy despite his almost forty years. "If they think you're a wealthy patroness of the museum, you're sure to be escorted to the front at the next lecture."

Her large eyes lit up with amusement. The next second she frowned. "I don't like being dishonest with people."

"You weren't. I was. Being put on the lecture circuit is both a blessing and a curse. Apart from being an archaeologist for the Egyptian Fund, I'm also expected to raise money for future digs."

"I should think that wouldn't be so difficult. The place was packed today."

His eyes scanned the lingering groups of people. "The fund will be pleased. The more we can generate interest in all things Egyptian, the more easily we can seek donations."

She nodded. "It sounds a little like missionary work. They both depend on funding from home."

"Yes, indeed."

He indicated the first display. Miss Norton looked over each artifact, marveling at things that had been preserved for so many centuries beneath the earth. She bent over the gold masks. He was pleased to note she didn't touch them, but looked at the brilliant surface painted with dark strokes to signal eyes and eyebrows, mouth and nose.

"What did you think of the talk?" Mr. Gallagher stood

close to her, keeping his back to the lingering crowd, hoping that would keep them from being interrupted.

"It was wonderful. I never realized there was so much to know about the ancient cultures. When I lived in Palestine, it seemed we were living in Biblical times."

She continued studying the artifacts, as he explained each one in more detail.

When they headed back to the lobby, a few people immediately came toward him. "Mr. Gallagher—" several voices began at once.

Ignoring them, he turned to Miss Norton, reluctant to end their time together so soon. "The lecture has left me quite thirsty. What about joining me for a cup of tea?"

She swallowed, and he was afraid for a moment she would refuse. "I'd love to," she finally said, before adding, "but I really need to get back to your aunt."

He nodded, surprised at the disappointment he felt. "That reminds me…you were very good with her the other day. I wanted to express my gratitude. I thought she was going to faint, and I wouldn't have known what to do."

Once again, Miss Norton's cheeks tinted pink. "By the sounds of it, you're used to much graver emergencies in the desert."

"But I'm only used to dealing with men in critical situations. I have no idea how to help an elderly female."

"Well, thankfully, it was no more than a passing moment and your aunt was perfectly fine afterward."

"Yes." His first impression hadn't been wrong. Miss Norton did understand his aunt.

She moistened her lips and glanced past his shoulder.

Before she'd think of another excuse for turning down his invitation, he held up his hand. "Now, what about that tea?

It'll only take a few minutes. There's a place right around the corner."

Instead of replying, she took out her watch. "I have a few minutes before having to return…." Her words came out slowly, as if still debating. "Lady Haversham generally expects me there for dinner at one o'clock."

He took out his own watch. "It's only half-past eleven. I'll make sure you're back in plenty of time…with time to spare." Understanding laced with humor underscored his words.

"All right."

"Good then." He felt lighthearted all of a sudden. He glanced back around him, knowing he'd have to tell the assistant curator something. "If you'll excuse me a moment, I'll be right with you. I just need to tell a few people I'm off." He marked his words with a touch to her elbow, as if afraid she'd disappear into the crowd again.

"Certainly. I'll get my things from the cloakroom."

"Good enough." With another brief smile, he headed away from her.

Maddie was left standing, wondering if she'd done the right thing accepting his invitation.

She retrieved her umbrella and coat, her mind in turmoil. Would she have enough time to swallow down a cup of tea and then walk all the way back to Belgravia? If she should be late for Lady Haversham…

Since she'd begun her employment a year ago, she'd never yet missed a day nor been late when Lady Haversham expected her by her side. Before she had time to wonder about the consequences, Mr. Gallagher returned and once again took her arm. How odd it felt to have a gentleman guiding her in such a protective manner.

Once out of the building, he turned to her. "Do you mind if we walk? I feel I've been cooped up all morning."

"Not at all. I walked to the lecture, as a matter of fact."

He stared at her. "You're joking. That's quite a hike from Belgravia to here."

Her cheeks warmed and she glanced down. "I enjoy walking. Too much of my time is spent indoors sitting, so I walk whenever I get the chance." No need to mention that she also did it to save the unnecessary expense of a cab or omnibus.

She sensed his scrutiny. "I imagine my aunt requires you at her side quite a bit."

She bit her lip, striving to answer honestly, yet not be critical of his relative. "It's the nature of my job."

"I suppose so." He didn't pursue the subject. No doubt his interest in the topic of paid companions had waned.

By the time they were seated in the tearoom and the waiter had taken their order, Maddie removed her gloves and decided to forget about Lady Haversham and enjoy herself. She couldn't remember the last time she'd been to a public eatery. She glanced around at the charming interior. Dark wood oak beams framed the low ceiling. They sat at a small, round table covered with a spotless white linen tablecloth. A small bouquet of forget-me-nots and daffodils was placed at its center.

Mr. Gallagher leaned forward. "Tell me about your time in Palestine, Miss Norton."

She folded her hands and looked down at the tablecloth. "There isn't much to tell. We lived in Jerusalem from when I was eight until I was fourteen."

"You said your parents were missionaries?"

"Yes." She was glad to be able to speak about them instead of herself. "Papa felt a call to the mission field when he was a young man—both my parents did, actually. They went to Palestine under the auspices of the Foreign Mission Society, when representatives of the society came to our church to speak one Sunday."

"I'm surprised they took a young child with them."

She couldn't help smiling. "Not only one. Three. I have two older brothers."

He shook his head. "I can't imagine being responsible for anyone but myself over there. And you all survived your time in the field?"

"Yes. I won't say it was without incident…." Her words slowed. "My parents probably wouldn't have come back when they did, but I had fallen ill with malaria."

"The Middle East can be a harsh place."

She found him observing her, his long fingers idly smoothing down the ends of his mustache. She could feel her cheeks redden under his gaze, wondering what he saw—a woman past her youth, with eyes that tended to look sad even when she wasn't, cheeks that gave away her emotions, a too-wide mouth. Her eyelids fluttered downward as the moment drew out.

"Most foreigners succumb to malaria at one time or another. I've gone through enough bouts to dread the symptoms."

She sighed. "I grew to know them quite well. It was after my third attack that my parents decided to return to England."

He continued stroking his mustache, studying her. He had such a direct way of looking at a person, she felt he could read her innermost thoughts.

"I'm still amazed that a European woman and her three young children survived the experience as long as you did."

"My two brothers were old enough that my parents would probably have braved it out longer, if they had fallen ill, but

I was younger, and somewhat frail when I was a child." She gazed out the window. Her parents had had to make so many sacrifices on her behalf. She turned back to him, recovering herself with a smile. "My two brothers are now missionaries in their place."

"In Palestine?"

"No. One is in Constantinople, the other in West Africa."

He whistled softly. "Your family is spread far and wide. Are your parents still alive?"

"Yes. Papa has a small curacy in Wiltshire." She steered the conversation away from her family. "Tell me how you came to be involved in Egyptology, Mr. Gallagher."

He eased back against the small wooden chair. "The question is more, How could I help not becoming involved? I lived a good many years in Egypt when I was growing up. My father was a diplomat. When I came back to England to school, my great-uncle—Lady Haversham's husband—took up where my life abroad had left off."

He was interrupted by the waiter bringing them their tea. Maddie absorbed what he'd told her, watching him as he spoke to the waiter. Although he addressed the man casually, seemingly as at ease in this quaint tearoom as in the great lecture hall, she continued to sense a man outside his natural element. Today he was as well dressed as he had been at his aunt's, in a starched white shirt, finely patterned silk tie and sack coat of dark broadcloth, yet she couldn't help picturing him in more rugged garb, such as he must wear in the desert.

As she stirred sugar into her tea, Maddie chanced a glance at her own navy-blue dress. It was the same one she'd worn the day he'd come to visit his aunt. Well, that wasn't surprising, being one of only three gowns she owned. It was certainly appropriate for a paid companion, but not up to standards to be seen in a gentleman's company. She must look like a nursemaid or governess beside him. What would the waiter or the patrons sitting around them think of such a handsome man escorting such a dowdy female?

The waiter moved away from their table and Mr. Gallagher turned his attention back to her. "I really wanted to thank you today for how you are taking care of Aunt Millicent. You seem to have a way with her."

"You have nothing to thank me for. I'm just her companion. She has a whole legion of servants to take care of her. As well as a fine physician," she added, thinking of how often Dr. Aldwin was summoned.

"She seems to rely on *you,* however."

Maddie removed the spoon from her cup and placed it on the saucer, uncomfortable with the compliment. "I'm only doing my job."

"How long have you been a…companion?" He hesitated over the word, as if unaccustomed to the term.

"Since I left home."

"When was that?"

"When I was eighteen." In the silence that followed she wondered if he was calculating how old she must be. On the cusp of turning thirty, she could have told him.

He only nodded, and again, she had that sense that he was evaluating her words, taking nothing at face value. He was probably cataloging her as a spinster securely on the shelf.

She shook aside the depressing thought and imagined instead that it was probably a painstaking attention to detail that made him a good archaeologist. She was still amazed he had remembered her name—or her, for that matter. He'd hardly glanced at her during the time he was at his aunt's for tea.

"How long have you been involved in archaeology?" she asked, returning to the topic she was really interested in.

Humor tugged at his lips, half-hidden by his mustache. "Oh, forever."

She smiled at his evident pleasure in the topic. "You said Lady Haversham's late husband was engaged in the field?"

"Yes. Good old Uncle George. It was he who gave me my love of archaeology."

She hadn't been with Lady Haversham long enough to know too much about her employer's late husband, although she knew he had often gone abroad. "Was he an archaeologist?"

"They didn't have them back then. He was more an adventurer and explorer. When he came to Egypt, he fell under the spell of the pyramids. He began to bring home anything he could find. It was all quite a free-for-all back then—any tourist or traveler taking what he could find; whatever the looters hadn't gotten over the previous centuries." His tone deepened to disgust.

Maddie rested her chin on her palm, glad to be taken away from her present world to one so close to that of her girlhood.

"By the time I came back to England, my father had been posted somewhere else. So, I began to spend my summers with Uncle George and Aunt Millicent. He was living in London by then. He'd show me parts of his collection. He had some incredible things—from Greek amphorae to Roman headdresses, but his real love was Egyptian artifacts. He had pottery, jewelry, bits of sculpture." He sighed. "I don't think I ever saw the whole thing. I wonder where it all is now."

"I haven't been with your aunt for very long. I know she has many things stored away. She often talks of her travels when she was younger. She was very excited when she knew you were coming home."

He looked sidelong through the window at the street. "I haven't considered Britain my home in many years."

Maddie bit her lip, afraid she'd said something wrong. But he turned back to her and began telling her about some of the digs he'd been involved in. Once again she was transported to another time and place, her present dreary existence swallowed up by that other world.

Suddenly a clock tower down the street struck the hour. She sat up and pulled out her watch. It was half-past twelve! "Oh, I really must get back. Thank you so much for the tea." She began to rise.

"Steady there." He snapped open his own watch. "You have plenty of time to get back if Aunt Millicent still dines at one. Wait, and I'll get you a cab."

Maddie sat back down, but felt the tension grow in her. She had wanted to avoid having to take the omnibus back. What would a hansom cost? Oh, dear, it couldn't be helped now. She had no time to cover the distance by walking.

Mr. Gallagher signaled the waiter and settled the bill. Maddie had to restrain herself from drumming her fingers on the tabletop. She gathered her bag and gloves.

Finally, he stood and she joined him immediately. "I can catch an omnibus a few blocks from here."

"Nonsense. You can catch a hansom right out front and it will be a lot quicker."

She bit her lip and said no more, thinking again how much the fare would cost. After they'd collected her coat and umbrella, they stood on the curb.

It didn't take Mr. Gallagher long to hail a carriage. When it arrived, she suddenly realized that their morning together was over. It seemed scarcely to have begun. She couldn't remember a time in her recent memory when she'd had such an enjoyable outing. Disappointment stabbed her.

"I—thank you again," she said, stumbling over the words in her effort to express her gratitude.

He held the door open for her. "The pleasure was mine. I really wanted to do something for all your kindness to my aunt."

Maddie held her smile in place, unable to help feeling just a bit disappointed that it hadn't been more for him than an act of kindness for an employee of his relative. It was thoughtful of him, all the same. Not many family members would take any consideration of a paid companion.

She placed her hand in his to bid farewell, and again she felt his strength and protection—which left her a little bereft when their hands separated.

She settled in the small space of the cab and placed her belongings at her side. Lastly, she took one more look out the window and gave a wave when she saw him still standing on the curb. He was a tall, lean man, his appearance that of a rugged adventurer and explorer, as he'd described his uncle, charmingly out of place on the London sidewalk.

He returned her wave with a small salute of his own, and she had another mental image of him in the desert, a camel as his mode of transportation, a host of Bedouins his companions.

As the carriage made its way from Bloomsbury across town to Belgravia, Maddie took out her purse and got her fare ready. She sighed, knowing she'd have to make up for the money in another quarter. She shook her head. There weren't many areas where she could cut back more than she already was. She couldn't *not* buy stamps for her weekly letters to her parents or brothers.

She was back at Lady Haversham's much more quickly than she was used to. A glance at her watch told her she still had time to wash up and tidy her hair.

When she descended the cab, she handed the coachman his fare.

"Oh, that's all taken care of, ma'am."

She blinked. "What do you mean?"

"The gentleman what hailed the cab for you. He took care o' your fare." He smiled. "And a generous tip, as well, to get you here quickly."

She stepped back on the sidewalk, astonishment leaving her speechless.

He tipped his hat to her. "Good day t'ye." With a snap of the reins, he was off.

Maddie looked after him a moment. She had underestimated Mr. Gallagher's attention to detail…as well as his kindness. She blushed, as it occurred to her that it only meant he understood the reduced circumstances of a paid companion.

Remembering her duties, she turned about and headed up the walk to the front door. She'd have to thank Mr. Gallagher the next time she saw him.

If there was a next time. Then she remembered his words, *At the next lecture.* All at once her steps grew lighter as she hurried up the steps.

Chapter Three

A few mornings later, Reid sat in his great-aunt's parlor for a second visit, this time in answer to a note from her. He'd been intrigued by her words that it was "about an important matter."

Aunt Millicent sat alone in her parlor, enthroned in her high-backed armchair. Despite her diminutive size, she appeared regal in her dark brocaded gown with several gold chains down the front.

He wondered briefly where her companion was and remembered the pleasant time they'd had over tea. The young lady had been a ready and willing listener, though he'd certainly never meant to go into such detail about his work.

"Thank you, my dear, for coming so quickly." Reid leaned down to kiss his aunt's cheek, which was soft and wrinkled but still smelled of the lavender water she'd used as long as he could remember.

"I was happy to oblige." He took a seat across from her. "Where's Lilah?" he asked, noting also the absence of the terrier.

"Miss Norton took her out for her morning walk."

He glanced toward the heavily curtained window. "It's a bit drizzly for a walk."

"Oh, Lilah's walks are very short. Miss Norton will protect her with an ample umbrella."

He tried to picture the willowy Miss Norton scurrying after the tiny dog, a large black umbrella over them both. He turned his attention back to his aunt. "And how are you on this damp morning?"

She made a face. "Not well, I'm afraid."

He leaned forward, clasping his hands loosely between his knees. "What is it?"

She patted her chest. "Oh, the usual, dear boy. My heart. Some days I feel I can hardly breathe."

"I'm sorry. Is there nothing they can do for you?"

"I think I've had every pill and potion invented, but to no avail. Dr. Aldwin says I must have total rest, but you know it's impossible not to worry about things. I find myself lying in bed at night just thinking of you off in foreign parts, and Vera with her children. Little Harry, you know, is going away to school this autumn." She shook her head. "I do hope they choose the right school for him."

Reid hid his smile. As long as he could remember his aunt had been a worrier. "Well, I'm glad you sent me a note. I would have come by soon at any rate."

"I hope I didn't disturb you at your duties, but I really felt I had to see you after the other day."

"Tell me what I can do for you."

"I've been thinking about what we discussed."

He tried to remember what they'd talked about. He hoped she wasn't still dwelling on the attack on their camp.

"It's about your Uncle George's collection."

Reid was immediately interested. "Yes, I was thinking

about it, too, since my visit. He must have some highly valuable pieces in it, from an archaeological standpoint."

"I'm sure everything in it is of the utmost value."

He hid another smile, remembering how protective his aunt was of Uncle George's reputation. "Yes, perhaps so."

"I would like to ensure that it is well taken care of at my demise."

He rubbed his hands over his trouser legs, uncomfortable with her behaving as if she was at death's door each time he visited. "Yes…I suppose it would be good to make some provision if…in the unlikely event…" He coughed, uncertain how to proceed.

"I'm glad you understand. Your Uncle George would have wanted the collection to be used for the advancement of science. He told me many times he wished to leave it to some museum or university, but he passed on before he could act upon his deepest desire, and has left me to dispose of his collection as I see fit."

"I see. Do you have anything in mind?"

"I'm much too ignorant of all he has to make such an important decision, which is why I wanted to consult with you." She folded her hands in her lap as if in preparation of an announcement.

"I'd be happy to advise you in any way I can."

"Your Uncle George was very fond of you. Alas, we never had any children of our own, so you were like a son to him." She smiled in recollection. "You'll never know how happy it made him when you decided to pursue his hobby."

"We spoke often of our mutual love for Egypt and its history." Reid had many pleasant memories of his uncle.

"Of course he could never pursue it full-time, what with his work in the consulate." She fingered the long chains around her neck. "Those were the days. So many parties, so much delicate negotiating with the government officials, the native sultans…" She sighed. "Once we returned to England, of course, his work with the Foreign Office again kept him so occupied, all he could do was put away most of his collection, in the hopes that someday he'd have the time to catalog it properly."

Reid nodded, remembering his many conversations with Uncle George on this very subject. But then his uncle had died suddenly in his early sixties, and Reid had gone abroad, so he'd never really bothered to think about the collection again.

"I've come to a decision." Reid waited, wondering what she was going to say. "I want you to take charge of organizing the collection and together we can then decide where to donate it. I was thinking of the University College."

Reid whistled softly. Although he'd never seen the entire collection, from what he remembered, this would be a sizable donation to the college.

"Of course, because it's such a large bequest, I want to make some stipulations."

"That is perfectly reasonable."

"Yes, I thought so. Firstly, I want you to have sole charge of it, and any decisions that are made by the institution have to be approved by you."

He sat still. "I don't know what to say." Her announcement certainly demonstrated a great degree of trust in him—an element in short supply these days among those working with ancient ruins, where so much pilfering and secrecy went on.

She smiled. "I'd hoped you'd be pleased."

Reid considered the enormity of the task. "I…am," he managed, still trying to take it in. "It will take some time. I haven't ever seen everything Uncle George amassed."

"Oh, it will take months perhaps. He left boxes and boxes

of things, all labeled, of course. I've had them brought down from the attic and the stables to his study and library."

He shifted in his seat. "I don't know how much time I would have to devote to it. I need to return to Egypt at some point."

She pursed her lips, and he recognized the signs of her displeasure. "Couldn't someone take over your duties there for the time being?"

"Perhaps I should have a look at the collection first. With the help of some assistants, it's possible we could manage to catalog the items more quickly."

She shook her head. "Oh, no. I couldn't bear to have the house invaded by strangers."

"It wouldn't be anything like that. Museum workers tend to be very quiet, and perhaps with only one assistant, I could manage, at least enough to have the collection moved."

"No, no. I couldn't have it. My nerves wouldn't bear it." She clutched her gnarled hand to her mouth and turned away.

"All right, no one need come," he assured her, not wanting to have to deal with a swoon. He wondered if Miss Norton would be coming back soon. She seemed to have a gentle yet effective way of dealing with his aunt.

Before he could rise, his aunt spoke again. "I knew you would understand. Would you like to look at the collection now or come back tomorrow?"

She seemed fully recovered. Reid flipped open his watch. "I have time now to begin to look at things, get a feel for the scope of the work. You said everything has been brought here?"

"Yes. You can go right into your uncle's study and the library. I'll ring for the maid to escort you."

Reid stood, preferring to come to no decisions until he'd seen the state of the collection. Time enough then to think what this job of cataloging would entail. Time enough to think what remaining so long in England would mean…

The moment Reid entered the study, memories of his uncle surrounded him. The scent of his brand of pipe tobacco lingered in the air. It seemed nothing had been changed from when his uncle had last sat here. The glass-enclosed book-shelves were crammed with leather-bound volumes and port-folios. The gilt-edged desk blotter still had ink stains on its green surface. Reid stepped farther into the room and examined the desk's surface. Even his uncle's pipe rested against the edge of an ashtray—a glazed piece of pottery from Crete.

He turned to the black-clad maid. "Thank you. I'll just look around."

She gave a brief curtsy. "Very well, sir. Just ring if you need anything."

The door shut behind her and stillness descended once again. Reid remembered his hours sitting on the straight-backed chair facing the large walnut desk, his uncle in the swivel chair in front of it. Uncle George would light his pipe and take a few puffs, the chair squeaking as he leaned back with those first satisfied puffs. Then with a conspiratorial grin, he'd show Reid an item or two and tell him the aston-ishing tale of how he'd come to acquire it. Then he'd finger the side of his nose and say with mock severity, "And not a word to your Aunt Millie about it!"

Reid would promise with all the solemnity of a boy en-trusted with a secret by so great a man as Uncle George.

His uncle's life had seemed one adventure after the other, and Reid had longed to grow up quickly to follow in his foot-steps.

Reid smiled to himself as he picked up a brass envelope

opener—a medieval knife from the early Ottoman Empire—
and fingered its sharp edge. He'd had a few adventures of his
own since then. It would have been nice to sit here once again
and swap stories with his uncle—but sadly he'd never have
the chance now.

He took a deep breath and straightened his shoulders, remembering what he'd come for. Behind him, against one
wall, were stacks of boxes. He peered at the topmost one:
Egypt: Saqqâra Pyramids, September 1839. He took out his
pocketknife and carefully cut the string holding the box shut.

Everything inside was tissue wrapped. Reid took out a
few items—vases, a female statuette, a broken piece of blue
porcelain tile. The box was crammed full.

He set the things on the desktop and entered the next room.
The library was also as he remembered it, but stacked in its
wide center were piles of boxes. He whistled as he looked
around.

This could mean months of work. He wasn't sure how
many notes his uncle had taken, but he'd have to uncover them
if he hoped to place and date the relics stored in the boxes.

He walked slowly around the room, reading labels where
they were available, opening some of the boxes and looking
at the samples inside. When he reached a smaller box, with
the word Notes scrawled across it in black ink, he slit it open
quickly. Inside he found leather-bound notebooks.

He leafed through one. His uncle's travel journals. He de-
ciphered the neat ink scrawl. Some pages were stained, many
were yellowed with age, while others were still clean and very
legible. Many had to do with his uncle's official functions, but
others detailed his archaeological endeavors. "Eureka…" he
breathed, his excitement mounting.

After skimming a few pages describing a harrowing climb
into a tomb, Reid closed the worn notebook. For all his ad-

venturous side, his uncle had been a meticulous recorder. A life's work summed up within the pages of a dozen or so notebooks. Uncle George had been a pioneer in a new branch of science. The few pages Reid had read reminded him a lot of his own work, but it also brought to the fore how primitive his uncle's foray into this new field had been.

He let his gaze roam around the room. Regardless of the enormity of the task, it had to be done. The record of the past needed to be cataloged and analyzed. The treasures needed to be brought to the light of day and shared with scholars.

With a sigh he eased himself down on the floor and positioned himself cross-legged on the soft Persian carpet. Opening the journal to the first page, he began to read.

August 12, 1840. Toured the inner chambers of pyramid. Intensely hot. Came to chamber of sarcophagi. Massive tombs. Crawled down narrow chamber, about two hundred feet lower… Air became thicker and staler the farther we went. Hoped no noxious gases lingering there. Wouldn't have wanted to join the mummies resting there, only to be found by a future explorer a century or so from now.

My dragoman almost left me. He didn't like invading a tomb… Can't be helped, I told him. Had to pretend an indifference I was far from feeling…

Reid wasn't aware how much time had passed when the sound of a throat clearing behind him brought him back to the present.

He looked up to see Miss Norton in the doorway, holding a tray. He stood, then immediately bent to rub the top of his legs, which had become stiff. "I'm sorry, I didn't hear you come in."

She smiled. "Please don't get up. I didn't want to disturb you, but when Lady Haversham told me you had been here since this morning, I thought you might like some refreshment about now."

The words made him realize he was both thirsty and hungry. He walked toward her to relieve her of the tray, appreciating her thoughtfulness.

He set the tray on a desk and flipped open his watch. It was just past noon. "I didn't realize I'd sat there so long, although my body certainly does," he added with a grimace as he rubbed the kinks out of his neck.

She poured a cup of tea, adding a sugar cube and placing a slice of lemon on the saucer. The simple task captured his attention. Perhaps it was the slim shape of her hands, or her graceful motions, or simply the fact that she'd remembered how he took his tea. She handed him the cup.

"Thank you."

"I brought a plate of sandwiches, in case you were hungry. Or if you'd rather, your aunt dines at one."

"Actually, I'd prefer just the sandwiches. That way I can work for another hour or so before leaving. I need to get back to the museum to continue with the other collection. If you could make my excuses to Aunt Millicent."

"Certainly. I'm sure she'll understand."

She offered him the plate of sandwiches and he took one. "Just seeing them makes me realize I'm famished."

She smiled, and he noted again how expressive her face was. His artist mother had dragged him through every museum in whichever country they'd been living in. Now he valued the lessons. It gave him an appreciation for the human form.

Miss Norton reminded him of paintings from the Italian Renaissance, he decided, with her pale skin and tawny hair.

She had a rather thin but mobile face, her caramel-brown eyes large and her mouth generous. Botticelli. Botticelli's *Birth of Venus* with its mixture of sadness and kindliness in the shapely eyes.

He hadn't realized he'd been staring until she moved away from the desk and gazed at the opened boxes on the floor. "My, I never realized there were so many things in storage."

"Nor did I." He leaned against the desk and took a bite from a sandwich quarter.

She peered into an open box but didn't take anything out, which also pleased him. Most people would grab anything unusual with no regard to its fragility. He had noticed the same thing at the museum. Although she'd asked a lot of questions about the mummy masks, she hadn't touched anything.

She paused at the open journal on the floor.

"Notes?"

He nodded. "Travel journals, but they contain quite some detail on the artifacts. My uncle did some extensive exploration in the years he was in Egypt."

Her eyes widened with interest. "When was he there?"

He calculated. "From the midthirties to the midforties."

"We were in Palestine from 1868 to 1874."

"I didn't go over until 1880," he told her. "Ten years ago."

She nodded, her expression pensive. "I remember our boat stopping in Alexandria. It seemed such a busy place filled with so many turbaned people. I was only a young girl, so it's a jumbled memory."

"I spent a few years as a boy in Cairo in the…let's see…early sixties. When I went back out this time around, I was much older, a full-grown man of thirty." He looked down at the remains of the sandwich in his hand. "Set on leaving England and never looking back." He looked up, embarrassed at the words that had slipped out, probably as a result of having gone back in time since he'd entered his uncle's study.

She didn't seem perturbed by his reply. Instead her gaze appeared to radiate empathy, as if she knew exactly how one sometimes cannot bear memories of a place.

He set down his sandwich and brushed the crumbs from his fingers. "Egypt was just the challenge I needed at the time. I sought action and adventure."

"Did you find it?"

He squeezed the lemon into his tea. "I found my fair share."

She took a few more steps around the boxes. "Your uncle seems to have been a man of adventure, as well."

"Yes, his journals make for some interesting reading. I wish I had the time to delve into them more fully." He set his cup down, frustrated once again as he thought of the task ahead of him. "My aunt wants me to catalog all these artifacts."

She turned her attention back to him. "My goodness. Can you do it all yourself?"

"Hardly. But she insists no strangers are to come to the house."

"I understand," she said. "Her nerves."

"Tell me, just how badly off is she?"

She folded her hands in front of her. "She is under regular medical care."

"Is she—" how could he phrase it politely? "—as serious as, well, you saw her the other day?"

"It's hard to say. I've been here scarcely a year." She pressed her lips together as if debating whether to say more. "She dismissed her previous companion, I'm told," she went on more slowly, "and the one before that." She gave him a small smile. "So far, I seem to have suited her, but I'm new yet."

He remembered how particular his aunt could be. It was unfair to ask Miss Norton to make any judgments about his aunt. She was only an employee, after all, her position at the mercy of Aunt Millicent's whims. "I apologize for my questions. I realize you probably don't think it your place to form any opinions."

"I may form opinions, but as to voicing them…" She shrugged and turned away from him to study something in one of the boxes.

"All right, fair enough."

She straightened. "I had better leave you to your lunch—and work."

"Thank you for the refreshment. It was just what I needed."

"I'm glad I could be of help." She paused a moment. "I— I wanted to thank you for…taking care of my cab fare the other day. It was most generous of you."

He waved away her thanks, having already forgotten about it. "It was the least I could do for keeping you so long over tea." He had no idea how much paid companions earned, but he imagined it wasn't much. He could hardly conceive of a life at the beck and call of another. He was used to the independence of working far away from civilization and its strictures. Occasional loneliness was the main drawback, and he'd learned to deal with that.

Miss Norton nodded, her cheeks bright pink, making her look more strikingly than ever like her famous portrait counterpart. What was such an obviously bright, not unattractive, young woman doing in such a position?

He looked away, having steeled himself over the years not to notice any woman's charms. There'd only been one woman in his life.

"I thank you, all the same, for your thoughtfulness. It was most kind of you."

Uncomfortable with her gratitude, Reid cleared his throat and picked up his teacup once again.

"Well, let me or any of the servants know if you need anything while you're here."

He frowned at the way she lumped herself with the servants. She was too intelligent and refined. Probably, as most paid companions, a gentlewoman down on her luck, reduced to the semiservant position. He remembered that she said her father was a curate. She was probably helping to support her elderly parents.

She had reached the door when he had a thought. Just before she disappeared through the doorway, he said, "You wouldn't be interested in helping me catalog some of this stuff, would you?"

As soon as he uttered the words, he already regretted them. He usually considered things carefully before making a decision.

What did this young woman know about ancient artifacts? He didn't need someone who would require careful supervision. It would be difficult enough sifting through his uncle's notes, trying to match them to the heap of antiquities.

As Reid watched the surprise in her eyes turn to excitement, something tugged at him. A sense of compassion stirred within him as he thought how narrow her life within these walls must be.

She had lived in the Middle East and had some knowledge of the ancient world. More importantly, she knew how to follow instructions and how to be silent, two qualities he valued highly in any assistant.

"Do you think I could be of help?"

He nodded slowly. It just might be the perfect solution. His aunt couldn't object to her as a stranger, and she was right here, available any time he chose to come by.

"I told Aunt Millicent I'd need help. I don't think she realized the scope of it. Since she balked at any suggestion of an outsider, I don't think she'd have a problem with someone in her employ lending a hand a couple of hours a few days a week."

"I'd certainly be willing to do anything to help." Her gaze roamed over the boxes around her. Then she drew her two eyebrows together. "I don't know if she will allow me to assist you, however."

"If you'd rather not, just say the word. It's no problem."

"Oh, no, it's not that at all. I think it would be fascinating work. It's just…well, perhaps *you'd* better broach the subject with your aunt."

He nodded. "If you're concerned about Aunt Millicent objecting, don't. I'll handle that aspect of it." If his aunt could force him to remain in Britain for a few months, she'd have to agree to some of *his* conditions, as well.

"I…" She hesitated, and he wondered again if she was having second thoughts about undertaking the work. "I—what I mean is…don't be discouraged if your aunt says no." She pressed her fine lips together and looked down, as if hesitant to say more.

He breathed a sigh of relief that that was her only qualm. "I've known her since I was a boy and learned how to get my way. Being a favorite nephew does have its advantages upon occasion."

A smile tugged at her lips, and he was heartened. She really had a most sympathetic face. There was something radiant in it when she smiled.

He rubbed his hands together, his eagerness to begin the

task starting to grow. "Very well, then. I'll let you know when you're to start."

Her eyes lighted up and he felt a tingle of warmth steal into his heart, as if he'd given a child something delightful on her birthday. It occurred to him there wasn't much brightness in her life. If he could give her a little bit, then maybe his time in England would not be altogether wasted.

Chapter Four

Maddie's gaze went from the small limestone fragment on her left to the battered notebook on the table in front of her. She compared the description:

Profile of king? Young prince? Standing on left. Sun God Ra with bird's head on right. Offering of bull, chickens. Seated monkey. Found at KV 2.

If this artifact matched the description in Sir Haversham's notebook, then it meant that everything in the box may have been found at the same location.

Maddie blew away the strands of hair tickling her forehead, sensing the excitement in her begin to grow. She scanned the fragments of pottery laid out on the long table before her. The last fortnight had involved painstaking work, first, unpacking a portion of the boxes and trunks and piling the remainder against one wall of the library. Then began the detective phase of deciphering the spidery handwriting in the stack of notebooks and various loose sheets of paper and matching descriptions to contents of boxes.

She glanced at Mr. Gallagher bent over a black stele covered in hieroglyphics. Her hunch that his attention to detail made for a good Egyptologist had been confirmed for her over the time they'd been working together. He had been uncompromising in his process of carefully unpacking each box and laying out the contents in a separate area, labeling what could be readily identified.

He'd given Maddie a quick training in some of the common artifacts from steles, sarcophagi fragments, plaster casts of wall reliefs covered in pictures, amulets, potsherds, faience vessels, wood carvings and basalt statue pieces. Mr. Gallagher had also given her a crash course in ancient Egypt, charting out for her the Old, Middle and New Kingdoms when the pharaohs had ruled. She'd gazed in fascination at the drawings he showed her of the massive tombs they'd built for themselves, some reaching skyward in the form of pyramids, others stone chambers underground, only recently rediscovered by the explorers and archaeologists traveling the length of the Nile River.

She realized how well he'd laid the groundwork before he'd ever set her to work to assist him with identifying the artifacts. It was only in the past few days he'd allowed Maddie to begin reading his uncle's notes.

She hesitated to interrupt him now with her discovery. She'd learned in the last two weeks how single-minded his concentration was once he began to work. It only took one instance, when she'd read the barely disguised impatience in his eyes, to keep her from disturbing him unnecessarily.

Her times of unhindered concentration were another story as she remained at the beck and call of her employer. She turned now as a parlor maid entered the room and motioned to her.

Maddie rose and removed the white apron she'd worn

when working among the artifacts. After folding it and placing it on the back of her chair, she left the room.

"Lady Haversham wants you, miss," the maid said.

Maddie no longer bothered to ask what the trouble was about or if it couldn't be taken care of by one of the staff of servants. Lady Haversham had made it clear when she called for Maddie, only Maddie would do, whether it was to pick up a fallen handkerchief or take Lilah out for a walk in the backyard.

"Thank you, I shall go to her at once."

As soon as Miss Norton left the library, Reid tossed aside his pencil and straightened on the tall stool.

In the scant hours he had Miss Norton's able assistance each day, it seemed his aunt couldn't do without her for more than half an hour at a stretch. He drummed his fingers on the tabletop, debating how to resolve the issue.

His concentration shot for the moment, he pushed back from the table and stood. Clearly, his aunt had no idea how much work was involved in what she'd set him to do. He gazed at the multitude of artifacts neatly laid out on every available surface in the large room. It wasn't even half the stuff. His eyes lingered on the gilded bust of a young Egyptian prince—one of the prizes of the collection so far.

He still didn't know where Uncle George had picked it up. He'd have remembered seeing it as a boy. It was most likely from the Valley of the Kings area. His uncle had spent several months in Thebes exploring the temples and tombs in and around Karnak and Luxor.

He wandered over to the space where Miss Norton had left her work. Taking up a pencil, he tapped it lightly back and forth against the tabletop between his fingers, his mind returning to his first thought. He hated the time wasted. He knew

Miss Norton's first duties were to his aunt, but he didn't think he was being unreasonable in requiring her services in the midafternoon hours when his aunt had her accustomed nap.

The sound of the door reopening interrupted his thoughts. He turned with relief to see Miss Norton. His relief was short-lived as her first words were, "Excuse me, I need to run to the post for a moment."

He merely nodded, realizing it would do no good to express his displeasure to her. She had no control over his aunt's whims.

She approached the table where he stood. "I—I'm glad you're up from your work. I didn't want to interrupt you earlier, but I think I found something." She pushed the notebook toward him.

He was immediately attentive, following her words as she read the journal's entry and showed him the fragment. "And look here, the entry before this one describes a wooden crocodile figurine." She held up a broken carving, her arm grazing his. She immediately moved away. "Well, this one was in the same box." Her voice rose, its lilting tone conveying her enthusiasm. Reid focused his attention back to what she was saying, his arm still feeling her light touch.

"I was just going to read the next entry when I was called out."

He took the notebook from her.

We found a cache of faience and terra-cotta cooking vessels, ornamental vases near the Theban necropolis.

Reid surveyed the articles before him, idly smoothing down his mustache with thumb and forefinger. His excitement grew the more he compared the journal entry descriptions with the objects ranged on the table. "I think a good many of these would qualify…yes," he murmured, examining a terra-cotta pot on legs. "And it would confirm my feeling that he found these near Karnak." He turned to her with a smile, his earlier displeasure dispelled. "Well done, Miss Norton, your first breakthrough."

She returned the smile, her face blushing. He thought once again of Botticelli's *Venus.*

Reid snapped his fingers, remembering something he had intended to do that day. Now was as good a time as any since Miss Norton would have little chance to do any more work that day. Her discovery made up for any lost time, however, and he could easily continue where she'd left off and gain a few hours' progress.

"Before you head out, I have something for you."

Her brows rose. "Something for me?"

He went to his portfolio and pulled out an envelope. "Your first fortnight's wages."

Her wide eyes grew rounder. "Wages?"

"Yes, I realize we never went over them. I thought what I usually pay a part-time assistant would be satisfactory."

Since she didn't reach out her hand to take the envelope, he held it out to her.

She took a step back. "Oh, Mr. Gallagher, I think you misunderstood. I never expected wages."

He laid the envelope beside the notebook. "I think it's *you* who misunderstood. I never would have requested your help in any capacity but a straightforward business transaction."

She moistened her lips, deepening their rosy hue, and turned her face away from the table. "Of course, I understand that, but I never expected you to pay me in addition to what I'm earning from Lady Haversham. I—I feel d-dishonest collecting what amounts to two salaries at the same time."

"No need to. They are wholly separate services you're

rendering. I made it clear to my aunt I needed an assistant and you've proved an able one. She agreed to share your services." Before she could protest further, he ended the discussion. "I don't expect to argue about this. It's a paltry enough sum and you deserve every penny. Much of this work is tedious but it's got to be done, and my time is limited. If you don't accept it, I'll have to find another who will." He folded his arms across his chest.

Still she hesitated. Finally, she picked up the envelope and held it by the corners. "Very well. I shall only accept it on behalf of my brothers' work in the mission field." There was something, while not defiant, yet firm, in her quiet words.

He shrugged, rocking back on his heels. "You can do whatever you please with the funds. They're yours."

She bowed her head. "Thank you." Without another word, she left the library.

After she'd gone, Reid sat at her place and continued with the notebook she'd worked on, glad that he'd hired Miss Norton. Aside from the interruptions, she was a most helpful assistant—quick to learn, interested in the subject matter, quiet and steadfast in her work habits. He couldn't think of a better work partner. He remembered her pleasure when he'd complimented her on her discovery. Her tawny eyes had lit up, color suffusing her cheeks, and her rosy lips had widened into a generous smile.

Reid shook aside the image. He had no business noticing Miss Norton's attributes other than those directly related to the work involved. He turned his attention back to his uncle's notes.

Little by little he matched more objects with those described in the journal. Several times, Reid stood and went to another part of the room, thinking he'd seen an object like the one described by his uncle. Little by little, piece by piece, he began to amass a picture of an excavation site. The thought flitted again through his mind of what an able assistant Miss Norton was.

Maddie paused at the top of the stairs, her hand on the newel. After a trying afternoon of waiting on Lady Haversham, the evening was finally her own. It mattered little that it was almost nine o'clock. She was grateful for at least one hour of peace and quiet before retiring.

She gazed down the length of the grand staircase, feeling the pull of the library. She could hardly wait until tomorrow to take up the thread she'd discovered in the late Sir George's notebook. She loved finding herself in the world of adventure Mr. Gallagher had opened up to her.

She debated a second longer. She didn't like going into the library outside of the daylight hours, feeling like an intruder, but her curiosity was too strong. Finally, she took a step down. Just another peek at the notebook, she decided, to reread the entry she'd stopped at.

As she approached the door, she perceived a crack of light under it through the gloom of the corridor. She turned the knob slowly, but as the door opened, she breathed a sigh of relief, seeing Mr. Gallagher.

Then she frowned. Had he been here all afternoon and evening…and everyone unaware of it? She cleared her throat softly. He looked up immediately. "Oh, you're back, Miss Norton."

"I didn't know you were still here. Or did you leave and return?"

Only then did he seem aware that night had fallen. He glanced at the darkened windows before rising. With a loud yawn, he took a leisurely stretch, making Maddie aware of the lean, taut length of him. She shifted her gaze to his rugged face. "No, I've been here all afternoon. I didn't realize it had gotten so late."

She gave a surprised laugh. "It's past nine o'clock."

"Is it?" He didn't seem unduly concerned. "Come, look what your discovery has led to."

She hurried to his side. Her wonder grew as he showed her all the artifacts that he'd labeled in the time she'd left him. He'd even pinpointed the area on a map tacked up to the wall.

"I was able to locate pieces from two other cartons of artifacts." He stood, rubbing the back of his neck. "Your careful observation this afternoon certainly helped me put a dent in this project."

She warmed at the brief words of praise then sobered, remembering the generous sum of money he'd paid her that very afternoon. "I'm sorry I had to leave so abruptly. I wasn't much help to you. My goodness, this represents hours of work." She shook her head at the array of meticulously labeled objects ranging from broken bits of pottery to carved masks.

"Don't worry about it." His low voice soothed her. "I'm just grateful you noticed the connection. It took some astute observation."

She said nothing. Suddenly she frowned. "Have you eaten? Did you ring for the maid for any refreshment?"

He shook his head, looking a bit sheepish. "To tell you the truth, I cleanly forgot all about the time of day—or night," he added with another glance at the dark windowpanes visible through the long, parted velvet drapes. "I could use something now. With your permission, I'll rummage through my aunt's pantry." A sly grin tugged at his lips. "I used to sneak down in the middle of the night as a boy. Let's see if I can remember where everything is."

"Come along," she said with a laugh. "You don't have to do any sneaking. I'm sure Lady Haversham would be upset if she knew you'd sat here so many hours without having something sent up." As they extinguished the lamp and exited the library, she said, "What were you doing up at midnight in those days?"

"Oh, I'd get to reading some adventure story and wouldn't be able to put it down even after I'd been told to put out my light. By the time I'd finished the book, I'd be famished."

She smiled in understanding. "That reminds me of how I felt this afternoon when I had to leave off reading your uncle's notebook, as if a good story had been snatched out of my hands at the most exciting spot."

He chuckled. "I would have left it for you, but I felt the same, like I had to pursue that lead. My own trail had grown frustratingly cold and I wasn't making any headway."

She pushed open the kitchen door. "Well, I'm glad I gave you some kind of start today." She turned up the gas lamps and headed toward the pantry. "What would you like? There's some cold roast from dinner."

"Nothing too much. If you have an apple, maybe a piece of cheese."

"Are you sure that's all you need?"

"Yes, I really should head back to my rooms. I need to get an early start tomorrow at the museum."

She nodded and ducked into the pantry. A few minutes later, she set a plate of thick slices of bread and cheese and quartered apples before him.

"Thank you," he said, from where he sat on a stool at the worktable. "This is more than adequate."

She offered him a glass of buttermilk.

"Won't you join me?" he asked with a gesture at the plate. Her heart skipped a beat at the invitation. Suddenly the cavernous kitchen took on intimate proportions. "No, thank you. I'll just have a glass of buttermilk."

"I hope I'm not keeping you up."

"Not at all. I had just read to your aunt and was going to head up to my own room. I couldn't help coming down to look at the notebook again. Just to be sure I hadn't fooled myself this afternoon." She smiled.

"I can understand perfectly. It's the reason I couldn't leave this afternoon."

"Your uncle must have been an interesting man."

He nodded, munching on an apple slice. "He was. You must have gotten a sense of the risks he took on his travels."

"I'm amazed at the number of times he barely escaped with his life." Maddie rested her chin on her hand, finding the same level of companionability with Mr. Gallagher that she'd experienced in the tearoom.

They continued speaking about Egypt and the discoveries made there over the last decades. Mr. Gallagher tore off a piece of bread. "Unfortunately, there has always been a spirit of competition amongst the different national expeditions— the Brits trying to beat the French, who are trying to beat the Germans—with who can unearth the most artifacts." He shook his head. "We'd have probably made more headway and prevented some of the needless destruction if we'd worked together."

When he'd finished the light snack, she offered him some more, but he declined. "I really must be going. Thanks for the fare. It should hold me till morning." He gave her another grin, and she realized for the countless time in the last fortnight how ruggedly handsome he was.

"A-are you staying far from here?" she asked, hoping the question wasn't too personal.

"Not too far. I'm at the Travellers Club in Mayfair. It's an easy walk."

She wondered at his staying at a club instead of with family or in a flat of his own. As if reading the question in her mind he said, "It didn't seem worthwhile getting my own rooms. When I come to London, it's usually for a short stay. It's more convenient just to put up at my club."

"Yes, I suppose so." She well knew how dismal a rented room could be. Did he have a place to call home in Egypt or did he live as a nomad in the desert? She wished she could ask but knew she'd never dare. He held the door open for her as they exited the kitchen together.

She escorted him to the front door where he'd left his jacket, thinking all the while that it was a pity such a man was so alone. She knew he had a sister in London in addition to his aunt, but he didn't appear terribly close to them.

The night was fresh but not cold when they stood on the stoop.

He took a deep breath, a look of disgust clouding his chiseled features. "I don't know how people live in this city. The air smells of sulfur and you can never see the stars."

She glanced up at yellow-gray aureoles of the gas lamps against the dark sky. "I guess we forget what clean air and a night sky are like."

"On the Egyptian desert you can begin to comprehend what a 'blanket of stars' really means. Between the cold dank winters and soot-filled air, I don't know why anyone would want to inhabit London."

She didn't know what to say. That not everyone had a choice? That not everyone had the freedom he seemed to have?

He grinned. "Don't pay any attention to me. I've never

liked this city and feel like a mule with a bit in his teeth every time I'm forced to step back in it."

"I—I hope for your sake then that your time here will be short." She said the words while fighting the wish that his stay would be lengthy.

"Thanks…though it looks like I'll be here for a while."

"May the Lord grant you the grace then to support it."

"I am grateful for the guidance He gave you today in making the connection in that journal." He took a step away from her. "I'd better let you get some sleep. Thanks for the snack. Thanks even more for your help in the library." He stood a few seconds longer, and she wondered if he was as reluctant to leave as she was to have him leave.

"Well, good night," he said at last, taking another step away.

"Good night, Mr. Gallagher."

With a wave, he turned and began walking briskly down the gaslit street. Maddie stood watching him until he'd disappeared into the evening mists. With a sigh she stepped back inside and closed the door behind her. Why did it seem she was enclosing herself inside a tomb like those of the pharaohs while Mr. Gallagher had fled to the only freedom available?

Had the last decade of her life been nothing but a futile servitude? She'd believed she was following the Lord's will for her life, but seeing it now through Mr. Gallagher's eyes awakened all the long-ago dreams of the call of the mission field in a faraway land. Had she missed her true calling?

Chapter Five

The next afternoon Maddie sat in the parlor, once again overseeing the tea service. This time not only did Mr. Gallagher sit with Lady Haversham, but also his sister and her three children.

Over the din of the two rowdy boys, Lady Haversham said to her great-niece, "Reid must get out in society a bit while he's home. You know I can't do as much as I'd like. I was counting on you and Theo to organize a few things."

"Of course, Aunt Millicent. You know we'd love to." Vera Walker adjusted the lace fichu at her neck. "What about a musical soiree here Friday a week?" She turned to her brother, her tone gaining enthusiasm. "I could invite your old school chums Harold Stricklan and Steven Everly. Did you know Steven was just made vice president of Coutts Bank? Theo just ran into—"

Before she could finish the sentence, her oldest son rushed by her and bumped into her knee, sending tea sloshing from her cup into her saucer and onto her silk dress.

"Harry! See what you've done to Mama's frock! You naughty boy!"

"I'm sorry, Mama." He didn't stop but whipped around the settee, closely followed by his brother.

"Timmy!"

At the same time his sister, who was sitting on the floor beside the sleeping Lilah, petted the dog too briskly and Lilah sat up and began to growl.

Lady Haversham leaned forward in her chair to see what was being done to her pet. "Careful, child! Madeleine, take the children to the garden, please."

"Yes, my lady." She rose immediately, knowing the command had been coming. Stifling a sigh, she rounded up the children, who jumped at the chance to be free of the confines of the parlor, and herded them downstairs.

"I had to let go their nursemaid. The woman was unreliable—" were the last words Maddie heard as she closed the parlor door behind her.

Harry, the oldest boy said to his younger brother, Timmy, "I bet I can beat you at jacks."

"No, you can't!"

The two continued arguing.

"Hush, children, until we're outside." Maddie took the two youngest firmly by the hand and began walking toward the staircase.

She herself wouldn't have minded a brief respite in the garden if it weren't for the fact she would have no peace for the next half hour.

Once in the backyard, the boys forgot their game of jacks and started running around the bushes.

Maddie clapped her hands, trying to get their attention, knowing Lady Haversham would be upset if any flower beds were trampled. "All right, children, what would you like to play? What about graces?"

"That's a girl's game!" The two boys made faces, their shouts drowning out their sister's assenting voice.

"What about hoops and sticks?"

"Blindman's bluff!" The boys jumped up and down until Maddie complied. It was no use arguing with them, she'd learned. She procured a large silk handkerchief from her pocket. "Who's to go first?"

"You! You! You!"

"Very well." She tied the scarf around her eyes. Before she could prepare herself, the older boy, an oversize ten-year-old, grabbed her from behind by the elbows and twirled her around. She groped the air in front of her to keep from losing her balance.

"You can't catch me!" Harry's voice came from a few feet away. Immediately they all copied him. Maddie swung around as each voice neared her but she was never close enough, and she didn't want to take the easy way out and catch Lisbeth, the youngest. She knew she was moving farther down the garden, as their voices rang out from that end.

From past experience, she knew the boys would have her at their mercy until they tired of the game and needed her attention for a new amusement. In the meantime, she needed to grit her teeth and play along, hoping not to trip along the uneven brick walk, and praying she wouldn't damage one of Lady Haversham's prized bushes.

Tired of the women's chatter around him, Reid wandered to the window, teacup in hand. He'd been sorely tempted to follow his niece and nephews out but Vera had insisted on his participation at that moment in planning her soiree. As the two women worked out the details of an afternoon musicale, he took a sip of tea and peered down into the garden, wondering what his unruly nephews were up to.

He spotted Miss Norton first, barely visible under an apple tree's bower of blossoms. Her hands were upraised and she appeared to be calling out to the children. He didn't see any of them at first, then one by one he saw them all up in the tree. His lips twitched in a smile until he discerned that Miss Norton was trying to get them to come down and not having an easy time of it.

Remembering the unmannerly behavior of the children the short time they'd been in the parlor, he set his teacup down on the tea tray and headed toward the door.

Vera broke off in midsentence. "Where are you going, Reid? We haven't decided on the guest list for the musicale."

He was already halfway across the room. "You and Aunt Millicent take care of it. Just let me know the date and time, and I'll show up. Now, if you'll excuse me, I'll only be a moment."

Before Vera could ask him anything more, he shut the door behind him.

When he reached the garden, he heard the children's shouts and laughter.

"You can't get us unless you climb up."

"You must get down immediately, Harry, and you, too, Timmy. Your sister might hurt herself. Where are you, Lisbeth?"

The six-year-old girl only giggled in glee.

"You know your aunt won't like it that you're in her apple tree. It's her best orange pippin."

"We won't come down till you come up!"

"You aren't playing by the rules. Now come down, Timmy."

In reply, the boy shook the tree branch at her and a shower of blossoms littered the ground. "It looks like it's snowing!"

"Oh, you mustn't do that. Your aunt won't have any fruit in the autumn if you knock the blossoms off now."

Reid reached the tree and spied Lisbeth first on a lower branch. "Whoever thinks he can beat me in a race around the square gets a half crown." He turned away from the tree, calling out over his shoulder, "Last one down's a rotten egg."

As he walked toward the garden gate, he heard scrambling and shouts as three small bodies shimmied down the tree.

"Lisbeth's a rotten egg!" The boys called over their shoulders as they caught up to Reid. Lisbeth began to cry.

Miss Norton removed her blindfold and smoothed her hair before going to crouch by the weeping child.

"There, Lisbeth, why don't you come along with me, and we'll show those boys you can beat them in the race?"

Reid's niece sniffed.

"Where's your handkerchief, honey?"

Leaving the child with Miss Norton, Reid herded the boys into the mews. They ran down the alley until they reached Belgrave Square. Reid took them to the nearest tree and marked out the starting place. "You'll run inside the square, all around and end back here."

Harry's chest puffed out. "That's easy."

"We'll see. Now, let's wait for your sister and then when I say 'go,' run with all your speed. Watch that you don't cheat by cutting the corners or you'll be disqualified."

As Miss Norton crossed the street and approached them, holding his niece by the hand, he smiled. "I thought you could use some reinforcements."

"Indeed, thank you." She shaded her eyes and looked across the large, tree-studded square. "Are you sure it's not too far for the children?"

"They needn't complete the course. I'm only hoping to rid them of some of their excess energy."

"Yes, I see." Her eyes twinkled, and he noticed again how exactly her eye and hair color matched, a rich, caramel color like the toffees he used to enjoy as a boy.

He cleared his throat and turned his attention back to the boys. "All right, on your mark." They lined up at the spot he indicated. "Go!"

He jogged alongside them, making sure not to overtake them. Lisbeth soon trailed behind and began to cry. By the second corner of the square, he glimpsed Miss Norton, who'd once again taken the girl by the hand and walked along beside her, encouraging her. Harry ran ahead of Timmy by a good lead, but as the older brother rounded the third corner, his foot tripped on a tree root, and he went flying headlong.

Reid ran up to him, the boy's sobs reaching across the large square. The fall hadn't looked serious enough to merit the boy's wails. Reid knelt by him.

His nephew clutched one knee in both hands. "I…th-think it's br-broken…!"

The trouser leg was torn and the knee scraped. Reid probed the area around it gently, but determined that no further damage had been done. Timmy leaned over his brother, panting heavily. "Does this mean I won the race, Uncle Reid?"

This only made Harry sob the louder. "You didn't win! That's not fair! Tell him he didn't win, Uncle Reid! I was ahead. You saw me!"

Reid smiled at Timmy. "I think it means there'll be a rematch once your brother's fully recovered. What do you think, Harry? Does that sound fair?"

He swiped a sleeve across his runny nose. "I would've won fair and square if that tree root hadn't been in my way." He glared at his younger brother. "I would've beat you today, just like I'll beat you by a furlong anytime we race!"

"I wasn't the one who fell on my face and then cried like a girl!" Timmy began hopping on one foot and then the other. "Waaa!" he bawled in imitation.

Miss Norton and Lisbeth reached them. Miss Norton knelt on Harry's other side. "Is he badly hurt?"

"Nothing more than you see. Come on, champ, let's see if you can stand." He held out a hand to his nephew. "'Attaboy."

Harry wiped his nose again. "It hurts something awful, Uncle Reid."

"Skinned knees always hurt. The trick is not to let on to the ladies." He winked in their direction. "Come on, let's show the others what a brave fellow you are." Draping an arm around the boy's shoulders, Reid urged his nephew forward. He turned to Miss Norton. "I'll take him to the kitchen and get him cleaned up if you take charge of the other two."

"Of course, thank you. Come along, Timmy, Lisbeth." She took them each by the hand and directed them back to the house.

Timmy resisted. "I don't want to go back yet."

She pulled him gently forward. "Your mother might be getting ready to leave."

Lisbeth tugged on her other hand. "I want to stay outside, too." Timmy took advantage of Miss Norton's inattention to break away from her and dart toward the middle of the square.

"Timmy!" The single word stopped the boy in his tracks. Timmy stared round eyed at Reid's sharp tone. "Take hold of Miss Norton's hand if you don't want to feel the palm of mine on your backside."

Timmy debated for only an instant. He dragged his toes in the dusty path but he didn't disobey. As soon as he was at Miss Norton's side, he gave her his hand and put the thumb of the other in his mouth, staring at his uncle as if he'd suddenly sprouted horns.

As they walked toward the house, Reid said to Miss Norton, "Don't let them forget who's in charge."

She gave him a quick look. But she said nothing, only pressed her lips together and looked down at the ground. "Yes, sir."

Wondering if he'd said something wrong, he walked alongside her and the children in silence to his aunt's house. He'd been only trying to help. Had he offended Miss Norton in some way?

Maddie reentered the parlor, clutching Timmy and Lisbeth, Mr. Gallagher's words still stinging. Although spoken softly, they'd made her feel incompetent and inadequate—the way she always did when put in charge of Mrs. Walker's children.

As soon as she entered the parlor, Mrs. Walker's glance went from one child to another. "Where is Master Harry?"

"He's with his uncle." Maddie hesitated to say anything about the scraped knee. Cowardice won and she kept silent. She immediately regretted her decision.

Lisbeth ran to her mother's lap. "Mama, Harry fell and cut his knee! He was crying and bleeding!"

Mrs. Walker's gaze flew to Maddie. "What has happened to my son? Tell me at once."

"He tripped over a tree root while running."

Lady Haversham leaned forward. "Whatever did you have him running for?"

"The boys were running a race."

Timmy pulled at his mother's arm. "You should have seen me, Mama."

Lisbeth reached up to get her mother's attention. "I was running, too."

Timmy thrust his chin out. "I would've beat Harry if he hadn't gone and fallen."

Mrs. Walker put her hands over her ears. "Please, children, don't interrupt your Mama when she is talking. Now, Miss— Miss—"

"Norton," Maddie supplied for her.

"Yes, will you please tell me why my children were involved in running a race?" Her glance swept over her daughter. "And why are they so disheveled?"

"It was Uncle Reid's idea." Timmy's voice wobbled. "He shouted at me, Mama."

"Shouted at you? Oh, goodness. Now, where is Harry?"

"He's perfectly fine, madam. Mr. Gallagher is looking after him."

"What is this about Master Harry?" Lady Haversham thumped her cane on the carpet. "Maddie, I demand to know what has happened to him!"

Sensing her mistress's agitation, Lilah jumped down from the old lady's lap and began dancing around her feet, barking in staccato bursts.

Mrs. Walker's voice rose over the din. "I placed the children in your care, Miss Norton, with full confidence that you would manage."

"Yes, ma'am." Maddie prayed for patience and hoped Mr. Gallagher would soon return to calm his sister down.

Mrs. Walker covered her ears again. "Can you please shush that dog, Miss Norton?"

Maddie fished out a treat from Lady Haversham's bag and gave it to the dog. Lilah gobbled it up quickly, leaving Maddie's palm wet, and immediately barked for another.

"Aunt Millicent, can something not be done to calm your pet?"

Lady Haversham fanned herself. "It's because she senses something is wrong. She's a very sensitive animal. There,

Lilah, dear, you mustn't worry. Now, Madeleine, please tell us what has happened to Master Harry."

"He's fine now."

Maddie whirled around in relief as Mr. Gallagher walked in with Harry.

"Look, Mama." Harry pointed to a plaster across his knee.

Mrs. Walker ran to her son. "Harry, whatever happened to your trousers?" Not waiting for his reply, she turned again to Maddie. "What is the meaning of this, Miss Norton? My son is not only hurt, but his best pair of trousers is ruined. Whatever have you done with the children?"

Mr. Gallagher went to pour himself a cup of tea. "Calm down, Vera. If you need to vent your spleen at someone, do it to me. Your darling boys were doing their best to disobey Miss Norton, so I took them to the square for a footrace."

Mrs. Walker let her son's arm go and turned to Reid. "To the square? In the midst of traffic? Reid, whatever were you thinking?"

"Attempting to wear out your unruly offspring."

"How can you say such a thing of your own flesh and blood!"

"That may be, but they need to learn to obey their elders."

Mrs. Walker knelt beside Harry. "Does it hurt very badly, darling?"

"It hurt awfully when I fell, and Uncle Reid put something on it that stung like the dickens, but now it's better. Uncle Reid told me how all the men in the desert buck up. They bite a bullet, isn't that right, Uncle Reid?"

"That's right, sport."

"We didn't have any bullets, so Uncle Reid gave me a wooden spoon to bite on."

"I should hope we don't have any bullets!" She shook her head at her brother. "Teaching him such vulgar things. Wait until your father hears about this." She fixed her gaze once more on Maddie. "In future, please be more careful with the children. Lisbeth is delicate and the boys need careful supervision. I don't expect them to be removed from the garden—"

"Vera, didn't you hear what I said? I took the boys from Miss Norton because they were acting like little dervishes."

She sniffed and resumed her seat. "Well, I never! I didn't expect you to insult my children. I'm their mother and ought to know them better than anyone!"

Mr. Gallagher poured another cup of tea and brought it to his sister. "Why don't you drink this and let it settle your nerves? As you can see, Harry has survived his ordeal." He turned to Maddie. "How about you, Miss Norton, could you use a cup of tea?"

Before she could reply, he frowned. "You look ready to collapse." He took her by the elbow and led her to her accustomed seat, then returned to the tea cart.

"Now, did you two ladies decide on an afternoon of torture—excuse me, musical delights—for me?"

His aunt gave him a reproving look. "Reid, you are incorrigible. Now, give me Lilah. She's had too much excitement."

He scooped the dog up in one hand and held a teacup and saucer in the other. "Here's your mutt, Aunt Millie."

She took Lilah onto her lap, still looking at her nephew in disapproval. "Your sister is putting herself out for your sake. You should be more appreciative of her efforts."

He approached Maddie and handed her the cup. "You'd best buck up, as I told Harry," he said with a wink.

"Now, Reid, pay attention," his aunt continued. "We've drawn up a list of twenty guests to invite, most of whom you are acquainted with. By the way, did you know Cecily Mason is widowed? Such a beautiful woman and still so young."

Maddie had met Mrs. Mason once at a similar tea in this parlor and remembered her as a very attractive, poised woman. Was Lady Haversham hoping to play matchmaker for her nephew? Maddie looked down at her teacup, realizing the thought filled her with dismay.

The conversation continued in a buzz around Maddie as the women discussed the guest list. Thankfully, everyone, including the children and Lilah, ignored her for the moment.

She thought of how Mr. Gallagher had so staunchly defended her and felt cocooned in a cloud of wonder at how one man—whom she hadn't even known a fortnight ago—could become her champion.

Finally, she lifted her teacup to her lips though her hand still trembled. Taking a small sip of her tea, she found he had sweetened it.

He'd remembered from their times of taking tea in the library how she took her tea…a lump of sugar, no lemon, no milk.

She glanced at Mr. Gallagher. He sat to her left, close to his sister. He was as handsome in profile as he was facing forward. He was still very much a mystery to her, a man who kept the few words he spoke to her during their times in the library strictly on the work at hand. She had learned so much on the subject of Egyptology from him, yet she had gleaned almost nothing about the man himself. His actions, on the other hand, spoke volumes. He was always patient in explaining the work to her. This afternoon, she'd witnessed compassion, camaraderie, a way with children, authority, a sense of humor.

What had compelled him to leave England and stay in the desert for so many years?

Maddie took another careful sip of tea. Mr. Gallagher's personal life was no business of hers, she reminded herself.

Like Lady Haversham, he was her employer, and her only obligation, besides fulfilling her duties satisfactorily, was to shine Christ's light into their lives, as was the duty of any man or woman of faith. She didn't know anything of Mr. Gallagher's faith, but she did sense a reserve that perhaps spoke of a wound not fully healed.

How she longed to offer a healing balm to that wound.

Maddie wrote to one of her brothers that evening at her desk.

Dearest Todd, I have the most wonderful news. The missionary society shall be receiving an additional bank draft this fortnight for your labors in West Africa.

You ask how I am able to manage this on my meager salary. Well, the Lord has blessed me with a bit of additional work.

You know Lady Haversham has a nephew? I think I wrote you about him, Mr. Reid Gallagher. He is an Egyptologist...

Maddie went on to describe how she had come to be his assistant. As she reached midway down the other side of the paper, she held her pen in the air a moment before continuing.

He is a most considerate and generous man. I had told him that any additional payment was not necessary beyond what Lady Haversham pays me. But he insisted. I told him the money would go to missions work. This didn't seem to bother him at all. I know you'd like him.

Maddie stopped and turned the sheet over to reread what she'd written already. It occurred to her halfway through that she had written almost exclusively about Mr. Gallagher.

She picked up her pen again. "He is an older man," she continued, then paused again. Her brother would probably form a picture of a sixtyish gentleman puttering about in a museum, when the reverse was true. Mr. Gallagher was a man in his prime, vitally alive, virile and the very opposite of a doddering professor.

Maddie chewed on the end of her pen. Was she misleading her brother? She hadn't said Mr. Gallagher was Lady Haversham's *great*-nephew, just her nephew. With that last sentence, she was deliberately implying he was much older than her almost thirty years.

Her glance strayed away from the page, picturing Mr. Gallagher's handsome features. She didn't know how old he was but didn't think he could be above forty. What would her brother think if he knew this and read her letters full of her activities at Mr. Gallager's side? Would he begin to suspect anything of her growing feelings for the man?

She swallowed, looking back down at her words. She hated deception and considered starting the letter over or crossing out the last sentence and inserting the word *great* to the reference to nephew, but finally she shook her head. That would look much too obvious. And as far as starting afresh, she really didn't want to waste a whole sheet of paper.

With a sigh, she continued writing, but this time made a deliberate effort to talk about Lady Haversham, her niece's visit and then went on to talk of last Sunday's sermon. She didn't close the letter until she was satisfied that other items filled as much space as all she'd written of Mr. Gallagher and her work with him.

The exercise was for her own good. She must put things back into perspective. She was only an employee of Mr. Gallagher's. In a few weeks, he'd be back in his beloved Egypt, and she…

She looked down at the envelope, which would soon be on a ship on its way to West Africa, while she remained behind, doing her small part to help those who were bravely carrying out the Lord's great commission.

Chapter Six

Reid paced the library, his steps muted by the thick pile of the carpet, as he dictated to Miss Norton.

"The faience vessels and fragments are likely from the area surrounding the small temple at Karnak. They are painted blue and have black lines and other markings. By their similar shape and color to those found at Gournah by Champollion on his Franco-Tuscan Expedition, I would place them in the Middle Kingdom—"

He broke off at the sound of a pen falling. He turned quickly to see Miss Norton fumbling for it. He noticed her other hand was rubbing her temple.

"Are you all right?" She looked pale, but only nodded and attempted to continue writing.

"Are you sure?"

"Just a bit of a headache is all. I'll be all right. Pray continue. You ended with 'Middle Kingdom'?"

"Never mind that. How long have you had a headache?"

"It's nothing, really."

In a few strides, he was at her side. "Look at me."

Slowly, she turned her face up to his and he was struck by

the shadows under her eyes. "Have you been getting enough sleep?"

Her gaze slid away from his. "I…I was a little restless last night."

He frowned, thinking how often she was summoned by his aunt. Did she ever have any time to herself? "How long has it been since you've been outside, getting some exercise?"

"I…I don't remember." Her voice was barely above a whisper now.

He stepped away from her and stroked his jaw. "Is this job too much? I know my aunt has you at her beck and call every moment of the day. If this job is taking away from your only time to get outside and get some fresh air—"

Her large eyes shot to his. "Oh, no, Mr. Gallagher. I'll be fine—"

He didn't let her finish but wheeled around and headed toward the door. "Come on."

"Where are you going?"

"Get your hat and shawl or whatever you need and come along. I'll meet you in the front hall."

She stood and began to follow him. "But your dictation—"

"It can wait. Now, I'm taking you for a walk before you become seriously ill."

"That's not necessary, Mr. Gallagher. I'm perfectly fine, I assure you. I can take a powder—"

He stood by the doorway, his hand on the knob. "I don't need my assistant to fall ill on me. Now, we do this my way, or I'll have to get myself another assistant."

She shut her mouth and preceded him out.

Once outside, Reid led her across the square at a brisk pace. "I'm not going too fast for you?" He slowed his pace as he realized her skirts might be hobbling her.

"Not at all," she said, keeping up with him. At least she didn't wear that ridiculous high bustle women favored these days. That contraption always reminded him of a one-humped camel. He glanced at her. She wore a nondescript brown skirt and tailored jacket. The colors offset the lighter shade of her hair. The outfit was similar in its simple lines to a riding outfit, although the narrow skirt looked hard to take long strides in. He slowed his steps some more.

He hoped he hadn't spoken too roughly to her. He really didn't know how to deal in the pleasantries women expected. With men, he was used to saying things straight-out, not wasting precious words. It had been too many years since he'd made time in his life for women.

There was something about Miss Norton, however, that brought out his protective instincts. Was it that his aunt seemed to take such advantage of her and she seemed so incapable of resisting the abuse? His aunt had always had some companion working for her whenever Reid had visited her in latter years, but he'd never paid much attention. They usually seemed faded women long past their prime and Reid hadn't given them a second look.

Why had Miss Norton warranted not only a second look, but a place in his work? Was it because she seemed much too young and attractive and lively? The words came to his mind thinking of her enthusiasm whenever they came upon a particularly choice artifact, or her willingness to play along with the children's games….

In short, Miss Norton seemed the least "companion" type he'd ever seen. He kicked at a pebble in the pathway cutting through the square. What did he know of companions?

"How—how—" Now he was being as hesitant as Miss Norton. He cleared his throat and began again. "How did you end up working for my aunt?" he asked her, fixing his gaze straight ahead.

"An old friend of hers lives in the same village as my parents. She happened to mention your great-aunt to my parents, and as I was looking for a situation at the time, I wrote to her."

He glanced sidelong at her. "Have you always been a companion? Why not teach?"

She seemed to swallow a laugh. "You saw me with your sister's children and you can ask that?"

"Not all children are as spoiled as my niece and nephews."

"They are not bad children," she said immediately. "I didn't mean to imply that. I merely lack the authority to keep them in control. It's not to say I don't enjoy children or teaching them. But somehow, the first situation that came to me when I was much younger was that of a companion." She smiled a faraway smile. "That was a good situation. The lady was a bit of an adventurer like yourself, except she confined her travels to Europe. When she wasn't in England, she would spend several months in France or Italy. I enjoyed traveling with her. She put me in charge of making all the arrangements. She had a wide circle of friends and acquaintances. She was a kind and generous person."

Reid wondered that someone in that circle hadn't latched on to Miss Norton…a gentleman, he admitted reluctantly. As he observed her under the dappled light of the tender green foliage overhead, he noticed her hair, pulled into a heavy knot at her nape, was definitely worthy of Titian. Her skin was porcelain—flawless, delicately tinted at the cheeks. And her eyes—a man could get lost in those soulful eyes.

He coughed, shifting his gaze back onto the street. "You must have met a lot of people."

"She—Mrs. Worthington, that is—enjoyed entertaining artists and writers."

"You never—uh—met anyone?" He felt annoyed at himself for fishing, but couldn't help it.

"I met many people through her."

He took her arm lightly as they crossed the street and made their way down Upper Belgrave.

"I mean…no one in particular…?" He stopped, embarrassed at his own ineptness at framing the question.

She looked at him. "You mean a gentleman?" She shook her head. "Oh, no, no one like that."

Subject closed. Served him right for prying. He certainly wouldn't appreciate anyone probing into his personal affairs. His family had long respected his silence on Octavia. "What happened to your employer?"

"She had such a youthful spirit that I often forgot how old she was becoming. She died peacefully in her sleep a little over a year ago. We'd been together for several years."

"I'm sorry. You must have been close."

She smiled gently. "Yes."

When she offered no more, he risked another question. "So then you went in search of a new position."

"Not immediately. I spent a fortnight with my parents. But then, yes, I wanted to seek employment. I…I didn't want to stop sending my brothers my support."

He narrowed his eyes at her, remembering her earlier reference to their missionary work. "Is that where all your income goes?" He immediately realized the impertinence of the question. "Forgive me, Miss Norton, I didn't mean to pry."

"That's all right. I help support my parents, of course. But as you see, I have no dependents, so yes, most of my income goes to the Lord's work in the mission field. There's so much need there. My brothers write to me about the work, and I only wish I could do more. My brothers are the ones giving their lives for the Lord's work. I'm just doing a very small part to help them carry it out."

Taking abuse from his aunt and scrimping and saving every penny didn't seem such a small thing from his point of view, but he said nothing.

"It's a lovely day, is it not?" she asked.

Sensing her wish to change the topic, he complied. "London does have its moments, though they are few and far between." He spoke the words, but his mind was dwelling on what she'd told him. "There are days, as today, when the wind is blowing in the right direction, houses aren't having to be heated so much, that one can almost see blue sky." He looked up, observing the sky through the trees. "The air has almost regained a sense of freshness...the stench of the summer heat hasn't yet begun."

She laughed. "I confess, I did enjoy the months with my first employer that we spent outside of England. The Italian countryside is particularly beautiful."

"Yes. I spent many summers when I was a lad near Florence. My mother fancied herself a painter."

She looked at him with interest. "Really?"

"Yes. She achieved some success, actually, as an illustrator of botanical books."

"What was her name?"

"Andrea Farringdale."

"Not Gallagher?"

He shook her head. "She kept her maiden name professionally."

"Is that unusual?"

"Yes." He smiled. "My mother was an unusual lady. A pioneer in many ways. She believed women should receive the same education as men and never let the fact that she was married and the mother of children stop her from pursuing her own career."

A light came into Miss Norton's tawny eyes. "Your mother sounds very special."

"Yes. She gave me an appreciation for art."

"Perhaps she influenced you in the direction your interest took toward ancient art."

"Undoubtedly to a degree."

They walked along in silence for several minutes until they reached another green spot at Eaton Square. He glanced over at her and was glad to see color in her cheeks. "Are you tired?"

"Not at all."

"How's your head?"

She smiled, surprise in her eyes. "The headache's gone."

"You've just been spending too much time indoors."

"I suppose so. I do get out a little, for Lilah's walks and a few errands for Lady Haversham, but those are short walks. It's difficult to find time for a long walk like I used to. But I'd hate to give up my work on the artifacts," she said quickly.

"I understand." Of course he did. Aunt Millicent was getting more and more difficult to please. She had always been a demanding woman, but it had not been so apparent when she had had a busy social life. It must be hard for her now to be so limited in her activities. It probably made it inevitable that she took her frustrations out on an easy victim.

"Please don't feel obliged to find another assistant, Mr. Gallagher. I usually don't suffer from headaches."

"You have to promise me you'll make the time to get out for a walk, even if it means shorter hours in the library." He held her gaze, not satisfied until he had her assent.

She nodded, her expression serious. "I promise to do my best."

A smile tugged at his lips. The words didn't mean total acquiescence. "If that's all you can do, I'll have to accept it for now." In the meantime, he'd have a talk with his aunt. There must be something that could be done. Miss Norton looked far too frail to continue under the strain of two demanding employers.

"All right," he said, taking her arm in his once again, "let's get back to work."

Reid spent the following days pondering the situation with Miss Norton, and believed he'd come up with a good solution. It only remained to convince his aunt.

A few afternoons later, returning with his aunt from a visit to old friends, he glanced at her in the carriage. The visit had gone well. She was in a good mood.

"Not too tired?" he said.

"A bit. I do want to thank you, Reid, for accompanying me. It has been a good while since I'd been to see Sally Thornton."

"I'm glad to have been of service."

"Cecily Mason is still quite attractive, is she not?"

"Mmm, hmm," he said, thinking of the beribboned lady who had sat too close to him, claiming an acquaintance from more than a decade ago, insisting he call her Cecily, as she kept referring to him as Reid.

"Cecily moved back with her parents when she lost her husband last autumn." His aunt clucked her tongue. "She was desolate with grief. Such a loving wife…I was glad to see her looking so well today."

"Yes." She didn't strike him as the grieving widow at all. Her cloying eau de toilette still lingered in his nostrils. He pushed back the window shade, deciding to bring up the topic uppermost in his mind. "With the weather so warm, I was wondering if you wouldn't like a little trip to the country. It might do you a world of good."

"A trip? Me? Oh, gracious, I couldn't possibly travel."

He looked across at the horrified expression on his aunt's face. "Pity."

"Where were you thinking of traveling?" she asked when he said nothing more.

"I have a friend at the club who has a house in Scotland. He's told me to make use of it for as long as I wish."

"Scotland! Goodness, as far as that? The trip alone would do me in."

"I don't know about that…with the train, it's not such a grueling trip. You'd wake up and be there. And once you're there, it would be to relax and enjoy the fresh air. It's a wonder you can even breathe in the city."

"You're right about that. I find myself gasping for air at times, it's become so noxious." She shook her head. "And growing worse each day."

"Why don't you think about it? Miss Norton and your maid would accompany you to see that you're comfortable."

She looked out the window and broke open her black lace fan. "Oh, I couldn't possibly consider it. Scotland is much too far."

Well, he'd tried. He'd just have to come up with another solution, his resolve stronger than ever to get Miss Norton out of the city for a while. When was the last time she had had a real holiday?

The quartet of musicians began the first strains of a Brahms violin concerto. After an hour of hustling about overseeing the serving of tea and cakes to the numerous guests at Lady Haversham's afternoon musicale, Maddie welcomed the chance to sit down. She glanced at her employer then at Lilah in a corner not far away from her mistress. For the moment, everyone seemed settled.

The music soon soothed her frayed nerves. After a few minutes her gaze strayed to Mr. Gallagher. He sat on the settee between two fashionably dressed, attractive ladies. Maddie judged them to be around her own age. Both were widows with a secure position in society and independent means. The fact alone of having been married gave them a cachet far superior to Maddie's, as if having procured one husband vindicated them for all time. Even if they never married again, the term *spinster* could never be applied to them.

Cecily Mason leaned over to whisper something to Mr. Gallagher and he smiled and gave a slight nod. At that moment his glance met Maddie's. She quickly looked away, feeling her face heat at having been caught staring at him. She clenched her hands together in her lap and tried to appear as if she were merely interested in the music.

When the musicians took a break halfway through, Maddie went to see if Lady Haversham needed anything, but she found the old lady engaged in a conversation. "You'll never believe what my nephew has convinced me to do!"

Her acquaintance, another elderly lady, leaned forward, her lace cap trembling. "I couldn't possibly imagine. Do tell me."

"He has prevailed upon me to accompany him to the Scottish Highlands!"

Maddie stared at her. Lady Haversham traveling to the Scottish Highlands?

"Never!"

Lady Haversham tapped her fan against the lady's arm. "I told him my constitution was much too delicate, but he insisted the outing would do me good. Imagine a month of that bracing air."

"Oh, goodness, I don't think I'd be up to the journey."

Lady Haversham glanced at Maddie. "Well, I have Madeleine. And my maid, of course. And Dr. Aldwin has given me his blessing. He even recommended a colleague of his in Edinburgh."

"Does this mean you've reconsidered my suggestion, Aunt Millicent?" Maddie started to hear Mr. Gallagher's low voice behind her.

Lady Haversham looked up at him with a mischievous smile. "I hope I don't regret this. But Dr. Aldwin thought it an excellent suggestion when I mentioned it to him."

"Well, I'm glad to have an ally in him." Mr. Gallagher took a cup of tea a maid offered him. He turned to Maddie with a smile. "Ever been to the Scottish Highlands?"

She wasn't used to seeing him in a dark frock coat. It set his tanned face off to further advantage. "No. I'm told they are breathtaking."

He stirred his tea. "They are. I haven't been up that way in years, but I have a friend who's offered me use of a place. Did Aunt Millicent tell you?"

"No." Her glance strayed to her employer, but her attention was on her old friend. "I'm surprised—but glad that she's agreed to go. The outing should do her good."

"That's what I'm thinking." He continued looking at Maddie, who felt herself blushing under his scrutiny.

"What about your work?" She frowned, remembering the reason he came by almost every day. What if she shouldn't see him anymore…? The thought brought her up short.

He shrugged. "A week more or less won't make much difference either way. Since the work is held up in Egypt indefinitely, there's no undue rush to finish things here. I don't mind the chance to get out of London for a fortnight or so, I can tell you that. You should enjoy it."

He would be accompanying them. On the heels of that thought came his last words. She would be going, as well. It finally began to sink in. A holiday away from London, with Mr. Gallagher…

It seemed almost too good to be true. Her heart began to sing with a lightheartedness she hadn't felt in a long, long time.

When the concert resumed, Reid found himself once again sandwiched between Mrs. Cecily Mason and Mrs. Augustina Drake, both of whom he'd known only slightly in his youth. He shifted on the hard horsehair settee, moving his thigh away from the one lady's, only to find his other brushing Cecily's. He hid a grimace when she immediately turned to him with a smile.

"How long do you plan to be in London this time, Reid?"

He smoothed down one end of his mustache with his thumb. "Not long," he whispered back. An older lady on a straight-backed chair in front of him turned to glare at them, and Reid wished he could offer to exchange seats with her.

"I'll be sure to invite you to a few functions. There's so much going on in London now. You must be famished for society."

He turned his attention back to the music, wondering how many more movements to the piece there would be. He folded his hands on his knees and felt like an accordion. The least movement to ease his muscles would bring him in unwanted contact with two females whose puffy sleeves, ruffled skirts and dangling jewels seemed to be everywhere he moved.

A soft sound in the corner drew his attention. He craned

his neck to the back and saw Lilah vomiting on the carpet beside Lady Haversham's chair.

His aunt motioned to Miss Norton, who had already risen from her place.

Grateful for any excuse to move, Reid stood and headed their way. Before Miss Norton had a chance to bend over the dog, Reid scooped up Lilah, thinking she barely weighed over a pound.

Once outside the drawing room, Miss Norton closed the door softly behind them. "Mr. Gallagher, you needn't have troubled yourself. I can take care of Lilah."

"Where should I take her?"

Without another word, she led him to his aunt's private sitting room and indicated the cushioned basket on the floor. Miss Norton knelt down and smoothed the dog's silky head, careful of her pink bow. "There, sweetie, that feels much better, doesn't it?" The terrier curled up and went to sleep under Miss Norton's soft strokes.

She met Reid's gaze across the small basket. "Lady Haversham feeds her too many rich treats and Lilah invariably gets sick."

He pictured the gaunt stray dogs roaming the streets of Cairo, their ribs prominent through their thin fur. "Spoiled mutt."

She smiled. "She does keep your aunt company."

He wanted to say, *So do you without being treated half so well,* but kept silent.

"You didn't have to interrupt your enjoyment of the music. Lilah will be all right now."

"If you call being jammed between two practical strangers enjoyment. I should thank Lilah for giving me a reason to stretch my legs." He did so now, easing his long legs in front of him.

With a glance in that direction, she resumed stroking the dog. Reid found his gaze lingering on her face. "Botticelli," he murmured, noting the tint of her cheeks, the downward sweep of her dark golden lashes—

"I beg your pardon?" Her lashes fluttered upward again.

Reid was held by those large tawny eyes, their expression tender, inquiring. He broke the connection and coughed. "Nothing…just a stray thought…"

He forced his attention on the small dog. What was getting into him? This was his assistant, not a painting in a museum… and *not* a single, attractive woman.

Before he could go any further with his train of thought, Miss Norton stood. "I suppose we'd better get back. Mr. and Mrs. Walker went to a lot of trouble to arrange this afternoon's entertainment."

"My sister loves nothing better than organizing entertainments, and as you've no doubt observed, my brother-in-law loves nothing better than snoozing through them." He rose to his feet more slowly and followed her to the door. "Although if I had the choice of facing down a hostile tribe of Bedouins or returning to the drawing room, I'd prefer the former."

She smiled in understanding and again he was struck by the soft expression on her face. "Definitely a Botticelli," he said to himself before turning away and holding the door open for her.

Reid endured another hour of music followed by polite small talk with a bunch of people he scarcely remembered and with whom he had little in common. It was early evening by the time he headed back to his club, walking through the Green Park and St. James's until he reached Pall Mall.

"Good evening, Mr. Gallagher." The porter took his hat and umbrella from him. "Fair weather, isn't it?"

"Yes, it's a fine evening, John."

Reid walked across the spacious lobby, nodding to the few gentlemen present. Most were still in the dining room. He decided to skip supper, having eaten more than he was accustomed to at his aunt's. He was getting tired of roast beef and Yorkshire pudding and similar heavy meals almost every evening. He missed the lighter fare of rice or couscous with a sparse serving of goat or lamb, and dates and almonds to finish with, usually eaten around a campfire in the dark desert night.

"Reid!" A tall gentleman with a beard headed across the carpeted floor. "By golly, man, is that you?"

Reid stared a moment trying to place the voice and face. "Cyril? Cyril Melshore?"

"The very one. How are you, Reid? Where the blazes have you been all these years?" The two clasped hands, Reid heartened to see an old friend, one with whom he knew he shared a lot.

"Mainly in Egypt. What about you? The last I heard you'd gone to the Far East."

"Been there and a whole host of other places. Now I'm an old married man, settled in the suburbs." Cyril laughed, a vigorous sound in the hushed lobby. The man looked the picture of health and well-being, his thick reddish hair waving back from a broad forehead, a neatly trimmed beard covering the lower part of his face. "I've become a family man."

"I see." Reid blinked, taken aback for an instant, remembering his friend's penchant for adventure. He shook away the surprise and held out his hand again. "Congratulations."

"Thanks. Listen, have you eaten?"

"No—yes, actually. I've just come from a relative's. I feel I've been fed the whole afternoon."

"Where're you headed then?"

"I was going up to the library."

"Mind if I come along? We have a lot of years to catch up on."

"Of course not." It would be good to talk with Cyril.

The two settled into leather armchairs by an unlit fireplace. A few other gentlemen sat reading newspapers in various corners of the large room.

"I always loved this place. A home away from home."

Reid looked around the book-lined room. "Yes, a fine haven from the rest of London."

Cyril grinned at him. "It does take getting used to once you've lived in the East."

Reid steepled his fingers under his chin. "Let's see…the last time we saw each other, you were heading over to China to clerk in some counting house. As I recall, you were quite anxious to leave Europe."

He chuckled. "Yes, I wanted nothing more than to explore far-off lands. Well, I ended up in Bangkok. I managed a trading house for several years."

A footman walked silently by, turning on the lamps.

"So, I'm here in London cooling my heels for a few weeks at least," Reid summed up after the two had spent a good hour bringing each other up-to-date. "My time isn't completely lost since I'm cataloging this collection left by my great-uncle."

"Sounds like a veritable treasure trove."

"It is an amazing collection."

"I must get over to the British Museum and see what their latest acquisitions are." Cyril's brown eyes twinkled. "You know I live a very staid life now, to work in the City every morning, home every evening."

Reid shook his head, still amazed at the change. "Well, I'd say you led a pretty adventurous life when I knew you. I guess you deserve to enjoy the fruits of your labors."

"Yes, I'm grateful I came back from my travels alive and

in one piece—and with a sizable fortune," Cyril added with a gleam in his eyes. "I had known Sarah growing up. When I saw her again, suddenly I was lost. Didn't stand a chance. I decided then and there it was time to settle down." He gave a satisfied sigh. "A man reaches a certain stage when life is no longer enjoyable if there's no one there to share the journey with." As if realizing how his words sounded, he looked away. "Sorry, old chap. I guess there's been no one since…"

"No, no one," Reid said quietly.

Cyril nodded. "Hey, did I tell you about the time I was chased down by a tiger in the jungles of Siam? Caught without my rifle!"

Reid listened as Cyril went on with another story. This time he found his mind wandering, feeling as if the two were a couple of schoolboys trading exploits just to feel good about themselves.

"You say you're living in the suburbs now?" Reid asked more out of politeness than any real desire to know. Suddenly he felt the full fatigue of a day spent making small talk.

"Yes, in Ealing. It's a pretty area. I take the train into Paddington every day. You should come out and visit us. We have a small villa, very comfortable."

"I'm not in London for very long. I'll be heading up to Scotland next week."

Cyril showed interest in that, and the two began talking about trout fishing.

After his friend left for the train station, Reid sat awhile longer in the library. He tried reading the paper, but found himself going over his conversation with Cyril. He shook his head, still amazed at the idea of his old friend a satisfied husband living in the suburbs.

In less than a month Reid would turn forty. He thought of the acquaintances he'd already lost. The rest seemed to be enjoying a comfortable middle age surrounded by family. He stretched out his legs before him, his gaze unseeing on the dark empty grate of the elegant carved-oak fireplace. He stroked his mustache absently. How much longer would he have? Would he, too, catch some fever on his return to Egypt or the Sinai and disappear into the tapestry of his generation?

He rose and stretched, shaking off the gloomy thoughts. He'd get an early night and hopefully be in better shape to accomplish some work in the morning. He remembered his aunt's surprising announcement this afternoon and wondered why she'd changed her mind about Scotland. He shook his head and smiled. Who could fathom the mind of a woman?

He went up to his room and turned up the gaslight. Everything looked neat, the bed made, his pile of books stacked on the bedside table. Oil portraits of past club members stared down at him from their shadowy positions along the damask walls.

He took off his jacket and hung it on the back of a chair then loosened his tie. He poured himself a glass of soda water, brought up earlier by a waiter who knew his habits. He riffled through the envelopes left for him on a silver tray. An invitation from Cecily Mason for a garden party in Chelsea. His aunt seemed determined to throw him in the company of women she deemed suitable for a lonely bachelor.

Reid donned the light cotton pajama pants favored in the Orient for daytime wear. He had grown to prefer the loose cotton trousers with their drawstring waist for sleeping to a nightshirt. He wound his clock and set it. Then he picked up his wife's photograph.

He kissed the framed photo as he did each night. "Good night, my dear." Octavia had been a beautiful woman. It was his favorite picture of her. It had been taken when she was twenty-eight, a year before she died. They had been at a party in London and a renowned photographer had been in attendance. So taken with her beauty, he'd asked her to sit for him and hadn't even wanted to charge a fee.

Octavia had agreed to the picture, saying she wanted Reid to remember her just like that. Her rich dark hair was worn high on her head. Her deep-set dark eyes looked back at him in that understanding way she had. How little the two of them realized her words would prove so prophetic. He rubbed the polished ebony frame.

She'd been his faithful companion for the past decade. Wherever he'd traveled, from India to Egypt, she'd been there every night to bid him good-night at day's end. "Good night, my love," he repeated, setting down the picture. She was his first and last love. And if he could offer her nothing more, he offered her his undying fidelity. It was the least he could do.

Chapter Seven

Maddie stood beside Reid in the library surveying their work of the past few weeks. Every surface was covered in bits of pottery, statuettes and bas-relief fragments. Sheets were spread on the floor and artifacts placed in neat arrangements on them.

Reid had managed to translate several fragments of hieroglyphics. She still marveled at the ease with which he uncovered the meaning of those strange figures on so many surfaces.

He was pointing to a piece of frieze now, his handsome features tilted in concentration.

"This shows Seti I paying homage to the god Ra. He's bringing him offerings of fruit and cattle after a victory in battle. Here he is seated on his throne, receiving homage from his own people."

Maddie studied the stylized figures, stiff and primitive. Reid had taught her to appreciate the beauty in the simple lines.

"So much idolatry." She traced an outline of the god-king.

"They had to worship something."

"But they had the truth so near."

"Moses?"

She nodded.

"It's easy to ignore the truth when it doesn't suit."

Was he being personal or speaking in that detached manner he employed when analyzing artifacts?

"It's amazing how God sent Joseph and Mary with the infant Jesus to Egypt into hiding. I wonder where they lived along the Nile," she mused, looking at the large diagram Mr. Gallagher had drawn and she'd helped fill in each time they'd identified a location from his uncle's treasures. The long river wound its way from the delta where the Port of Alexandria was located, past Cairo and the Giza pyramids then down along several other locations of temples and pyramid ruins until it arrived at Karnak and Luxor.

"There's a small basilica in Cairo dating back to the fourth century where they allegedly came for a short period."

Maddie looked at him in wonder. "Is that so?"

"Tradition has it so. If hiding was their main intention, they'd probably stick to one of the more populated areas." He shrugged. "But we'll probably never know."

She smiled. "Don't you think an archaeologist may someday discover something?"

"It's hard to say. The humbler a person's station, the more anonymous what he leaves behind. The Egyptian pharaohs made sure their names were carved everywhere. A fragment of a poor man's clay pot could have belonged to anyone."

She nodded.

They continued working in silence several more moments. Maddie at her end of the room, copying in a fine, neat hand Mr. Gallagher's notes about each identified object.

Mr. Gallagher hunched over his end of the table, studying the hieroglyphics on a vase and jotting down notes.

When she rose, Mr. Gallagher looked up. "Is it noon already?"

"Nearly. I've gotten to the end of this section." She showed him her morning's work.

"Good." He tapped his pencil against the tabletop. "Has my aunt told you we're to leave for Scotland on Monday?"

"Yes. Her mind is quite occupied with the arrangements."

"I told Aunt Millicent she needn't worry too much. My friend's house is fully staffed."

She smiled. "I think your aunt plans to take anything including bed linens and tablecloths she feels might not meet her standards."

"I'm hoping the weather holds so I can spend most of the time out of doors. Make sure you bring warm enough clothes. It's always cooler and damper up there."

"Yes, I'll be sure to, thank you."

"I used to go up to Scotland quite frequently when I lived in England, though usually only as far as the Lowlands." He glanced toward the row of windows. "Octavia's family had a place near the border along the River Tweed."

"Octavia was your…wife?" she asked.

"Yes." He said no more, his head bent over his notes again.

Maddie couldn't help adding, "You still wear your ring."

The only sign that he'd heard her was that his pencil stopped in midmotion.

"That's because I'm still married to her." The words were matter-of-fact, yet they made Maddie feel like a child who'd spoken out of turn.

Feeling chastened, she bowed her head and left the room, closing the door softly behind her. When she was alone, she took a deep breath, leaning against the solid door of the library. What had she been thinking to ask such a personal question of her employer? It had been the first time he'd talked about his late wife. But his closed expression and his clipped words showed her he did not welcome any conversation about her.

As she walked down the corridor, she remembered his tone of voice. *That's because I'm still married to her.* He spoke in the present tense. Hadn't he been widowed at least a decade?

What devotion. She'd rarely, if ever, seen it in a man. His wife must have been very special. Maddie tamped down her own feelings. Mr. Gallagher was her employer, nothing more.

As she entered the parlor, she saw Mr. Gallagher's sister sitting there conversing with Lady Haversham. Mrs. Walker leaned forward. "You saw him yourself. Poor Cecily was doing everything she knew to be entertaining, but it was as if she was talking to one of those stone tables Reid spends hours poring over. I was distressed for her."

Maddie moved as quietly as possible to take her usual place, trying not to listen to the conversation but unable to shut it out. She picked up her needlework, focusing on the stitches before her. But the more the ladies spoke, the more she resented hearing anyone, even his closest kin, discussing Mr. Gallagher's personal life.

She pulled her silk thread through another hole, her mind conjuring up the late Mrs. Gallagher, a woman no doubt fine not only in feature but also in temperament, a woman noble of soul. She'd have been sweet tempered—

"Well, then, why don't you come along with us to Scotland?" Lady Haversham's voice broke into Maddie's thoughts, bringing them to an abrupt halt. Her glance shot to Mrs. Walker.

"Me?" Lady Haversham's niece looked taken aback. "Why, I'd never considered it…."

Lady Haversham clasped her hands together on her lap. "Think of it now, my dear. Why, it's just the thing. The children will benefit from the good mountain air, you can organize our activities and see to it that Reid doesn't spend all his time in the library."

"Yes…" She nodded slowly, listening to her aunt's arguments.

Maddie's heart sank. She bent more closely over her needlepoint, trying to shut out her thoughts. She had no business thinking of Mr. Gallagher at all—not as anything more than her part-time employer. If he should be there during their holiday, what better than to have his sister and her children along? He got to see them so little.

"Maybe I could invite Cecily up for a few days," Mrs. Walker mused.

Maddie's mood plummeted even further.

"That's a wonderful idea. I hear from Reid it's a large estate."

"Yes, I shall talk to her about it and see if she can manage to get away from London for a few days," Mrs. Walker continued with a brisk nod, satisfied that she had hit upon a wonderful solution. "She's such a busy lady with her various charities."

Maddie tried to blot out the image of Mr. Gallagher with Mrs. Mason…visiting, hunting, riding…

She pricked herself with her needle and started. Goodness, she was going to ruin this seat cover if she wasn't careful. Taking herself sternly to task, she set another stitch, but already her excitement over the upcoming holiday was severely dampened.

Without her work on the artifacts, there would be no reason for her to be in Mr. Gallagher's company. Would she see him at all?

The trip she'd been so looking forward to now only seemed another extension of her dull days in London.

Chapter Eight

Her fears began proving true as soon as they left for Scotland. During the overnight train trip, Maddie hardly saw Mr. Gallagher. After settling them in their private compartment, he left them, presumably to sit in the smoking car in the company of men.

She could hardly blame him, as she had to endure the restlessness and noise of three young children, the chatter of the women and the yap of an excited terrier. Thankfully, with the services of a new nursemaid, Maddie was not responsible for the well-being of Mrs. Walker's offspring.

Maddie admired the sturdy young woman who seemed unfazed by the children's boisterousness. Just when the noise of the children threatened to upset Lady Haversham, Mr. Gallagher reappeared and took them off to tour the train, the nursemaid bustling along after them. Maddie tried to stifle the feeling of abandonment. She couldn't help remembering her time in the square with Mr. Gallagher and the children, when he'd been her champion.

Early the next morning, they arrived in Edinburgh's bustling station to take a local line to Stirling and from there to Aberfeldy. Amidst a bath chair for Lady Haversham, porters' carts piled high with their luggage, Maddie carrying Lilah in her basket, the nursemaid herding the awestruck children, it was a miracle they all made it in one piece to their next stop. The last leg of the journey was completed in two hired coaches to the village of Kenmore.

Maddie drew in her breath at the countryside. Kenmore was situated at one end of Loch Tay. The long lake reflected the pristine blue of the clear sky. Tree-covered hills rose above it, the outline of a higher mountain ridge behind it. Their coaches crossed the bridge over the River Tay, leaving the small village, and continuing along a dirt track through the forest. On one side, she caught glimpses of the lake as the road climbed higher up the hillside.

Suddenly the carriage entered a clearing and Maddie couldn't help but gasp. It was like a fairy-tale setting. A large, gray stone turreted structure like a miniature castle stood half-hidden against the heavily forested hills. Far below them lay Loch Tay. Puffs of white cloud floated against the trees, offering a magical aspect to the scene, as if they were halfway to the heavens.

Maddie had little time to admire the setting. As soon as she descended from the carriage, her attention was taken up with Lilah. She secured the yapping dog to her leash. "I know you want to run about, dearie, but we mustn't lose you," she murmured to the squirming animal in soothing tones.

Lady Haversham motioned to her from the chair being pushed along by a footman. "Be careful of Lilah. I feel a distinct chill in the air. I don't want her catching cold."

Maddie bent down to adjust the collar before the dog wriggled away. "She won't. I'm sure the fresh air is good for her."

She looked around for Mr. Gallagher, but she saw he was occupied with the footmen with the cases and trunks.

"Maddie, I feel faint." Lady Haversham leaned against her chair, the back of her hand to her forehead.

Maddie pulled on the leash and hurried to her employer's side. "Just hold a moment longer, my lady. We'll soon have you settled in your room."

The next hour was filled with confusion as each one of the carriage's occupants demanded the attention of the awaiting servants. Maddie admired the housekeeper's calm manner in directing the guests to their rooms. The children and their nursemaid were dispatched to the nursery, with instructions for porridge to be sent up for their supper.

Maddie sat with Lady Haversham over her supper tray and then read to her. By the time she came downstairs, everything was once again quiet. She wandered down the wide curved stairway lined with stuffed animal heads, to the spacious flagstone foyer below. As she passed one door, she heard a murmur of voices behind it. She quickened her pace away from it.

She opened the heavy front door and shivered at the drop in temperature. The early June sky was still light…the gloaming, the Scots called it. The horizon was tinged lavender. She tightened her shawl around her shoulders and ventured onto the gravel walk.

She breathed deeply of the evening air, feeling with each breath that her very lungs were being cleansed of the polluted London air, where tiny black particles dusted every surface. She reached a stone balustrade, which fronted the house, and marveled at the view of the lake far below. She didn't know how long she stood gazing at it when she smelled cigar smoke.

"Silence is indeed golden."

She turned to see Mr. Gallagher crossing the space separating them. Her heartbeat quickened with each step. He had changed out of his traveling clothes and wore a tweed Norfolk jacket. The slight breeze ruffled his thick blond hair.

"I didn't know anyone was out here," she said, afraid of intruding on his own quiet time, while longing to draw closer to this solitary man.

"It's a large enough space and I know you are not a chatterbox." Humor laced his low voice, as he turned to tap the cigar against the stone balustrade.

She clasped her hands in front of her, falling silent, not wanting to do anything to make him wish her gone.

"I'm glad to see you survived the journey." His blue eyes swept over her.

"Survived? Oh—yes, thank you." She brushed back a tendril of hair.

He cleared his throat and looked away, as if aware he'd been staring. "I'm sorry I took the coward's way out and made myself scarce most of the time. I figured you were well looked after with the legion of servants at our disposal."

She swallowed, reminding herself she was one of those servants. "You were very good with the children."

He shrugged and looked over the landscape. "As you said, they aren't bad children, just high-spirited, as is natural, and a trifle overindulged. Vera seems to have found them a good nurse."

"Yes, she struck me as very able."

He leaned his elbows against the wide balustrade. "She seems to know all their tricks and refuses to fall for any of them."

Maddie looked down, remembering her own ineptitude. "Yes."

He turned to her. "I didn't mean to imply you were any less capable with them."

Her glance met his. His perceptiveness was uncanny. How could he have sensed how incompetent she felt?

"You're not used to being around children, and you had the added disadvantage of having to answer to both my sister and aunt."

She blinked away the tears that threatened, realizing how long it had been since she'd experienced such thoughtfulness. "You're not used to children, either."

"No, but I can give my sister a hard time about her unruly children." His mouth tugged upward and she couldn't help smiling back.

Maddie said nothing more, too affected by the man's sensitivity. What did he care what she felt?

He flung the cigar down and crushed it out. "Excuse the smoke. I rarely indulge but it has been a trying day," he said.

She gave a look around her. "It's a beautiful spot. Thank you so much for including me in the invitation."

He shrugged. "I thought you could use a change of scenery. Tomorrow I'll show you some of the landmarks." He pointed to the west where the sun was beginning its slow descent behind the mountains beyond the loch. "See the peaks?"

"Yes."

"The highest is Ben Lawers. It's almost four thousand feet."

"It's majestic."

"I've always wanted to climb it."

She looked at him curiously. "Why?"

He turned to her. "Why not?" He smiled, a smile that began in his blue eyes and slowly reached his lips. "Think of the view from the summit. On the other side of the range lies

Glen Lyon, which I'm told is one of the loveliest glens in all the Highlands."

"It sounds spectacular." She was no longer looking at the mountains but at Mr. Gallagher's profile. He was a man of action, she saw, like her brothers, and her parents before them. While she was…what? What did she have to show for her life?

"Wouldn't you like to climb it, too?" His eyes met hers once more.

She? Her gaze traveled up the mountain's fluted silhouette and over the lower peaks beside it. They were massive, dwarfing the scenery below. "Yes," she found herself breathing, hardly aware of what she was saying. "Has any woman ever climbed it?"

"I don't know. I don't imagine so, but what does that matter? You could be the first." There was a challenge in his blue eyes.

She continued looking at the mountain range. He never seemed fazed by the idea of a woman accomplishing anything. It must be the influence of his unconventional mother. She wondered what his wife had been like. Had she been just as remarkable?

She drew in a lungful of the sharp air. "The thought is appealing, I'll admit."

"Think about it, Miss Norton."

She said nothing more, hardly capable of imagining herself scaling that peak.

He yawned. "I think I'll head in and make it an early night."

"It has been a tiring day."

"Are you coming in?"

"I'll be along in a minute," she replied.

"All right, take your time. You've earned some peace and

quiet." He tapped the stone balustrade with a fist before finally moving away. "Well…good night."

"Good night." She watched his silhouette until he'd disappeared through the door, feeling a pang that she couldn't have thought of something more interesting to say to hold him a moment longer. Was he disappointed in her response to climbing Ben Lawers? If he could only see how her soul had soared within her at his suggestion.

With a sigh she turned back to the mountains. The pink-and-lavender tinge along the horizon was deepening as the sun fell below the highest peaks. Down below, the loch looked a silvery lavender.

Thank you, Lord, for bringing me here. "You know my downsitting and my uprising," she quoted from the psalm *You knew this was just the place I needed to come.* Her glance strayed back to the Ben Lawers. Who knew? Maybe someday she would scale its summit. She smiled at the remarkable thought.

Maddie didn't see Mr. Gallagher at all the next day until dinnertime. He entered the great room where the rest of the family had already assembled and glanced about. As soon as he spotted her in one of the far recesses, he smiled.

He looked rested and refreshed, and she felt a twinge of envy at his freedom to be out and about enjoying the hills and dales, while she'd been cooped up most of the day. It wasn't that she'd had so much to do. Lady Haversham had spent most of her time with her niece, so Maddie felt at loose ends more than anything. Even her duty of walking Lilah had been co-opted by the children, under the watchful supervision of their nursemaid. When Lady Haversham had discovered that the young woman had grown up on a farm with dogs, she'd entrusted her precious pet to her.

Before Mr. Gallagher could make a move toward Maddie, Vera approached him with a drink. "Where have you been the whole day, while we've been sitting around trying to amuse ourselves?"

He rubbed his hands together before the massive stone fireplace, his cheeks ruddy from the outdoors.

"Exploring the region. I talked with the local gillie and found out the best salmon beats along the river and where to hire a boat to fish on the loch. I also scouted around a bit and discovered some good walking trails on the property."

Vera frowned. "I hope you discovered some local families, as well. I don't mean to spend all my time in my own company."

He took a sip of the amber liquid. "I thought I'd leave that part of the exploration in your capable hands, Vera. There's a good brougham and wonderful stables. You can ride into Kenmore or farther afield to Aberfeldy and make the rounds."

His sister's lips firmed in a distasteful line. "You are impossible. You expect me to leave my calling cards without your lifting a finger to help."

He grinned. "That's right, my dear. I'm here to enjoy the river and loch."

"I hope you don't mean to become a hermit. I expect you to accompany us on a few of those visits."

"As long as it's only a few. I don't mind talking with some of the local anglers." He turned to Maddie. "Do you fish?"

"Does she fish?" Lady Haversham spoke up for her. "What kind of a question is that for a lady's companion? Of course she doesn't fish. I hope you don't plan to spend all your time at the river."

"No, Aunt Millicent, I propose to rise early and spend the mornings there."

Once again, Maddie had to swallow her disappointment that she couldn't share a moment with Mr. Gallagher.

As they were walking into dinner, however, he approached her. His eyes narrowed as he studied her face. "You look pale. Didn't you get outside today?" His tone was stern.

"No." Was he angry with her?

His frown deepened. "Did my aunt keep you too busy?"

"Not at all. I just didn't want to stray too far in case she might need me."

"I never did hear whether you fished or not."

"I used to…with my brothers." She was taken aback by the quick switch in topic. "That was a long time ago and in a little mud hole near home, so I don't know if that qualifies."

"You'll find it a bit more challenging here. The area has the best salmon fishing of any in Britain. If you'd care to have a go, I'll be leaving at sunrise, if that's not too early for you."

She stared at him. He was inviting her to go along with him. "No, it's not too early."

"In that case, you can meet me at the front door. Don't worry about breakfast. I'll have the cook prepare us some sandwiches." He glanced toward his aunt as they entered the oak-paneled dining room. "And don't worry about Aunt Millicent. We'll most likely be back long before she's up."

She nodded her head, again grateful that he seemed to know her concerns without her having to voice them.

She found it hard to swallow at dinner and every once in a while took a surreptitious glance Mr. Gallagher's way. He had singled her out and invited her fishing. She knew from her brothers and father that fishing was not a social activity. Those passionate about the sport enjoyed the peace and quiet of it. It would be no more than working alongside Mr. Gallagher in the library. Yet, she knew from those moments the sense of companionableness she'd experienced with him.

Why had he invited her along? She couldn't fathom an answer.

* * *

Maddie woke to the shrill sound of birdsong. A second later she remembered Mr. Gallagher's invitation. Was she too late? She breathed a sigh of relief when she read the clock face. It was just past four.

The sky was still dark, although a pale tinge along one horizon signaled that daylight was not far off. Maddie closed her casement window and hurried to dress.

Hoping he hadn't left without her, Maddie walked softly down the stairs toward the front door. Mr. Gallagher was already there, looking properly like a country gentleman in his tweed jacket and trousers tucked into high leather boots.

"Good morning, I hope I haven't kept you waiting."

"No." He eyed her gown with a frown and she bit her lip, wondering what was wrong with her old black serge skirt and bodice. She pulled her knitted shawl more tightly around her shoulders.

"Let me see your shoes."

Beginning to worry, she lifted the hem of her skirt just enough to reveal her low walking boots.

"What you really need is a pair of Wellingtons." He gave her skirt another critical glance. "You won't be able to do any wading in that. Why women's dress has to be so impractical is beyond me," he muttered. "Here, this might keep you warmer." He handed her a folded woolen square.

"Oh!" She took the tartan shawl. "Thank you."

"Wrap it around yourself like the local women do. It'll keep off the morning chill."

She discarded her own smaller shawl and did as he suggested. She felt immediately cozier.

"Let's see if we can find you a pair of better footwear in here." He led her to a small room that held an assortment of cloaks, mackintoshes and umbrellas. A row of boots was ranged along a low shelf. He inspected one pair of boots, then another, glancing at her feet as he did so. He finally approached her holding a black pair in one hand. "Here, try these, they're the new rubberized Wellingtons."

She sat on a bench under a rack of coats along one wall and bent to unbutton one of her boots. Her fingers fumbled in the dark, aware of his gaze on her. He was probably regretting having to wait for her.

"Let me." Before she knew what he was about, he crouched down in front of her and gently moved her hands out of the way. "Your fingers feel like ice," he said, his own nimbly undoing the row of buttons. The next second he slipped her boot off, his fingertips gently brushing her heel. "All right, let's see how this fits." He held out the knee-length boot and she grasped it by the top edges and pulled it on.

She wiggled her toes in the space in front.

"It seems fine."

"Good. Now for the next one." This time, without asking her permission, he took her other foot in his large hand and undid the top button. In a few seconds, he had that one off, as well, and was holding out the second boot. Maddie was glad of the dark, afraid he'd see how ruffled the contact left her.

"Well, at least they should keep you from getting pneumonia," he said, looking down at her feet. "If we could do something about those long skirts, you would be in fine shape to wade. Have you ever worn a pair of those bloomers?"

Her eyes widened at the mention of the controversial female garment. Only suffragettes and sporty women wore the wide, knickerbocker-like garment, to the scandal of respectable females. "No."

"Pity. Well, come along then, the morning's advancing."

He picked up a collection of long rods and baskets he'd left by the door. She offered to carry one of the baskets.

She had no time to do more than take a deep breath of the cool morning air before he was disappearing down the drive. She hurried after his long strides, the memory of his gentle hands touching her feet lingering in her mind.

He glanced over his shoulder. "Do you mind a bit of a walk?"

"No. I'm used to walking."

"Good. We'll head toward one of the pools on the river this morning," he said, his tone clipped from his stride. "It's one of the gentler areas. It's said even a lady in long skirts might fish it without having to wade." He waited for her to catch up and held a branch to one side to allow her passage.

The vegetation around them was wet as if it had rained in the night, although she hadn't heard anything. More likely just the mist Scotland was known for. The air smelled of earth and leaf mold and green vegetation. Swirls of white mist drifted upon the trees and over the lake below them. All around them birds lifted up a cacophony of sound as if impatient for the day to get under way.

After about a mile of walking, they reached the village of Kenmore and heard the rapids at the head of the River Tay. The sounds of rushing water drowned out the birdsong. They bypassed the village and continued along a narrow track along the river, which flattened and widened as it meandered through the forest.

A short walk along the north bank took them away from all signs of civilization. When they reached a bend in the river, Mr. Gallagher stopped.

He set everything down on the damp grass and she followed suit with her basket. "We'll try this pool today. The gillie tells me the salmon are running. There are also plenty of trout and grayling. Have you ever fly-fished?" He glanced up at her from where he squatted by an open basket.

She shook her head.

He held up a feathery object. "These lures mimic the insects the trout and salmon are accustomed to feeding on in these waters."

Maddie peered over his shoulder at a colorful array of feather-clad hooks. "How pretty."

He held one out to her and she took it. It was an intricate design of feathers tied around a hook. "Mayflies, dragonflies, stone flies, midges, take your pick," he said, turning to survey the river. He was quiet a long time and Maddie knew better than to speak. Too much commotion would scare the fish away.

He inspected the flies again. "I think…a nymph for you." He selected one of the smaller hooks and picked up one of the rods from the grass.

She crouched beside him and watched as he attached the fly to the line. "The trick is to tie one of these flies to this thin line called the leader, which then attaches to the heavier line." As he spoke, he demonstrated what he was saying, amazing her with how deftly his fingers managed to tie a knot in the thin filament. She thought once again of his fingers undoing the small buttons on her boots.

He proceeded to select a fly for his own rod and secure it to the line. As he prepared his own rod, she stood quietly, enjoying the break of day. "Bless the Lord, oh my soul, and all that is within me, bless His holy name," she recited to herself. Suddenly she felt freer than she had in a long time.

He stood and motioned for her to follow him to the edge of the bank. "The next thing is to learn how to cast." He pointed forward. "See the insects hovering on the surface?"

She nodded, seeing the dancing insects above the dark waters in the pale light.

"You want to emulate them. Watch." He set his own rod down and took hers from her. "Instead of flicking your wrist as you normally would, you need to use a longer, slower movement in order to get the line to go in a wide arc into the water. Unlike a lure, the fly won't offer any weight to aid you, only the line."

His arm arched behind him then moved forward in a long, smooth curve. Unaware she held her breath, she watched the line flow out in a smooth curve and land halfway out in the river, upstream from them. She let out her breath, scarcely making out the fly on the barely rippling river surface. Then it floated with the current downstream. A moment later, there appeared a tug on the line.

"Yes…" She glanced at Mr. Gallagher, detecting the slight smile playing beneath his mustache. "Now, to make sure he's well secured on the hook." His wrist barely moved as his other hand came up to switch hands on the rod. He used his right hand to play the line in. In a few moments he had reeled in a good-size speckled trout. Handing the rod to Miss Norton, he waded in to land it in a net.

He hefted it in his hand. "Half a stone, perhaps a bit lighter."

She beamed at him, enjoying his satisfaction. "Wonderful."

After depositing the fish in the creel, he came back to her. "All right, now it's your turn."

She gave a nervous laugh. "You make it look so easy. I'm sure it's not."

"It's not as complicated as it might seem if I try to explain it to you. It's best you just try it and then keep on practicing it." He handed her the rod and stood away from her.

She could feel herself grow nervous under his observation.

Her first attempt landed the line somewhere close to the bank. She turned to him shamefaced. "It doesn't go where I want."

He approached her. "That's because there's no real weight on the end. Here, let me guide you through it." The next thing she knew, he stood just behind her, his hand covering hers. She couldn't breathe, feeling the length of his strong arm against hers. His other hand held her gently by the opposite shoulder. Before she could react, she felt him take her hand and the rod it held and move it swiftly up and behind, then forward. She watched, openmouthed, as the line made its wide arc far above the water and land.

"Not perfect, but you get the general idea." Mr. Gallagher's voice sounded somewhere above her head.

He let her go and stepped away from her. He cleared his throat. "Keep an eye on the fly. Let it drift with the current. If nothing happens in a bit, take it up and cast it once again."

She was too overwrought to hear much of what he said, much less follow his instructions. She blindly moved her wrist, but that only jerked the line.

"Easy there or you'll scare the fish." He took the rod from her and reeled in the line. Then he guided her through the casting just as before. "Let gravity do its work once you let it go."

She nodded, hardly knowing what he meant.

He stepped away from her and watched her do it on her own. "That's better. All it takes is a little practice. I'm going to move a little farther upstream but within sight. Just call me if you need any help."

She nodded, feeling half-relieved that his too-observant eyes would be away from her, and extremely sorry to lose his closeness.

Reid selected a spot about twenty-five feet away from Miss Norton. He knew he liked to master something without someone hovering over him. From where he stood, he could easily watch her if she got in trouble, but still remain far enough removed to give her a sense of solitary peace.

He tried to dismiss the sensation of holding her while guiding her through the fly casting, yet, like the mysteries the artifacts he dug up produced, it teased him, compelling him onward to discover more thoroughly the reason for its origin.

The feel of her smaller hand in his, his larger frame so close behind her had been... He searched for a word to describe what he'd felt. *Unsettling* came to mind. He still felt unsettled.

He realized he hadn't held a woman in a very long time. The rare times he'd come home he gave his great-aunt and sister a mere peck on the cheek and moved away from them.

He waded out a bit and cast his line, determined to shake off the memory. It was merely the strangeness of it. Unsettling, he repeated to himself for the third time before relegating the word and sensation to the outskirts of his mind, like an unsolvable but insignificant mystery.

He felt a tug on his line and, with relief, concentrated on the fish caught by his hook. It was hardly a challenge, but it was satisfying. The fish were biting and they were plentiful.

After landing a few more trout, he began to feel the kind of calm that he hadn't experienced since arriving in England, the kind that came only with solitude, the kind he was used to in the desert. He gazed around him. The morning was glorious. Light and shadow began to dapple the area as the sun rose above the trees.

He felt a sense of satisfaction that he had accomplished what he'd set out to do with this trip to the Highlands. He had Miss Norton away from the stuffy atmosphere that surrounded his aunt. He hadn't liked the pale look of her last evening. He wouldn't have this trip be in vain even if he had to personally escort Miss Norton on a daily fishing or hiking excursion.

The notion wasn't in any way displeasing, the more it lingered in his mind. For one so used to being in the company of men, the thought of her presence was at once peaceful and gentle.

In a short time Reid had caught half a dozen respectable trout. He removed the hook from his last trout and placed the fish in the creel when he heard Miss Norton shout. His gaze flew to her and he saw her body jerk forward.

He dropped everything and sprinted toward her. She must have hooked a good-size salmon for that kind of force on her line.

"Mr. Gallagher! I think I've caught something!"

A few seconds later he was at her side. Seeing her in danger of being dragged off the edge of the bank, he didn't think but wrapped his arms around her and grasped the rod with her.

For the next several moments the two fought the fish. "Keep a firm hold, play out some line." His voice remained calm, even as he gripped the rod.

He loosened his hold a fraction to allow her to land the fish herself, but no sooner had he slackened his grip that she jerked forward again. "Help!" she called out.

His hands tightened once more on the rod.

Even as his rational mind remained cool, using his experience and knowledge to land the fish, another part of him felt ripped apart. This time it was no slight touch, but the greater impact of Miss Norton fully in his arms.

His senses felt bombarded with light and sound and color—the feel of Miss Norton's shoulders against his chest, the splash of the fish as it surfaced and receded again, the tug of the line, the sheen of the water now that the sun's rays had hit it, awakening its dark depths just as his own senses were being forced awake.

"He's a big one," he murmured. "And strong." Miraculously his voice came out sounding steady and normal, and not as if he were being punched in the gut, knocked in the head, inundated with a sweet taste in his mouth, a roaring in his ears, light and sound exploding in him like a rocket launched in the desert night.

Miss Norton's straw hat fell off and his chin bumped into her soft hair, its feminine fragrance hitting his nostrils like a potent elixir spreading to every particle of his being.

Oof! Her body hit his and he absorbed the impact, his arms involuntary tightening around her. He felt chilled and burned wherever his body touched hers. Dear heavens, what was happening to him?

Maddie fought the sensations assailing her even as Mr. Gallagher and she fought the salmon. They pitted their strength against it for several more minutes, and then as suddenly as it had begun, it was over. The fish, spent from its valiant struggle, was reeled in and trapped in a net. Mr. Gallagher didn't look at her, his attention fixed on the salmon, his fingers deftly removing the hook.

"It's beautiful," she said, her voice coming out breathless as she leaned over him.

"Yes." He took the fish up in his hands. "I'm surprised it didn't break your line. It looks a good two stone. Congratulations."

For a second their gazes locked, hers lost in his deep blue one. "I—we both caught it," she managed.

"He was on your line. He's yours."

She chuckled, the sound nervous to her ears. "Beginner's luck?"

He looked away from her. "Whatever you want to call it, it's still your catch." He rose and placed the fish into the creel. "How about some breakfast?"

"All right." She set down the fishing rod as he fetched the hamper, and she wondered if he was as intent on finding a task as she was. Did he feel as self-conscious as she did after the moments they'd just experienced? Now, it hardly seemed real. Had she actually been held tightly in his arms?

He laid out their simple breakfast of oatcakes and a flask of tea. She watched him furtively as she spread a plain linen cloth on her lap and received the oatcake he handed her.

He began to raise the food to his mouth, but froze in mid-movement when she bowed her head. "Dear Lord," she said, "We thank you for this beautiful morning, the bountiful fishing and for this meal we are about to partake of. Please bless it, in Jesus's name."

"Amen," he repeated with her.

She bit into the cold oatcake, its hearty texture satisfying. As the two sat silently eating their breakfast, she replayed in her mind the feel of his strong arms around her. It had been more than the physical wonder of the contact. As she remembered the moments, she thought how wonderfully protected and how bound to this man she'd felt.

As the sensations receded, they were replaced by the quiet companionability of two souls in harmony. She sighed, glancing sidelong at Mr. Gallagher. How long would this interlude last?

How would she survive its end?

Chapter Nine

Try as he would, Reid couldn't get the memory of Miss Norton in his arms out of his mind. Almost every morning the two went fishing together, but no other opportunity presented itself in that realm. Miss Norton proved an apt pupil and was soon almost as competent as he with rod and reel.

He'd never had a female as a fishing companion and found her all that he could wish for in an angling partner. Together the two would return with a laden creel, well satisfied with their catch, knowing they would enjoy the fresh trout and salmon for dinner. Without any conscious consent, neither mentioned Miss Norton's participation in the fishing. His aunt and sister assumed the catch was solely his and the local gillie's. He didn't enlighten them and was glad Miss Norton kept silent, as well.

It wasn't in his nature to deceive. Yet, he sensed his aunt wouldn't approve of Miss Norton's having some recreation time to herself. He observed how demanding his aunt was whenever Miss Norton was with her.

Thankfully, his aunt depended more on Vera now, and the two spent a good part of the afternoon in the carriage making calls on the neighboring lairds. Reid avoided these calls as much as he could. Whenever he managed to remain behind, he usually invited Miss Norton on a hike. The hills behind the manor beckoned, and he told himself he was doing his own Christian duty by making sure Miss Norton got a real holiday.

He found himself wondering at the oddest moments of the day—reading a fishing journal or a volume from the library shelves, staring out on a misty yard, taking tea with his aunt—what it would feel like to have his arms about Miss Norton again.

Would it be as shocking to his senses? Or would the familiarity of being with her almost every day diminish the impact? The only sensation he could liken it to was the keen anticipation he experienced at the beginning of an archaeological dig, when the promise of uncovering some long-buried pottery of an ancient civilization faced him, but that excitement appeared monochromatic in comparison to what he was feeling now.

After Octavia had died, he'd never thought to experience these kinds of feelings for any woman. Perhaps that's why he'd avoided the company of women and buried his needs as deep as any ancient treasure.

But now he'd stare into space, his thumb and forefinger smoothing down his mustache, reliving the moment he'd held Miss Norton, until someone's voice would bring him back to the present and he'd start, and blurt out something about the weather.

It was during a rainy afternoon as he sat in a warm parlor, the peat fire glowing in the huge stone hearth, his aunt and sister entertaining a local gentlewoman and her daughter that he hit upon a perfect solution to his dilemma.

In a lull in the conversation, he ventured, "Do you ever hold any dances here locally?"

His aunt and sister stared at him as if he'd just asked if it snowed on the moon. Mrs. Campbell, their visitor, turned to him with delight. "We haven't had one in an age, but we do so love a dance, don't we, Priscilla?" She turned to her daughter, who had been silent until that moment.

The young lady blushed and nodded. "Oh, yes, Mama."

Reid's gaze drifted to Miss Norton who sat by a window embrasure, working on her embroidery as usual. She hadn't looked up during the exchange, and he wondered if she forswore dancing as some of the stricter evangelicals did. The dance plans would be for naught if that were the case. He braced himself and continued on, feeling like a plodder in the fine desert sand.

"We have a nice-size drawing room here." He consulted his aunt. "It would serve for a dance floor. What do you think?"

"I—well, I hadn't thought about it, but..." She turned to Vera. "What do you think, dear?"

Reid's sister clapped her hands together. "A dance is just the thing. There are some ever so agreeable families in the valley. I could write to Cecily, as well, and ask her to come up for the weekend. Theo could accompany her."

Aunt Millicent nodded her approval. "That's a wonderful idea. Now when should we hold this dance? Mrs. Campbell, you must help me draw up a list of the local lairds and their families to invite."

The women grew more animated in their talk. Reid rose, having no interest in the particulars of the dance. If Cecily Mason were to come, it would prove a tedious time. But he was determined to make himself agreeable if it meant an opportunity to hold Miss Norton in his arms once again. Like a scientist designing an experiment, he was single-minded in his effort to replicate the conditions.

He ambled over to the window embrasure and glanced down at Miss Norton's work, some sort of dark red tapestry.

"That's very intricate," he said.

She glanced up at him. "Thank you. It's…it's for a set of chair cushions for my parents."

"I see. Do you dance?"

She raised her head again. "Dance? I…"

He seemed to have taken her unawares. He smiled slightly, feeling suddenly like a nervous schoolboy. "Yes, dance… waltz, polka, quadrille…if my memory serves correctly. It has been some years since I hosted a dance."

Her cheeks were tinged a pretty pink. "It's been some years for me, as well…since I danced."

"I'm told it's one of those skills one doesn't forget."

"I'm…not certain."

The topic seemed to make her uncomfortable. He didn't blame her. It wasn't something he was easy conversing about, either. At least she hadn't said anything disapproving about dancing. He tried another tack. "Do you have any—" how to word it? "—party outfits?" She always dressed quite severely in plain, dark gowns, which was appropriate for a paid companion he supposed, though he thought it a pity, that one of her years and…complexion should have to dress like an elderly widow.

"Party outfits?" She made it sound as if the words were foreign to her.

Before he could explain further, his aunt's shrill voice interrupted them. "What are you two discussing? Reid, I need your help with this guest list."

He turned to the other ladies. "I was just asking Miss Norton if she danced."

"Miss Norton dance?" His sister's horrified laugh irritated

him. "Miss Norton is Aunt Millicent's companion. She isn't paid to dance."

When had Vera become such a snob? "That doesn't mean she can't enjoy an evening's entertainment, does it?"

"Reid, don't be silly." His sister's voice took on that note he recognized whenever she took offense. "Now, come and help us invite some *suitable* guests."

He didn't argue further, knowing it wouldn't do Miss Norton any good. For some reason, he felt she wouldn't approve of his defense of her, either. With a murmured "excuse me," he moved away from her. He'd make sure she felt welcome at the dance, but he wouldn't do anything to draw attention to her.

Maddie sat perfectly still after Mr. Gallagher had moved away, her hands clutching the linen and needle, her head bent low over it. But her heart thudded with deafening rhythm in her chest.

He'd come expressly to ask her if she danced. Her face warmed in chagrin. He'd asked if she had any party dresses. She looked at the faded cloth of her skirt. For a man who didn't seem to take note of the beautifully dressed women around him, he had noticed how unsuitable her garments were for such an occasion.

The only fancy dress she had brought with her was a gown several years old, given to her by her first employer.

Maddie raised her eyes and looked across the room. Mr. Reid sat with the ladies but spoke little. He seemed distracted. Probably thinking how he'd rather be hiking in the hills.

These last few days had been a paradise for her. Fishing trips in the early-morning hours, like being at the dawn of creation, everything untouched, unspoiled. Afternoon hikes through forest and hillside, over moor and meadow to stand far above the world.

She had never known such a wonderful companion. Quiet yet strong, sensitive to her every need, whether to stop and rest, or have a drink of water, or break for lunch. Her mind went back to that first morning when she'd landed the salmon. She'd been so happy to show him he hadn't brought her in vain, that she wouldn't be a millstone around his neck.

Somewhere, tucked deep down where no one and nothing could disturb it, was the memory of his arms around her. Enveloped, protected…cherished… The words rose unbidden.

Of course, she was sure he didn't harbor any of those feelings for her. She could never forget the ring he still wore on his left hand. But deep, where no one was privy to her thoughts, she could dream it was so.

Her feelings sank back down the next moment when she remembered his last question. Did she own something suitable for the dance?

Well, if she were expected to make an appearance at this dance, and if…her glance went once more to Mr. Gallagher…*if* Mr. Gallagher were to notice her, the old faille and crepeline would have to do. She had no alternative. Besides, Mr. Gallagher was used to seeing her in her everyday gowns. He wasn't prone to notice what a woman wore. She thought back to their first morning fishing and the close scrutiny he'd given her then. But that had been for strictly practical reasons.

Maddie sighed and poked her needle into the cloth. She'd best put all thoughts of balls and gowns out of her mind. Likely Lady Haversham—or Mrs. Walker—wouldn't permit her to attend.

The thought brought her no relief.

* * *

Scarcely a week later, Maddie stood at the head of the massive curved stairway in the manor's main hall. She touched the golden fringe along the pull-back drapery of her gown and swallowed. One last glance at the mirror in her room had not reassured her. She hadn't worn such formal attire in years. She brought a hand up to her throat, feeling almost naked.

The gold silk faille with the bronze underskirt in crepeline had been the height of fashion at one time. The low-cut square neckline with its narrow lace frill edging and tight cap sleeves felt inadequate. She wished she had a shawl to drape around her shoulders, but she'd had nothing appropriate.

She heard Lady Haversham from the drawing room. Maddie could hardly swallow from nerves, but knew she must join the family before the guests arrived. *Lord, be with me.* With that prayer, she finished descending the stairs.

The others were already gathered in the drawing room. A fire blazed in the stone fireplace against the cool evening.

"Madeleine, is that you?" Lady Haversham eyed her through a lorgnette. "Good heavens, where on earth did you get that gown?"

Maddie stiffened, crossing her arms as if to cover herself.

"What's wrong, my lady?" she managed with difficulty, feeling everyone's eyes on her. If only Mr. Gallagher didn't have to be among them.

Lady Haversham approached her, still examining her toilette through the glass. "Too many furbelows, for one thing." She walked behind her. "Doesn't suit you. Much too youthful for someone who's on the verge of thirty. You must begin to dress more soberly."

Maddie dearly wished she could sink into the floor beneath her, but the solid oak held firm. Her glance went across the room to Mrs. Walker in her plush burgundy velvet skirt and cream lace underskirt with its large appliquéd flowers in deep crimson. She must be at least Maddie's age, if not older.

Before Maddie could disappear into some corner of the room, Mr. Gallagher approached her and offered her his arm.

"I think she looks charming, Aunt Millicent." He smiled into her eyes, his blue ones offering warmth and support.

Maddie pressed her lips together, afraid they would tremble otherwise.

"Thank you," she said, the sounds coming out in a whisper, before she looked away.

He led her to a side table. "What can I get you to fortify you before this revelry begins?"

"A…a lemonade would be fine," she replied, hardly aware of what she was saying. He looked breathtakingly handsome in his black evening attire.

He stepped away from her and went to the sideboard. She fingered the lace at the edge of her bodice, feeling ridiculous. She touched her temple. Her hair was dressed differently, too, a few tendrils curled around her face and the rest drawn back loosely to the crown of her head, exposing more of her neck than she was accustomed to. Now, she wished she had a cap.

"Here you go." She started at the sound of Mr. Gallagher's voice.

She took the glass and napkin he held out for her and bit down on her lip to see her wrist shake. If Mr. Gallagher noticed, he didn't let on. He had turned away from her but remained standing beside her. She almost wished he would walk away. She felt humiliated and his presence only bespoke pity.

"Am I late?" A feminine voice floated from the doorway,

and Maddie's heart sank at the sight of Mrs. Mason, who had made the journey from London the day before.

"Not at all, Cecily." Mrs. Walker gave her two airy pecks on the cheeks. "You look lovely."

"Indeed you do," Lady Haversham echoed.

Mrs. Mason remained in the doorway a moment longer, her confidence in direct contrast to Maddie's urge to hide.

Mrs. Walker nodded her approval. "Your gown is the latest fashion." The teal-blue gown with its puffy sleeves reaching to the elbows, its wider skirt, the bustle in back less prominent made Maddie feel all over again how dated her own was.

"Who are we awaiting, every laird in the region?" She smiled at her witticism, then slowly entered the room, as if to give everyone in it the chance to admire her.

Mrs. Walker laughed. "I suspect we shall be swarmed by every respectable family from here to Inverness."

Mrs. Mason stopped before Mr. Gallagher and eyed his glass significantly. He asked her immediately what she would have.

"A sherry, if you please." As he moved away from them, Mrs. Mason glanced at Maddie's gown. With her lips pursed, she ran her eyes over its length but said nothing. Instead she turned to wait for Mr. Gallagher.

When he returned, she thanked him. "I vow, I had my doubts about coming all the way up here for merely a dance, but now I begin to feel recovered."

"I'm relieved to hear it."

Mrs. Walker came to stand with them. "I do hope you're not too tired to enjoy this evening's festivities."

"A nap has restored me, thank you." She raised her glass. "Here's to good food, good drink and good company." The others followed suit.

Maddie quietly moved away from them before they would

notice her. She needn't have worried as Mrs. Walker began describing the local families to her friend.

The next moment, her three children trooped in with their nanny. They were clad in dressing gowns and slippers, their faces scrubbed and shiny.

Harry spoke for the group. "We've come to wish you good-night, Mama and Papa." Their father had traveled with Mrs. Mason to join his family for the weekend.

Maddie had to admire the way the children's manners had improved in the short while the nursemaid had been with them. Mr. Gallagher also spent a good portion of each day with them, taking them on horseback rides or organizing ball games out on the lawn.

"Good night, my darlings." Mrs. Walker bent down, offering each one her cheek for a kiss. Their father patted their heads as each one approached him.

Lisbeth reached up to put her arms around her mother's neck.

"You look ever so pretty, Mama."

"Thank you. Careful, sweetling, with Mama's coiffure."

"You smell good, too."

Her mother eased away from the girl's embrace. "That's because your mama is going to a ball."

Maddie felt a pang at the sight of the children's affection for their mother.

"Good night, Great-aunt Millicent and Uncle Reid," they chorused when they had finished bidding their parents good-night.

"Good night, children." Lady Haversham smiled regally. "Now, mind you get to bed on time and tomorrow you shall hear all about the ball."

Mr. Gallagher knelt down and gave them each a hug.

Soon the first guests arrived. Maddie forgot about her

earlier discomfort as the hall filled to overflowing. The local gentry appeared a mixed bag, with titled dignitaries from Glasgow, Edinburgh and London mingling equally with the local lairds, whose pride came from their living in the area for many generations.

She wasn't formally introduced to anyone but when the orchestra began to play, she found herself asked onto the dance floor by a local laird named Duncan McGee. He appeared to be in his fifties, with steely gray hair and muttonchop whiskers. He wore a dark frock coat and kilt in a blue-and-green plaid.

After being led in a vigorous Highland jig around the dance floor, he didn't wait for her permission but took her hand and swung her around for another tune. Maddie hadn't danced in years, but she preferred dancing to standing or sitting along the sidelines, knowing no one there except Lady Haversham's family.

After the fifth or sixth dance—she'd lost count—she could hardly breathe and felt she would faint if she didn't sit down. She glanced at Mr. McGee's florid face, amazed at the man's stamina. Of course, he didn't wear a corset, she told herself.

"A fine pair we make, eh, lassie?" His gray eyes twinkled into hers as his rough palm squeezed her hand. She managed a wan smile, wondering where his wife was.

"I believe I'll sit this one out," she said.

He was ready to take her in his arms again but stopped and peered down at her. "Deen oot, are ye?"

When she managed to ascertain that he asked if she was "done out," she nodded. "Indeed."

"Well, coom along, then, we'll get you a wee dram. That'll fix ye up straightaway."

"If I may just sit this one out, I should be fine."

But he insisted on getting her some refreshment. She finally prevailed upon him to get her plain lemonade. He came back after a few moments with a glass of iced lemonade for her and a tumbler of whiskey for himself.

He took a healthy swallow and smacked his lips. "Finest malt in the land," he said with a wink. "Distilled right here along the Tay." He drained the glass and wiped his mouth with the back of his sleeve.

Maddie took a careful sip from her glass, wondering how she could excuse herself politely from this energetic gentleman.

He signaled a passing waiter. He placed the empty tumbler on the man's tray and took two more. "Best be prepared." He winked again. Before the waiter had moved more than a few paces away, McGee downed one of the glasses. He held the other one in his weathered hands between his knees and leaned forward.

Maddie inched back in her chair, away from the smell of the whiskey on his breath, her knees tightly locked, and wondered yet again where his wife might be.

"Ye hail from down south, do ye?"

"Yes, London."

"Bet yer happy to be up here where you can breathe some pure air."

She smiled. "Oh, yes. The air is very fresh here." She took another small sip and looked past the laird to the crowded room. She hadn't seen Mr. Gallagher since the music had begun. Perhaps she could excuse herself to check on Lady Haversham. She craned her neck, but didn't see the older lady, either. Reluctantly, she turned her attention back to the laird. "Are you family of the present owner of Taymouth Castle?" she asked, referring to the largest landowner of the region.

He scowled. "Ech, nay. I be of Clan Mackay."

Maddie glanced at his tartan. "Oh. I thought it was the Campbell pattern."

"Nay, lass." He smoothed the tartan over one knee. "The Mackay has the blue line, see. The Campbell is a broken black thread."

"Ah, yes." She noticed the difference in the two blue-and-green plaids.

He finished downing the third tumbler. Grabbing her by the wrist, her lemonade scarcely touched, he pulled her to her feet again. "That should do ye for the next round. Come along, lassie, the music's awastin'."

"Mr. McGee—" She barely managed to set her glass down before it spilled over her gown. Protesting against more dancing was useless. The man was either hard of hearing or willfully deaf to her weak protests.

Maddie's heart sank. The dance was a waltz, and she felt an aversion to being held in this stranger's embrace. But he held her close—too close—the rough wool of his coat chafing the exposed skin of her upper arms. She bit back a wince as one of his rugged shoes stepped on her slipper.

"Ouch." She pulled back but he didn't seem to notice. Her toes throbbed as he tugged her along to the music.

Suddenly a large hand clapped onto McGee's shoulder, separating him from Maddie. Her gaze traveled up the black-clad sleeve to Mr. Gallagher's forbidding features. "Excuse me, sir, but this dance was saved for me."

Reid set the laird firmly aside, making certain he didn't fall. Seeing the man hauling Miss Norton around, oblivious to her discomfort, had angered Reid beyond reason, and he was struggling inwardly not to cause a scene.

Reid had stayed away from the dance floor most of the evening, remaining in the billiard room after dancing an obligatory dance with his sister and enduring another with her talkative friend, Cecily. But finally, he'd returned to the great hall.

Not wanting to appear too anxious or eager, he'd begun a circular tour of the large room, his progress slowed by the crowd. His eyes scanned the dancers, in search of titian hair and a bronze-colored gown that complimented it so well.

He'd stopped in midstride, catching sight of Miss Norton before she disappeared behind another couple. He wove through the dancers as he made his way toward her.

She was held—crushed seemed a more accurate description—against—what was the fellow's name? McGee? Reid had met him earlier. Although Miss Norton smiled, her expression seemed strained. Her color was high. Then he caught a flash of pain in her features when the laird lurched against her. Reid pushed past the remaining couples and grasped McGee by the shoulder.

Reid disengaged Maddie's hand and enfolded it in his own. Her large tawny eyes went from alarm to relief. He frowned, taking in the sight of her flushed cheeks. "Are you all right?"

She nodded. "Only a bit of a headache."

He glanced around the crowded room. "It is infernally hot in here. Would you like to go outside for some air?"

"Yes…please…" She rewarded him with a grateful smile, a smile that never ceased to turn something around inside him. He stifled the desire to hold her in his arms, and instead, took her by the elbow and began negotiating a way out of the room.

When they finally gained the garden, he found her an empty bench. He remained standing and silent, giving her time to recover herself. In truth, he was afraid to look too closely at her. The first sight of her earlier in her evening gown had stunned him. There was no denying she was beautiful…and wholly feminine. The gown revealed a creamy neck and perfectly sculpted shoulders, slim bare arms, a small waist.

He swallowed, his mouth as dry as the Libyan Desert, and shifted his gaze off into the dark yard behind her. "Feel better?"

She nodded. "Much."

"It was pretty smoky in the billiard room and not much better in the hall."

She agreed. "It was getting harder to breathe."

He eased himself beside her on the bench and glanced sidelong at her. "Mr. McGee seemed to be holding you in a death grip."

A small laugh erupted from her, and he felt pleased to have made her laugh. "Yes, a little."

"Couldn't you escape him?"

"Well, he asked me to dance and then just kept dancing. He seemed not to hear anything I said. I didn't want to hurt his feelings."

"So, you risked being crushed by the drunken lout?"

"I…I kept hoping his wife would show up and claim him."

"I'm told the good laird has been a widower of some years and is in eager pursuit of a second Mrs. McGee."

Her smile died. "Oh."

"He's said to be worth quite a fortune." He eyed her in the dim light, wondering how she'd react to the information.

"I'm sorry I shan't be able to accommodate him."

He sensed a feeling of relief. "By the time we return, he'll probably have found himself another hapless young lady."

She made no reply. Dusk enfolded them and only muted sounds followed them from the ballroom. "You know you're really too nice for your own good."

She looked down at her gloved hands. "There is too much unkindness in the world as it is."

"I'll agree with you there. But many times people will interpret a person's kindness as weakness and take advantage of it."

Her gaze was steady and serious. "That's a chance I'm willing to take. In the end, the Lord's love is stronger than any ill treatment I receive at an individual's hands."

Reid said nothing, not sure if he wholly agreed with her but admiring her all the more for her convictions. "It sounds like you're soon to have a birthday," he said instead, remembering his aunt's words to her earlier. He cleared his throat. "When is it to be, if you don't mind my asking?"

She looked away from him. "It hardly matters."

He'd probably done the unpardonable, broaching the subject of a woman's age. Nevertheless, he was curious, all the more so at her reticence. "You should at least have the day off."

"I feel as if I've had every day off since I came to Scotland." She half turned to him on the bench. "I want to thank you again for the holiday, Mr. Gallagher."

Even though the light was dim, Reid felt her smile radiate toward him. He was coming to know that smile well. It was wide and generous, always grateful, as if she was not used to receiving good things of people. The thought gave him pause. He stared at her in the gathering twilight, the notion growing in him that he wanted to make her birthday a special day.

His ears caught the strains of another waltz through the open doors, and his thoughts turned back to his earlier purpose. "Are you up to dancing one more dance? Perhaps if we dance out here, it won't be so uncomfortable?"

He waited, his breath held.

She looked at him. "I—"

He stood and held out his hand.

"Yes, I'm…quite recovered."

She placed her hand in his and stood.

He wrapped one hand around her slim waist, feeling the satiny texture of her gown. Her other hand came up to rest on his shoulder, her fingertips brushing his collar.

At last she was in his arms. He had to restrain himself from drawing her too close. After all those days of dreaming and imagining, he was finally reliving the experience. The memory had not exaggerated the reality. She felt fragile, like the most precious treasure. The cool air caressed them and the music floated out to them as they went around in time to the music. They could have been all alone in the world.

He had not held a woman in this manner since he'd danced with Octavia.

He wouldn't think of that. He refused to think beyond the moment. What was his intention in this folly? All he knew was that he had had to feel Miss Norton once more in his arms, to…what?

To see if the sensation he had felt some days ago had been real or imaginary. But now that he had succeeded…what would follow?

He glanced at her face to discover if she was feeling anything near to what he was feeling. But her eyes were focused somewhere over his shoulder. Back and forth, round and round they went, and he wished the music wouldn't end.

Because he knew he wouldn't allow himself another moment like this one. It was too dangerous. This woman threatened to destroy the carefully erected life he'd built for himself for the past decade. At the center of that life stood Octavia, his beloved wife, soul mate, the woman he was bound to love.

He took Miss Norton around again as the music came to

its conclusion and then slowed as the last chord died out. Reluctantly he stopped and held her an instant longer. Their arms fell away from each other, and they stood like a pair of shy schoolchildren, with tentative smiles and awkward gazes.

Laughter and voices came through the open French doors as couples broke apart. "I—thank you." She murmured the words, her head bowed so he couldn't read her eyes. Then she was moving away before he could stop her. His every impulse wanted to follow her, but he restrained himself, watching the crown of her titian hair until it disappeared out of sight.

Maddie hurried away from Mr. Gallagher, skirting the crowded hall until finally finding an empty room where she could remain unseen. She put her hands up to her warm cheeks, glad of the darkness. The muffled strains of the orchestra reached her ears, and unconsciously she began to sway to its rhythm, reliving those moments in Mr. Gallagher's arms.

Even though she hadn't dared look into his eyes once during the dance, she had felt his gaze on her. She'd been afraid to raise her head, afraid he'd read what her eyes would convey to him—her yearning…and love.

She'd felt cherished in his arms, more cherished than she'd ever felt since she'd left home so many years ago. Since then she'd been a lonely pilgrim, in the employ of strangers, sometimes appreciated by them, sometimes not, but there had always been that wall of separation between employer and employee, that invisible line that couldn't be crossed.

What was it that was happening between Mr. Gallagher and her? Was she the only one experiencing it? Why had he asked her to dance—and such an intimate one? He could have asked her for a polka or quadrille, but he'd chosen the waltz. Was it only his innate sense of politeness, that sensitivity he displayed not only to her but to every human being he came in contact with?

She swallowed, afraid of the emotions he awoke in her. For if they weren't reciprocated, she was in for a nasty fall, far more devastating than what she'd felt when the only suitor she'd ever had had jilted her. She'd been only eighteen then. She made a small, strangled sound. If she'd thought herself brokenhearted then, what would she feel now that she was a woman, a woman who had been alone so many years, who knew the cold, hard ways of the world?

And if her feelings *were* reciprocated? No, it couldn't be. Mr. Gallagher had made it plain to her he loved his late wife. She remembered his words with chilling clarity. *I'm still married to her.* They'd rung a death knell to any hopes Maddie might have. And if there were any chance of her forgetting the words, the wedding band he wore was a fresh reminder every day of where his heart lay. And yet, the way he'd rescued her tonight and danced with her, his touch unmistakably tender…

Maddie shook her head in the darkness. She mustn't let her hopes rise, nor could she permit herself to give even a hint of her own feelings to Mr. Gallagher. She would on no account put him in an uncomfortable position. He'd been so kind to her already. She wouldn't make him feel that she had misinterpreted his generosity.

Oh, dear Lord, she prayed, *help me!* Only the Lord could give her the grace to accept the inevitable.

That evening, after Reid had prepared for bed, he went to his bedside table. Since the fishing episode he had kissed his wife's portrait as he'd done every night for the last decade, but it had felt hypocritical, as if for the first time in his life he had something to hide from her. He knew what an adulterer must feel who is trying to maintain an outwardly normal relation to his wife, but knows inwardly how false he is being.

He pulled down the covers and got into bed without glancing at his wife's photograph. But he felt its presence there in the dark as if she were looking at him with pity in her eyes, able to see and read into his very soul.

Without meaning to, he fingered the wedding band on his finger, slipping it up and down past his knuckle. He'd worn it since making his vows to Octavia that long-ago day. To love, honor and cherish her. Her death had released him from those vows. But since he felt responsible for her death, he'd never felt released. He owed her his allegiance. It was the least he could do to make amends for having cut down her life prematurely.

Maddie tossed and turned for hours before falling asleep. She lay in the dark, staring at the canopy above her and remembered being held in Mr. Gallagher's arms.

Her mind relived the dance. Once again, she couldn't help dreaming what it would be like if her love for Mr. Gallagher were reciprocated…if she could help him get over the pain and loneliness of a decade of widowhood.

Would she read something new in his eyes tomorrow— anything that let her know he was beginning to see her as a woman? Would she ever see his finger bare of the wedding band?

Chapter Ten

The next day, Maddie came into the breakfast room and saw only Mr. Gallagher seated there. She paused on the threshold, feeling a shyness come over her. How would he react upon seeing her?

He looked up and gave her his usual smile. "Good morning, Miss Norton. Sleep well?" His tone was pleasant, nothing strained or awkward in it.

She stifled a sense of disappointment and crossed the room to the sideboard. "Yes, thank you. And you?"

"Very well, thank you."

He continued eating, so she took a plate and served herself, chiding herself for getting herself all worked up about a simple dance. Was it a sign of an aging spinster when she began having delusions about a gentleman being attracted to her? She seated herself halfway down the table from him, unsure she could keep her own demeanor from betraying her. After a short blessing, she unfolded her napkin. When Mr. Gallagher lifted his coffee cup for a sip, Maddie couldn't help glancing at his hand.

Even down the length of the table she could distinguish the wedding band he still wore. If she needed any further proof that his feelings remained unchanged, the wedding band was irrefutable evidence.

His eyes met hers. "You're not too tired from last night's festivities?"

"No. I didn't go to bed too late." She strove to match his matter-of-fact tone.

"You never did tell me yesterday when your birthday is to be."

She blinked at him, surprised that he'd remembered the topic. She was foolish to make anything of it. "It—it's next Saturday."

"We were born a decade apart. I'll be celebrating my fortieth on the twenty-ninth."

She wondered how he'd celebrate. Before she could think of anything to say, he changed the subject. "We've been having quite a spate of good weather."

"Yes." She stirred a spoonful of sugar into her porridge, unused to the Scottish custom of unsweetened porridge.

"I've been thinking we should attempt Ben Lawers before the weather turns."

She paused. Had he said "we"? She cleared her throat. "You said you wanted to climb to the top."

"That's right. Do you still want to attempt it?" He grinned. "As a milestone to mark your thirtieth and my fortieth?"

The idea began to grow on her. To scale a mountain peak to mark her birthday would certainly be better than thinking of herself as being forever on the shelf. She nodded. "Yes." But what if she slowed him down? "That is if you still think I could—should…." She stopped, waiting for him to back out of his offer.

He shrugged. "It's up to you. I'm told it's anywhere from

a five- to eight-hour hike there and back. We'd need to leave around dawn to return by midafternoon or a bit later."

She moistened her lips. He hadn't tried to get out of the invitation. Did that mean he really wanted her to go? His tone sounded noncommittal, yet, he was leaving it up to her. If he didn't want her, he certainly needn't have issued the invitation. He hadn't invited his own sister, for one thing. "Do you think Mrs. Walker would care to go along?"

"Vera? I should hope not. She'd probably expect me to provide a means of conveyance and stop every half hour."

"Yes, of course." He was paying her a compliment if he thought she would be little trouble. "When would you like to go?"

"I thought tomorrow, if you're sure you're sufficiently recovered from the dance by then. Vera mentioned something about taking Aunt Millicent to Aberfeldy. They should be gone till early evening. I don't think Aunt Millicent expects you to go along."

"No." It seemed perfect. She wiped her mouth with her napkin and set it down. "Then, yes, I should like to attempt the climb, if you're sure I won't hinder you."

"Good. We can leave around dawn, as I said." His tone conveyed no sign that her acceptance had either pleased or displeased him. "The gillie will accompany us. He knows the best trails from this side. I'll speak with him about what we need to take."

She nodded.

"There's one other thing…." He continued regarding her.

"Yes?" Was there something wrong? He was looking at her a bit strangely.

"It's just…your outfit."

She stared down at her starched blouse and dark skirt.

"You'll need suitable garments." He cleared his throat.

"You certainly can't attempt a hike of that nature in a long skirt and—and—"

For the first time, she sensed his discomfort with the topic and took pity on him. "That's all right. I'm used to walking long distances in London."

"This is a lot different from walking the London streets. What you really need is a pair of...trousers—" His eyes shifted away from her.

She could feel the color stealing up to her cheeks and she remembered the previous time the topic had come up and he'd mentioned the word *bloomers*. But...was he talking about *gentleman's* trousers now?

He gave her no chance to reply, for which she was thankful. "I know it sounds shocking, but it's not as unusual as you might imagine. Women in India regularly wear loose silk trousers called pajamas. They're infinitely more practical than what western women wear in the name of fashion."

She bit her underlip, trying to assimilate what he was saying. She had been brought up with very strict ideas of what was proper and improper for a lady to wear.

"Chinese women, too," he was saying, but she hardly heard him, too concerned with what she was going to wear herself. Would this one detail keep her from accompanying Mr. Gallagher up the mountain?

"What do you suggest I wear? Those bloomers you mentioned the other day?" She strove to maintain her tone and gaze steady, despite the flush she could feel on her cheeks.

"Yes, precisely." He sounded relieved that the topic was settled. "Except...I don't know where you might procure a pair so quickly. Perhaps if we could just furnish you with a pair of borrowed trousers, a young boy's from here in the house?

"My mother would sometimes don a pair of men's trousers

when she was painting a mural." He smiled, his expression reminiscing. "She painted a few on the walls of our rooms. We'd catch her gazing at a wall, and Father and I soon came to know that look. A few days later, we'd find her high on a stepladder, palette in hand. She'd borrow a pair of trousers from my father. She finally purchased a pair of her own, tired of having to cinch up the waist on a pair of Father's."

She couldn't help smiling at the picture she envisioned of this unusual, creative woman.

He rose from his chair. "So, I'll meet you at the stables at dawn then tomorrow. Wear comfortable boots, as well."

"I will," she promised. He was gone before she realized she didn't know what she would do about the trousers. What would Lady Haversham say? Her heart sank.

An hour later, when she went to her room to retrieve some thread for her needlework, she found a package had been delivered there and lay on her bed. She removed the brown paper and gasped when she saw a pair of corduroy trousers in it.

She unfolded them and stared. They looked worn but smelled clean as if freshly laundered. Gingerly she held them up to her waist, hardly able to imagine donning them. But they didn't seem too wide or long. Where had Mr. Gallagher found them for her? A stable boy's, most likely. Even a pair of suspenders was provided with them.

At tea she heard Mrs. Walker and Lady Haversham making plans to visit a family in Aberfeldy that had attended the dance. Maddie breathed a sigh of relief. She dearly hoped she and Mr. Gallagher returned before the two ladies came back from their visit.

It was still dark the next morning when Maddie came down the back stairs and headed for the stables. She felt strange walking with her legs encased in the soft thick material and was glad of the darkness. The trousers did feel warm, she admitted, in the cool air. She had also donned her warmest undergarments, a blouse, a warm jacket and the plaid.

Mr. Gallagher stood by the stable door with Ewane, the gillie, who was holding a pony's lead. They were to ride in the cart hitched to it, as far as the hamlet of Lawers a couple of miles along Loch Tay. From there they'd proceed northward along a track familiar to the gillie to the foot of the mountain.

"Good morning." She greeted each man with a brief nod, afraid of drawing too much attention to herself.

Mr. Gallagher gave her the once-over, bringing heat to her cheeks. "Good, I see the trousers fit." He turned abruptly back to Ewane. "I guess we're ready."

"Yes, sir." The gillie didn't seem to find her appearance in any way remarkable and she wondered if he was used to seeing tourists of every stripe.

Mr. Gallagher gave her a hand into the farm cart as the gillie took the reins. Maddie was glad of the semidarkness as she climbed aboard. It felt too unnatural to have her shape so revealed by a pair of narrow trousers.

Once seated, though, with a blanket wrapped around her legs by Mr. Gallagher, she felt better. She soon forgot her appearance as they began their journey along the loch. White mists rose from it and birdsong erupted from the tree branches above them.

After a little while, Mr. Gallagher handed her an oatcake. "Hope that'll do for breakfast. There're plenty more if you get hungry." His white teeth flashed in a grin.

"Thank you, this will do fine." She munched quietly as the cart rattled along the dirt road.

The small hamlet was silent as they passed through it and took the narrow path away from the loch. The path soon disappeared into a grassy sheep track, which began to rise steadily northward. Alongside they heard the gurgle of a brook.

Ewane gestured to it with the stock of his whip. "Lawers Burn."

About three-quarters of an hour later they reached a small lake. Maddie gazed upward to the west and gasped. A massive peak loomed before her, the first glimmers of sun lightening its green surface.

"There she is," the gillie said, noticing her admiration. "Ben Lawers, the highest peak in the central Highlands." He turned to Mr. Gallagher. "We'll leave the cart here by Lochan nan Chat. There's a crofter nearby."

"Very good." The two men led the pony and cart toward a small thatch-roofed hut tucked away on one side of the small lake. Maddie waited, continuing to gaze up at the sloping mountain peak. Was she really going to ascend it today?

"Ready?" Mr. Gallagher asked when the two men returned a few minutes later.

She returned his smile, her excitement rising. "Ready as I'll ever be."

"Good, come along then."

The gillie led them through a stile and onto a stony farm track. She walked abreast of Mr. Gallagher, behind the gillie. Nobody spoke. Maddie didn't find the going hard as the slope rose gradually and was mostly grassy with only an occasional rock visible. Stone walls outlined some fields where sheep grazed. The air was cooler up here. She hugged the tartan shawl around her, glad of its warmth.

Mr. Gallagher lifted an eyebrow. "Cold?"

She shook her head. "Not at all. This plaid is very warm."

Once in a while they passed a heap of square stones. They looked too structured to have fallen that way naturally and she asked Ewane about them.

"Those be shielings. When I was a wee lad, we'd spend summers in them and bring our cattle up here to graze. That was afore the lairds began taking over all the land for sheep." The gillie kicked at the hard, stubby grass and spat. "They eat everythin' down to the dirt, leaven' the land fit for nothing but bracken to grow."

Once in a while they passed a shieling that still stood. Maddie spotted one in the distance, smoke rising from the center of the roof. A small, dark-haired child stood in the doorway, barefoot and ruddy cheeked. Maddie waved but he didn't respond.

"They be tenants, looking after the laird's sheep up here for the summer," the gillie said.

After a couple of hours' silent marching, they stopped to rest. The way was beginning to grow rockier and the grade steeper. The walking sticks they each carried came in handy.

Mr. Gallagher turned to her. "All right?"

"Yes." She was breathing deeply but had never felt more alive. She was also grateful for the trousers she was wearing. She'd become strangely accustomed to wearing them and they certainly made the climbing easier. She slipped a glance at Mr. Gallagher, another thing to be grateful to him for.

She surveyed the distance they'd come, shading her eyes from the rising sun. "My goodness." Below them lay thick dark green forest to the south and above it the grassy meadows they'd climbed. She could barely distinguish the thin curving line of the burn from where they'd started.

After a few more miles' march, Mr. Gallagher suggested they stop for lunch. She nodded. He turned to the gillie and exchanged a few words with him.

Maddie looked above her. The hill continued upward, but now the stubby green grass was giving way to craggy gray stones. They settled on some lichen-covered boulders and broke open the lunch packet of more bannocks, some fruit and flasks of tea. The gillie moved off a distance to eat his meal.

They ate in contented silence for a few minutes. Maddie felt as if she and Mr. Gallagher were all alone on top of the world.

"Are you still game to climb higher?"

She smiled at him, experiencing the most freedom she had in a long time. "That's what we came for, isn't it?"

"How're your shoes holding up?"

"Not a blister." She shook her head. "It's funny, when I was a young girl, I suffered quite a few bouts of illness. It seems I've grown quite hardy in old age."

"I wouldn't call thirty old age."

She blushed at the reference to how old she was to be in a few days. "It's not exactly youth. It's more the age of maturity," she said, attempting to make light of the fact.

"It appears youthful from my vantage, believe me." He crumbled the remains of a bannock between his fingers. "What would you call turning forty?"

Her gaze traveled from his hand to his blue eyes watching her steadily. "A man's prime."

She was rewarded by the grin beneath his dark golden mustache and she felt a warmth spreading through her like the camphor oil her mother used to rub over her chest when she had suffered from congestion during her bouts of illness.

"Diplomatic answer."

"Truthful, nonetheless."

He said, "Excuse my impertinence, but I'm surprised you never married."

She was stunned by his bluntness for a moment. "I was almost engaged...once."

"What happened?" His voice was gentle, inviting confidences.

It all seemed so silly now. "The gentleman found out that I was obliged to work for a living." She shrugged. "He backed off before formally declaring himself. Who knows, maybe he never had any intention to."

Mr. Gallagher frowned. "If you believed he was going to, he must have taken things to a point where you would not have been unreasonable to expect him to. Courtship follows certain steps, and a man is no gentleman who raises a young lady's expectations without following through."

She looked away again, afraid of the sympathy in his voice and eyes. "It was so long ago, I can scarcely picture him. So it no longer matters."

The gillie walked over to them from where he'd been standing. "Excuse me, sir, we best be leavin' if we're to make it back afore nightfall."

"Right you are." Mr. Gallagher stood and they stowed their things back into a pack, which he shouldered.

She glanced above them. "When will we be able to see Ben Lawers?"

The gillie pointed. "If we reach that rise there, we'll have a good view of Lawers and Ben Glas."

"And when we reach the summit of Ben Lawers, we'll be able to see the entire valley, Loch Tay and Glen Lyon to the north," added Mr. Gallagher.

"It sounds spectacular."

After that there was little distraction. The slopes became steeper. Maddie was glad of all the miles she'd walked in London. Even so, she was grateful to rest when they reached a forbidding line of crags. The air had a distinct chill to it.

They were silent, looking at the vast landscape all around them. Bluish-purple mountains strung out to the west and north of them across another valley. The valley they had come from lay to the south, the river scarcely visible between the smoke trails of clouds and thick forests. Maddie drew in her breath, seeing the vast lake connecting to the River Tay.

As if reading her thoughts, Mr. Gallagher said over her shoulder, "Loch Tay."

"It's beautiful, so blue against the forests."

He touched her lightly on the shoulder, directing her view to the opposite side. "On this side lies Glen Lyon." He turned to the gillie. "Isn't that right?"

"Aye. Glen Lyon, the bonniest glen in all Scotland. Thataway ye see Ben Lawers."

Maddie looked to where he pointed to the west and admired the mountain range, immediately distinguishing the grandest peak as Ben Lawers.

They soon recommenced walking, though the going was much slower. Maddie was more grateful than ever for the trousers when she found herself forced to crawl on her hands and knees up narrow, rocky ridges.

"Best keep to this side o' the dike. There's a nasty hanging corrie up ahead," the gillie advised as he reached a narrow ridge and pointed to a hollowed-out portion of the mountain-side.

Maddie edged closer to the dike. At the end of the stone barrier, the path leveled off somewhat and began to weave through jagged vertical crags. She had to focus all her thoughts on her steps. Tiny pebbles crunched under her boots and went rattling down the cliffs.

"Watch your step here." Mr. Gallagher held out a hand to her and she grasped it gratefully as they negotiated a tricky pass.

They reached a spot where another ridge joined the one they were on and stopped a few minutes to admire the view below. Mists floated between them and the valley.

"Almost to the summit," the gillie said with a motion of his walking stick.

Mr. Gallagher adjust the knapsack on his shoulder. "Come on then. The view is better from there."

They did no more talking, each one intent on maneuvering the steep rocky hillside. In places, they faced great mounds of boulders that they had to climb over. At others, they had to walk single file along narrow ridges.

Maddie climbed through a fissure in a large crag only to find herself on another treacherous course of boulders and sheer drop-offs. She'd taken a few steps when abruptly her ankle twisted under her. Before she could utter more than a cry, she was falling, slipping down the rocky slope, the smaller rocks falling with her.

"Miss Norton!" She heard Mr. Gallagher's shout above her but she could do nothing to stop her fall. Suddenly her head hit something sharp and the world went black.

Chapter Eleven

"Miss Norton!" Adrenaline coursed through Reid's body as he lunged for her, but he was too late. He watched her topple down the steep incline. A second later he was after her, scrambling down the rocky slope.

There was nothing for her to reach for. If she fell any farther, she'd be lost to them. "Miss Norton, I'm coming!" Trying to make haste and not lose his own footing, he worked his way down the rocky slope at an infuriatingly slow pace.

When he was able to turn around, he saw her lying still, her fall broken by a jutting rock. A new worry replaced his fear. He didn't like the way she looked so motionless. What if her neck was broken? Cold sweat erupted over his body, fear gripping his heart until he felt strangled by it.

When he reached her body, he hardly dared touch her. She'd lost consciousness and her face looked deathly pale. He wasn't aware of Ewane until he heard the other man's heavy breathing at his side. "Is she alive?"

Reid placed his fore and middle fingers at the base of her neck. Relief flooded him. "I feel a pulse." *Dear God, thank you*. He looked above them. She'd fallen about thirty feet. "We've got to get her out of here."

"Aye. Trouble is there's naught around here to fashion a litter with."

Not a tree or twig graced the landscape this far up. "I'll just have to carry her."

"Aye." The older man nodded. "I'll help when you get winded. Best thing is to take her to the last shieling we passed mebbe half a mile back."

"Yes." Reid turned his attention to Miss Norton and frowned. She hadn't yet regained consciousness. He wished he had some of the smelling salts his aunt always had at her side.

Just then her eyes fluttered open and she stared at him. The tension began to ease from his frame. Never had he been so glad to see someone looking at him. "Miss Norton?" Would she know him?

Recognition lighted her eyes. "Mr. Gallagher." Her voice was a broken whisper. "What happened? I was—" She fell silent as if remembering the fall. She reached up a hand to the back of her head and winced as soon as she touched a spot on her skull.

"Easy there. You must have hit your head against this rock. It's the only thing that kept you from falling farther." He wondered whether she had suffered a concussion. It had to have caused quite a blow at the speed she'd fallen. But he voiced none of this.

"I'm going to have to help you get up the hillside."

She heaved a deep breath. "All right. Just give me a moment to catch my breath." Her voice sounded strained.

"First, let's make sure you've broken nothing. Try to move your limbs and tell me if you feel any pain anywhere other than your head."

She did as she was told. "Everything feels fine except my head."

"Good. Now, if you just lie still, I'm going to lift you in my arms to get you back up this slope."

Her eyes showed immediate alarm and she clutched at his forearm. "Oh, no, that won't be necessary. Truly, Mr. Gallagher."

He stilled her agitation with a touch to her hand. "We'll take it slowly. Just relax." He spoke as if to a child, still not liking how pale she looked. Gently, he placed one arm under her shoulders, trying to cushion her head, and the other under her knees. He focused on her as an injured person, and not a woman. How many times had he given similar aid to an injured man in the desert?

Bracing himself on one knee, he took a deep breath then lifted her up. She didn't weigh much, her form slim and delicate in his arms, but he knew it wouldn't be easy going. Ewane stayed at his side to catch him if his foot should slip.

One careful step at a time, Reid made his way back up the mountainside. When they reached the ridge, he only paused a moment to get his breath and ask, "How are you doing? Are you in any pain?"

"No. I'm fine. I just wish you'd let me walk."

"Don't exhaust yourself protesting over something that you have no say over." He gave her a slight smile to make light of the situation. Then he shifted her weight in his arms, and with a nod to Ewane, indicated he'd follow the gillie's lead.

The man turned and began the long trek back.

Miss Norton made no more protests. She was silent all the way back and Reid was afraid she must be in some discomfort. As hard as he tried, he couldn't help jostling her as he maneuvered past the crags and half slid down certain slopes.

He was getting winded but wouldn't let Ewane carry her when the older man offered to help shoulder the burden. If only Reid hadn't brought her up here. If only he'd listened to reason and kept her down below where she'd be safe. What had possessed him? Couldn't he see how fragile she was?

Ewane turned to him again. "Let me take her, lad."

Reid just shook his head, trying to keep from gasping for breath. Despite the cool air, his shirt was damp and he could feel the perspiration trickling down the sides of his face.

Miss Norton no longer insisted she try to walk and rested quietly against his chest. She still looked ghastly pale to him.

They had finally reached the grassy slopes when she suddenly pushed against his chest. "Please, let me down. I feel like I'm going to be sick."

He let her down as gently as he could. She scrambled away from him on her hands and knees and began to retch. He opened their pack to retrieve a bottle of water and a napkin, unable to keep the worry from his thoughts. It looked more and more as if she'd suffered a concussion.

He handed her the water and cloth. She took them from him, turning away again, and he felt bad for her, realizing she was probably feeling embarrassed in addition to being physically unwell.

"It's likely the knock on your head that's brought on the queasiness to your stomach," he said quietly when she'd finished washing off. He took the things from her and repacked the satchel. Ewane took it from him and shouldered it.

"We're not far from the shieling now, ma'am."

"Come on then. Let's go." Without meeting her gaze, Reid bent over Miss Norton once more and lifted her up, feeling awkward at the close contact. He'd wanted to feel her in his arms before, but not at this price. He wished he could make it easier for her but knew the most important thing was to get her to some sort of shelter.

"Are you feeling any better?" he asked, her soft hair rubbing his chin. Despite the difficult circumstances and the exhaustion he was feeling, he couldn't help being aware of her body curled so close to his, her head tucked under his.

He snapped his attention back to the trail. It wasn't the time or place to harbor such thoughts. If anything happened to Miss Norton he'd never forgive himself—

The realization brought him up short. Was he being punished for having had the kinds of thoughts about her he'd had lately? He should never have brought her to the Highlands.

First Octavia and now Miss Norton. If anyone deserved to die, it was he.

"There it be." The gillie pointed ahead of them far down the grassy slope.

Reid shut off the chaos in his mind and concentrated once again on the task at hand. First things first. There would be time enough later for self-recrimination.

Maddie remembered little of the next moments. After her initial distress at being such a burden to Mr. Gallagher, she felt too ill to think of anything much. Mr. Gallagher carried her so surely, she never once feared he'd drop her or lose his footing the way she so stupidly had.

She prayed for the Lord to give him the strength to carry her to wherever they were going. She knew she wasn't that light and no matter how much stronger or bigger he was, it was no easy task he'd undertaken. She could tell by his labored breathing and the damp patches on his shirt what an effort it was.

He'd been so kind and considerate, even when she'd been sick, as if he'd known exactly what she was going through.

She was hardly aware when they arrived at one of the small stone huts they'd passed earlier, until she heard the gillie conversing with someone in Gaelic. Then Mr. Gallagher let her down and she was finally able to try standing on her own two feet. She felt light-headed and clutched his arm. He immediately steadied her about her shoulders.

"We're going to stay here," he told her. "I just need you to crawl through the opening into the shieling. The opening is too low to walk through upright. Take your time."

"Stay here?" She didn't understand what he was saying.

"I'll explain once we have you inside."

"All right." She bent over to enter through the tiny square that served as a door into the hut. The space inside was high enough to stand in, but wasn't much bigger than a small room.

Mr. Gallagher appeared beside her in the hut. A woman led her to a crude bed, thin bedding over some wooden boards. Mr. Gallagher arranged some pillows behind her head and removed her boots before covering her with her own plaid and another blanket the woman brought him.

"Thank you, ma'am," he said, taking it from her.

He tucked it in around Maddie.

"I'm sorry to be so much trouble—"

"None of that, Miss Norton." His voice was low and soothing. "I just want to be sure you make it back down in one piece."

She met his earnest gaze and realized he was worried about her. She wished she could reach out and smooth the lines from his brow. Then she realized something worse than everything else that had occurred. "I kept you from reaching the top of

Ben Lawers." She pressed her lips together, looking away from him. "I'm so sorry."

He shook his head. "It's been there thousands of years. It'll keep until we have a chance to have another go."

She swallowed. Once again he'd included her. Her eyes misted. She knew very well she would never have another opportunity for such an adventure. This holiday would soon be over. Mr. Gallagher would return to foreign soil. And she? She'd return to London and taking care of Lady Haversham. If Mr. Gallagher did return to the Highlands someday, it wouldn't be with Maddie.

Mr. Gallagher had turned back to the entrance of the hut and was conferring with the gillie. Maddie was thankful for having a moment to compose herself. She attributed her emotional state to the blow she'd received. The back of her head pained her and she felt more exhausted than if she had hiked all the way down herself. She brought her hand up to her skull only to find a large lump.

"You took a nasty fall." Mr. Gallagher had returned to her side and crouched beside the bed. "I've sent Ewane on down to let them know about the accident so no one will worry when we don't show up this afternoon."

"We…we're staying here?" Oh, dear, what was Lady Haversham going to say? Would Maddie lose her job?

He nodded. "I don't think you should attempt much movement for a while."

"I'm better, I assure you." She tried to sit up.

His hand immediately closed over her shoulder and held her back. "You might feel better, and I'm glad. But your head sustained some injury. You could have a concussion."

She stared at him. "Oh." She wasn't sure exactly what that was except that it meant a serious injury to one's head. She knotted her hands together. *Oh, Lord, forgive me for being so foolish, coming up here on some sort of adventure when my duty was by Lady Haversham's side. I didn't even tell her.*

"What's the matter?" Mr. Gallagher's blue eyes narrowed as if he could sense her agitation.

"I'm sorry for all the trouble," she whispered, this time unable to hide the quaver in her voice.

He covered her hands with his large one. "Steady there. Just be thankful you're alive and in one piece. When I saw you fall, it looked like you were going to roll all the way down to where we'd begun our trek this morning."

Her laugh sounded weak and watery to her own ears. He chucked her under the chin. "That's better."

"Will your—your aunt be very angry?"

"Don't worry about Aunt Millicent. I'll explain to her how foolhardy I was in dragging you up here."

"Oh, no. It wasn't your fault. Please don't take the blame."

"Shh. Worry is not good for head injuries." A gleam of humor in his eyes belied his serious tone. He removed his hand from hers and adjusted the blanket around her. She kept her hands still, already missing the warmth of his touch.

The woman approached the bedside with a tin mug in her hands. "I brewed a bit o' mint tea for the lady."

Mr. Gallagher took the cup from her. "Thank you. That's just the thing."

With a quick bob of her head, the woman retreated. Two small children hovered behind her, staring at Maddie. She smiled at them and the youngest, a ruddy-faced girl of about six, smiled back.

"This might help settle your stomach," Mr. Gallagher said.

The words only reminded her of having been sick in front of him. She wrapped her hands around the cup, glad for the warmth against her cold hands.

"Careful you don't burn yourself."

She smiled at his attentiveness. "All right."

He readjusted the pillows so she could sit up higher then he left her, telling her he'd be just outside.

She sipped the tea slowly, afraid of upsetting her stomach further. At the other end of the room, the woman and children went about their tasks, stirring a pot on the open fire pit in the middle of the room, bringing in a pitcher of water from somewhere outside, setting a few meager utensils on a rough wooden table.

Outside she could hear the baaing of sheep. She sighed, taking another sip of her tea. Under other circumstances, she'd enjoy the cozy hut, which reminded her of some of the dwellings she'd been to with her parents outside of Jerusalem. Much different from her life in London with Lady Haversham.

Just when she started missing Mr. Gallagher's company, he came back in, accompanied by another man. Mr. Gallagher approached her bedside. "I've been talking to the crofter. This is his family. They're spending the summer up here to pasture the sheep on these meadows."

"I hope I'm not taking their bed."

"They are glad to offer you anything they have. He and his son will sleep outside. He says he does so on many a fine night. The woman and the little one will share the other bed."

"And you?" She could feel her face warm at the question.

"I'll catch a few winks outside, then I'll come in and rudely wake you up at some point."

She tried to discern if he was serious. "Why is that?"

"Just a precaution. If it is a concussion, you must be awakened regularly the first night."

"Why do you suppose it's necessary?"

"I haven't a clue. Head injuries can be tricky things, I'm told. I knew a chap once who fell from the pyramid at

W e'd like to send you two free books to introduce you to the new Love Inspired® Historical series. Your two books have a combined cover price of $11.00 in the U.S. and $13.00 in Canada, but they are yours free! We'll even send you 2 wonderful surprise gifts. You can't lose!

Each of your **FREE** books is filled with engaging stories of romance, adventure and faith set in various historical periods from biblical times to World War II.

FREE BONUS GIFTS!

We'll send you 2 wonderful surprise gifts, worth about $10, *absolutely FREE,* just for giving Love Inspired Historical books a try! Don't miss out— **MAIL THE REPLY CARD TODAY!**

GET 2 FREE BOOKS!

HURRY!

Return this card today to get
2 FREE Books and **2 FREE Bonus Gifts!**

Love Inspired
HISTORICAL
INSPIRATIONAL HISTORICAL ROMANCE

YES! *Please send me the 2 FREE Love Inspired® Historical books and 2 FREE gifts for which I qualify. I understand that I am under no obligation to purchase anything further, as explained on the back of this card.*

affix
free
books
sticker
here

302 IDL ERYH

102 IDL ERXT

FIRST NAME	LAST NAME

ADDRESS

APT.#	CITY

STATE/PROV.

ZIP/POSTAL CODE

Steeple Hill®

Offer limited to one per household and not valid to current subscribers of Love Inspired Historical books. **Your Privacy -** Steeple Hill Books is committed to protecting your privacy. Our Privacy Policy is available online at www.SteepleHill.com or upon request from the Steeple Hill Reader Service. From time to time we make our lists of customers available to reputable third parties who may have a product or service of interest to you. If you would prefer for us not to share your name and address, please check here ☐.

Saqqâra. He didn't even lose consciousness like you. Just said he saw stars. He got up right away and seemed fine, went back to work—" Reid stopped, realizing too late this wasn't the right story to be telling her at this time.

"What happened?"

He hesitated. "A few days later he keeled over, dead."

She drew in a sharp breath. "I'm sorry."

"Yes, so was I. He was a good man."

She was silent a moment and he wondered if she was worried about her own fate. But she sighed. "I'm glad, in that case, that I no longer live for myself."

Her calm tone intrigued him. "You don't worry about the future?"

"Not about my eventual end, if that's what you mean. I only worry if I feel I'm not in the Lord's will. I don't want to be like the man who was given only one talent and went and buried it instead of using it to multiply it."

He marveled at their different perspectives of multiplication. Did she feel she was using her talents buried alive at an old lady's side? "I'm sure the Lord is very pleased with what you're doing."

She turned away from him. "Yes, leaving my employer's side to traipse up a mountain in men's trousers. I'm sure He's very pleased indeed."

He clenched his hand to keep from reaching out and smoothing the hair from her brow. "I'm sure He's especially lenient with first-time offenders."

"You speak as if you think I never do anything wrong. Nothing could be further from the truth."

"No? I can't imagine you ever being naughty when you were a child. I bet you never disobeyed your parents like my niece and nephews for instance."

"I assure you I was as naughty as any child. Let's see…I

remember once I wanted to go with my brothers to a fair, but I was always told I was too young, or too frail, or too something. This time I hid in the wagon and when they arrived, I sneaked out and tried to follow them. But then I got lost. I must have been five or six, like the little girl here." A smile warmed her tone. "Then I got so scared. I didn't think I'd ever be found or find my way back."

"Did you?" He drew a stool over and sat down, wanting to hear more of her story.

"After what seemed like hours, my brothers did find me. They were so angry. Of course, they were afraid of what they'd have to say to our parents if I hadn't been found."

They both chuckled.

"Well, if that's all you did as a child, your slate is very clean indeed."

Her hands knotted the blanket. "I wish it were so. But I'm afraid my shortcomings were a lot graver than mere disobedience." Her tone was so serious, he was afraid she would cause herself unnecessary distress.

"I hardly think you capable of committing any grievous offense."

She was silent a moment and he began to wonder what awful thing she imagined she had done. Fought with her siblings? Stolen a sweet?

"If I hadn't been so awfully weak as a child, my parents would undoubtedly still be following their calling on the mission field in Jerusalem."

He stared at her through the gathering gloom of the hut. "I hardly think you would be the cause of changing their life's work."

"It was because of my repeated illnesses that they were finally forced to come back to England."

Was that why she had undertaken such a life of servitude

herself? To compensate for what she imagined she'd done to her parents? "I'm sure your parents felt it no sacrifice to do what was best for you."

"Yes, I always felt their unconditional love for me." She looked down at her fists. "Sometimes that made it harder to bear…knowing how much they'd done for me. I know if I'd been as healthy as my brothers, they would still be in the field."

He was beginning to understand the enormous burden she carried. "You don't know that. Life is too full of uncertainties, especially in a place as harsh as Palestine. It could just as easily have been one of your parents to have fallen sick."

She made no reply. But he felt her resistance to his argument. He knew well what it was to carry such guilt. Except in his own case, it was well-founded.

The crofter's wife approached them at that moment with a wooden bowl of porridge but Maddie hesitated. She looked at Mr. Gallagher. "I don't think I'd better eat anything yet. I'm not sure…" Her voice trailed off.

He turned to the woman. "Thank you, but I think all Miss Norton needs right now is some rest." He turned back to Maddie. "I'll leave you for a little while to do just that."

She nodded, grateful for his sensitivity. "Thank you."

She watched him walk away and sit with the family at their simple meal. With a sigh, she turned her back on them all and gazed at the rough stone slabs on the other side of her bed. She felt inordinately tired but not sleepy. The base of her head was throbbing. What a disaster. *Lord, please see us through this calamity. Help us to explain to Lady Haversham tomorrow. Deflect her anger from her nephew. If she would dismiss me, please help me find another position.* Tears filled her eyes once more. What a muddle. She mustn't give in to self-pity. She focused her prayers on her brothers and the lives they were touching, but it was hard to concentrate and she realized her words were sounding like nonsense.

She began reciting a psalm. Before she had finished it, she drifted off to sleep.

Reid made his way through the dark hut toward Miss Norton's bed, careful to bypass the other sleeping occupants.

He leaned over to touch her shoulder and paused, listening to her even breathing, noticing the way the slivers of moonlight offset her features. He pressed his fingertips to her shoulder, hating to wake her.

She didn't stir and he began to fear her sleep was too deep.

"Miss Norton," he whispered.

Her eyes opened. "Wha—"

"I'm sorry to wake you like this, but I wanted to make sure you were all right."

Her glance darted about her. "Where—?" She finally focused on him in the dark. "Mr. Gallagher."

He breathed a sigh of relief that she had recognized him. "Can you remember anything? Who are you?" he asked softly.

"Maddie," she whispered back immediately. "Maddie Norton." Then she thought a moment. "I…we…we were climbing…Ben Lawers, and I fell. I ruined it for you!" She turned stricken eyes to him.

"You ruined nothing," he said, her name resounding in his thoughts. *Maddie.* The name fit her. He pictured a carefree girl, vulnerable and tenderhearted. How he wanted to pull her to him and keep her safe.

But how could he keep anyone safe? He hadn't managed to keep Octavia safe.

"How am I doing?" He could hear the smile in Maddie's whispered voice through the dark.

"So far so good," he said, seating himself on the stool by her bed.

"You seem to know an awful lot about doctoring." Her voice was barely above a whisper.

"It comes in handy when one is miles from the nearest clinic. I've had to do my share of doctoring."

"In the desert?"

He nodded, then realizing she wouldn't be able to see him clearly in the dark, said, "Yes. Knowing how to dig out a bullet is always valuable. Setting a bone can be complicated but I know enough about making a splint until a proper physician can be had."

"How did you learn so much?"

Seeing she was wide-awake, and finding it better to keep her so awhile, he continued. "A doctor traveled in our company once and I watched him and asked a lot of questions. He said I made a good nurse. Taught me a lot of useful tricks, like waking a concussion victim in the night."

They sat quietly for some minutes. When he began to wonder if she had fallen asleep, she suddenly spoke. "Tell me about your wife."

He froze. Nobody ever asked him about Octavia, too respectful of his silence on the subject of his wife. He felt as if Miss Norton had intruded onto sacred ground. He shifted on the hard stool, making a conscious effort not to take offense, seeing Miss Norton's silhouette lying there in the dark, her eyes closed. She might not even be in her right mind, woken up in the middle of the night after suffering a concussion.

He cleared his throat, not sure where to begin. "She was a very special woman."

"How did you meet her?"

Her eyes remained closed and he found he didn't have the heart to rebuke her curiosity. "At a garden party. I had just come down from Oxford and my parents had thrown a large party. There was Octavia, at nineteen, as beautiful and fresh as one of my mother's just-opened roses." He couldn't help smiling in the dark, remembering the moment. "I was a blushing, stammering twenty-one-year-old. I don't know how I got through the introduction."

"I can't imagine you losing your poise. You seem so worldly and sure of yourself in every situation."

How little she knew of him. "Well, I assure you, I was none of that on this occasion. Not only did I stumble over her name, but later, as we were walking through a garden path, I tripped over a flagstone and went sprawling."

She laughed softly, and he chuckled at the memory of his most embarrassing moment. "What happened next?"

"By the time I managed to get on my knees, my best trousers torn, the palms of my hands scraped, I was planning to emigrate to India and never return to England, my humiliation was so great."

She stifled her laughter with a hand. "Oh, you poor dear! My own story pales in comparison."

Feeling something strange at the sound of the endearment on her lips, he went on with his story. "Well, thankfully, the situation improved. When I looked up, there she was, kneeling beside me, concern written all over her pretty face, begging me to tell her I was all right. I fell in love at first sight and haven't ever recovered from it."

He could feel her gazing at him through the dark.

"How soon before you were married?"

"A year later. Her father wanted her to wait until she reached her majority, but after a year of my constant presence at the house, he relented." He chuckled again. "So we enjoyed a decade together." He sighed. "Those were the happiest years of my life. We traveled a lot...until she fell ill. I don't remember an unpleasant moment with her."

"You never had children?"

Reid's lips firmed into a hard line, not expecting such a forthright question.

"I'm sorry, that was indelicate of me to ask."

His anger evaporated. How could she know? No one did. "No…we never did." He looked down at the outline of his folded hands, not ready to tell her about the circumstances of that subject. He'd never be ready to talk about that.

"That's the one thing I regret most about never marrying…not ever having children…." Her voice drifted off. "I would have loved to have been a mother…."

The words cut him to the quick. She'd have no idea how much.

She yawned. "I think it will be light soon. Do you think I'll survive the night if I go back to sleep now?"

He dragged his thoughts back to the present. She must be exhausted. "Yes, I believe so. Ewane will probably be up around noon with some help to carry you down the rest of the way." The words came out automatically, his tone steady, revealing nothing of the pain her words had reawakened in him.

"Surely I'll be able to walk by then."

"Not yet. You need to take it easy and let your head mend. Just for a few days at any rate or however long a real doctor recommends." He rose from the stool, feeling his stiff legs. His arms ached from the distance he'd carried Miss Norton.

"I'll catch a few more winks myself," he told her, although he wondered whether that would be possible, now that he'd awakened the past so thoroughly.

Maddie waited until she heard the sound of Mr. Gallagher's footsteps retreat. Only when she was sure he'd left the hut did she allow herself to react.

Although she'd made him believe she was ready to drop off again, in truth, sleep was the last thing on her mind.

She went over their conversation in her head. All Mr. Gallagher's words, his whole tone of voice when talking about his late wife, expressed complete devotion. Reid Gallagher still loved his first wife, as deeply and purely as on the day he'd first met her. Maddie stared dry eyed through the dark. With each word of his, every inflection of tenderness in his voice, she'd felt all her hopes snuffed out.

He'd been candid about his love. She had no reason to doubt it. No wonder he'd never remarried in all these years. No wonder he still wore his wedding band. No woman could ever hope to compete with such a sacred memory, least of all a penniless, aging spinster with nothing to recommend her— no connections, no looks and no charm—none of the attributes of Cecily Mason and any other lady his aunt and sister threw in his path.

Her future stretched before her, one colorless day drifting into another as she continued her servitude to Lady Haversham. Somehow she'd have to bury her growing feelings for her…employer. She hesitated over the word, which sounded too cold and formal for the man who'd carried her down the mountainside in his arms today and sat by her side and made her smile and in a matter of seconds had broken her heart so thoroughly….

What did one call that kind of person?

A man with whom one had fallen desperately, hopelessly in love?

Dear Lord, don't let him know, never let him suspect how I feel about him.

Chapter Twelve

The next day the gillie, Ewane, arrived with another man. Feeling like someone feigning illness, Maddie protested against being carried all the way down to the glen in a litter, but Mr. Gallagher was adamant. She was not walking more than a few steps.

Now she lay on the litter, once again tucked into blankets by Mr. Gallagher, and felt its gentle sway. She bit her lip, stewing in her sense of powerlessness. She hadn't felt so helpless since she was a girl in the Holy Land, suffering bouts of illness. She remembered how she'd hindered her parents' work overseas, and now she had destroyed this man's climb to the summit. The comparison might seem ridiculous but Maddie couldn't help drawing the parallels as she watched his strong back at the front of her litter. He'd insisted on carrying one end of it.

They arrived back at the house by early evening. Both Lady Haversham and her niece stood at the front entry when Maddie was carried in.

Lady Haversham leaned on her cane and glared at Maddie.

"What is the meaning of this? You caused me the utmost worry yesterday. I couldn't sleep a wink the whole night, isn't that so, Vera?"

"Yes, indeed. I had to sit up with her. Reid, where in the world did you take off to with Miss Norton?" She turned shocked eyes onto Maddie. "And Miss Norton, I'm amazed at you, sneaking off like that, leaving your employ—"

Mr. Gallagher interrupted his sister. "That's enough, Vera. Can't you see the woman is injured? Now, clear the way, everyone," he told the hovering servants in a stern voice.

Maddie sat up on the pallet, horrified at the accusations. "I can make it up the stairs on my own." Before Mr. Gallagher could stop her, she'd swung her legs over the side. It was only in the shocked silence that followed that she remembered her garments. She swallowed, staring down at the trousers she still wore.

Lady Haversham's sharp intake of breath told Maddie all she needed to hear.

"Excuse me, my lady." She faltered then turned and stumbled from the area, her only wish to disappear from the looks of disapproval all around her. She clutched the stair rail, her legs feeling weak, but determined to mount the flight of steps.

She ignored Mr. Gallagher's "Miss Norton—" Instead of insisting on accompanying her, she heard him give a sharp order to one of the maids, who hurried to her side.

"Here, miss, take my arm and I'll help you to your room."

"Thank you," she mumbled, hardly daring to look the woman in the eyes.

By tomorrow she knew she'd be on a train heading back to London, unemployed. She had no one to blame but herself. Did all spinsters on the verge of turning thirty do such foolish things?

* * *

Reid refused to discuss Miss Norton with his aunt and sister until he'd sent for a doctor. Only then did he escort the two ladies into the library and shut the door behind them.

"Really, Aunt Millicent, did you have to light into the poor woman like that? Didn't you see she was injured?"

His aunt sat down in the wing chair and took deep, gasping breaths, one hand over her breast. "What did you expect me to do? You and the woman go missing yesterday and then I see her carried in on a stretcher, and her outfit!" She turned to Vera. "Did you ever see such a scandalous thing?"

At her niece's vigorous shake of the head, her attention returned to Reid. "Can you blame me? Here I thought Miss Norton was a respectable lady. I brought her to live under my roof." She closed her eyes and shuddered.

"Auntie, are you all right?" Vera asked. "Do you want me to get you your maid?"

"Give me a moment." Her voice was faint. "I've had such a shock."

Reid raked a hand through his hair, at a loss of how to deal with his aunt's hysteria. How long before the doctor arrived? Miss Norton had slept much of the way down, so he was more convinced than ever she had suffered a concussion. He wished he could go up and see how she was but was afraid that would only make things worse. If he'd known their entrance would cause such a disturbance, he'd have brought Miss Norton in through the back. Then he swore under his breath, disgusted at this subterfuge. He was tired of the way Maddie was treated—

"Haven't you heard a word I've said, Reid?" He swiveled around to face his aunt, who didn't look any too well herself.

"What?— Excuse me, Aunt Millicent, I'm simply concerned for Miss Norton. She suffered quite a blow to her head and I'm anxious for a doctor to see to her."

"A blow to her head? Whatever did you do to her? Oh, my goodness, my nerves can't take anymore—" His aunt began to fan herself.

"We were merely hiking up to the peak of Ben Lawers when she lost her footing and fell several feet. She hit her head on a rock and lost consciousness for a few moments."

His sister gasped. "Is she all right?"

"I don't know. I've known men to suffer less profound blows and be seriously injured. It can even prove fatal."

"But…but she's all right now, isn't she? She appeared fine," Vera insisted.

"She might *appear* fine, but we have no idea what internal injury might have befallen her. She could have a skull fracture, for all we know. I'm almost certain she suffered a concussion."

His aunt fanned herself more vigorously. "Oh, my heavens. How could you take her up there? I've suffered enough."

Vera went to her aunt. "There, Auntie, Reid is scaring us unnecessarily. He's used to talking to men and has forgotten the sensibility of ladies. I'm sure Miss Norton will be fine. Her color was good and she walked up the stairs herself."

"I must consider what is to be done once she is fully recovered. I really can't have such behavior under my roof. Think of your children, Vera. What will Theo say?"

"Yes, I know. There'll be time enough to deal with Miss Norton once she is up again."

Reid stared at her. "Are you thinking of dismissing her, Aunt Millicent?"

"Reid, dear, consider my position. What were you thinking, taking an unmarried woman—my paid companion—up a mountaintop? How could you do such a thing?"

"I was thinking of her good. She spends most of her time cooped up in a stuffy house in London—"

"In my ample house in one of its best quarters—"

"You can hardly breathe the air in that city—"

Aunt Millicent closed her fan with a snap and tapped it against the chair arm. "Her behavior was improper, to say the least. What is everyone going to think?"

"I thought the fresh air would do her good—"

"Fresh air? Fresh air?" She waved the fan around her. "There's all kinds of fresh air around us."

Reid paced the room, frustrated. They were clearly talking at cross-purposes. "The poor lady is as pale as a sheet and suffers headaches."

"Nonsense. She's as strong as a horse and gets out on plenty of my errands. And how do you know so much about her, anyway?"

Reid stopped. "She works for me, too, or don't you remember Uncle George's collection?"

"I should never have agreed to that arrangement. I regret ever hiring the woman. Well, she won't be with me much longer, I can tell you that."

Reid's resolve hardened. He'd done Miss Norton enough harm. "If you dismiss her, I'll hire her to work with me at the British Museum."

Suddenly Aunt Millicent slumped forward. "Oh, Reid, I feel…it's my…heart…it's just tripping. Help me!"

Reid and his sister were at her chair instantly. "What is it? What can I get you? Where are your pills?"

"Ring for Mad—for my maid," she amended, clutching her chest.

The maid, when she arrived, immediately got her one of her pills and handed it to her with a glass of water. "There, ma'am, that should fix you up."

Vera rose to look out the window. "I wonder if the doctor has arrived. He can take a look at you, Auntie."

"Yes, please," Aunt Millicent whispered, lying back against the chair now, her breathing steadier.

Reid headed for the door. "I'll go see." He felt torn between worry for Miss Norton and causing his aunt further upset. Her attack of nerves seemed almost too convenient, but he couldn't doubt it. He'd done enough damage as it was already.

Women! He was better off returning to the desert and the company of men. He knew how to deal with them there.

The doctor confirmed that Miss Norton had indeed suffered a concussion and was to take it easy over the next several days. He gave Lady Haversham a sedative with instructions to the others not to worry her with anything.

By midafternoon the next day, when Lady Haversham was sitting up in her bed, her niece came to share tea with her.

"How is that woman?" was Lady Haversham's first question after replying to Vera's inquiry over her own health.

Vera made a moue of distaste. "I've seen neither hide nor hair of her. Hiding out in her room, it seems."

"What are we to do? I don't like it, not at all. You saw the way Reid blew up at me over her."

"I know, Auntie. I agree the situation is of concern." She tapped her teacup with a fingernail, looking at her aunt with troubled eyes. "But do you really think Reid would give a woman like that a second glance...I mean, with *serious* intentions?"

Lady Haversham firmed her lips. "I wouldn't have thought so until yesterday. But remember how he was with Octavia? One look and he fell hard for her. What if he were to do so with this...this creature?" She shuddered.

Vera gave an incredulous laugh. "Miss Norton and Octavia? Why, the two are nothing alike. What does Miss Norton have to offer? Oh, I grant you, she's passably attractive, but she's no longer young, she comes from who knows where. She's a *paid* companion, for goodness' sake!"

"Nevertheless, she's wily," Aunt Millicent reminded her. "She has insinuated herself as an assistant to poor Reid. It's all my fault for allowing her to work some hours with him on your uncle George's artifacts. To think of her closeted alone with Reid. The poor man has been beguiled."

"Yes…I see."

Lady Haversham squeezed her niece's hand. "Don't forget, you and Reid are my only heirs. Miss Norton is no fool. She's looking out for her future." Her eyes hardened. "I won't have some gold-digging servant get her claws into my nephew who's too gullible to know he's being taken in. I told Reid I'd dismiss her, and I meant it."

"You must be careful, Aunt Millicent. You heard what Reid said about hiring her himself."

"Oh, don't even mention that! I won't have it!"

"Yes, I know. I like it as little as you do, but we need to consider things carefully. We wouldn't want to precipitate anything."

Her aunt regarded her niece. "What do you suggest, then? I can't have her under my roof anymore."

"Perhaps it's better to have her where you can keep an eye on her…keep her so busy she'll have no time to be in Reid's company."

Her aunt considered and slowly nodded. "I see your point, my dear." She gave a deep sigh, lying against the pillow. "I shall have to think about your suggestion."

"Well, there's no undue rush. The woman has to convalesce awhile, it seems, according to the doctor."

Her aunt's look soured once again. "Yes. She certainly arranged that conveniently."

"Don't fret, Aunt Millicent. As long as she's confined to her room, Reid can't see her, either."

"Yes, there is that. It will give us time, too, to decide on our course."

Maddie awoke on her birthday feeling every one of her thirty years.

After washing and dressing, she examined herself in the mirror—an activity she wasn't in the habit of doing. She didn't look any different. No gray threads running through her hair yet, but it was only a matter of time.

She swung away from the glass. Enough of that nonsense. At least the pain in her head had subsided. The doctor had explained to her that her brain had been jolted around a bit and was most likely a bit bruised. "Best to let it settle and heal," he'd said with a final snap of his bag after instructing her to take it easy and to indulge in no strenuous activities for at least a week.

She didn't see the family until dinner. She'd spent most of the intervening days in her room, having her meals sent up. It wasn't that she was afraid of confronting Lady Haversham, but neither had she felt up to facing an immediate dismissal without references. She had no doubt that was what awaited her as soon as she saw her employer.

She'd also not seen Mr. Gallagher. Her feelings there were more complicated. She had received a brief note from him, delivered by a maid. He urged her to rest and take it easy. She wondered if he, too, thought it best that she stay out of his aunt's way for a few days. Torn between desiring to see his dear face and afraid of depending on him too much, she'd finally kept to her room in order to avoid him, as well.

Maddie had packed most of her few belongings. Now she stood a second, hearing the murmur of voices in the dining room, telling her the others were already assembled.

She opened the door and immediately they all fell silent. Everyone around the table turned to look at her.

Lady Haversham held her fork aloft. "You've decided to grace us with your company, I see." Not waiting for Maddie's reply, she turned away and continued eating.

"Yes, my lady." Maddie stepped to her place. A footman came immediately to pull out her chair. "Thank you."

"Good afternoon, Miss Norton." Maddie turned to greet Mr. Gallagher, who stood. She returned his smile with a tentative one of her own. At least he did not regret their outing to Ben Lawers. "It's good to see you up and about again."

She took her seat. "Thank you."

Lady Haversham turned her attention to Maddie again. "I can't say *I* have fully recovered. I have suffered countless lost hours of sleep and a terrible strain to my heart on your account."

Maddie's smile disappeared. "I'm sorry for any—"

Mr. Gallagher set his fork down with a clatter. "Now, Aunt Millicent, do we really need to begin our meal in this manner? We've been over this already."

"You are right, dear boy. This is not the time nor the place for what I have to say."

Whatever appetite Maddie had had upon entering the room shriveled up and she shook her head at the tray of sliced meat the footman held before her. Instead she took a sip of the crystal goblet of water.

Lady Haversham turned to her nephew. "Reid, I'm told there's a beautiful castle we really must see. I do hope you can accompany us before we leave."

Maddie's heart sank, not wanting to be reminded of having to leave Scotland.

"Just let me know when you'd like to visit, Aunt Millicent, and I'll arrange an outing."

"Thank you, my dear." Lady Haversham sighed. "It's hard to imagine that by next week it will be time to return to London. Poor Cecily Mason was desolate to have to depart so soon."

"I, for one, look forward to our return," Vera said. "Not that I haven't enjoyed this holiday, but there's something about the vigor of city life I miss."

"It's a pity Theo couldn't stay longer," Lady Haversham said.

"Yes, another reason I must return. I'm sure my poor husband is pining."

Maddie sighed. What would it be like when they returned to London? Would Maddie ever see Mr. Gallagher again? Where would she go? She could only count on her unpaid wages.

"Aren't you hungry?"

She lifted her head at Mr. Gallagher's sharp tone.

"Not too much, I'm afraid." Her stomach already felt twisted in knots.

Lady Haversham looked at her fork. "This lamb is delicious, so tender and well seasoned. The cook has outdone herself with the new potatoes and peas. What a shame to have it go to waste."

Mr. Gallagher motioned for the footman to pass Maddie another platter. "If you want something lighter, we can have them bring in some of the potato-and-leek soup from the first course."

"No, this is fine, thank you." She took some of the vegetables offered her, determined to make an effort to eat, if only to please Mr. Gallagher. She could see he was trying hard to be agreeable to everyone and at the same time shield her from his aunt's barbs.

Finally, the dishes were cleared away and the dessert plates brought in. Mrs. Walker's three children marched into the room, their nursemaid accompanying them.

Harry came up to his uncle, his face eager. "Are we in time, Uncle Reid?"

"Just in time." He placed a finger to his lips. "Hush, now."

The boy nodded vigorously. All three children seated themselves at the foot of the table, at the place where their nursemaid indicated.

Lady Haversham smiled at them from the opposite end of the table. "What brings all of you here?"

"A surprise!" her oldest nephew answered, barely able to keep his excitement contained.

Before she could react, a maid appeared in the doorway carrying an enormous round cake topped by dozens of lit candles. Amidst the children's chorus of "Happy Birthday," she headed toward Maddie.

Maddie's hands flew to her cheeks, unable to believe what was happening.

The maid smiled and set the cake before her. "Happy birthday, miss."

"Th-thank you." Maddie hardly knew what to say. The children clapped, and she noticed Mr. Gallagher clapping, as well. She looked around her in question, but both Lady Haversham and her niece seemed as surprised as she. Maddie's gaze landed on Mr. Gallagher who gave her a small nod of acknowledgment.

Before she could decide if he'd been responsible for her surprise party, the butler brought her a tray of wrapped packages. "Oh, my, what's all this?"

Lisbeth stood up. "Happy birthday, Miss Norton. The presents are from us—and Uncle Reid."

Her gaze flew once more to Mr. Gallagher. He shrugged. "Just a small token to celebrate this special day."

"Oh, my." It was almost too much to absorb. She stole a look at Lady Haversham, and her joy evaporated when she saw the woman's pursed lips.

"Aren't you going to blow out your candles, Miss Norton?"

"Oh—yes!" She looked from Lisbeth's shining face to the candles which had burned down at least halfway.

"As I recall, today you're officially an old maid."

At the acid tone, Maddie turned to her employer, surprised by how much the words hurt. "Yes, your memory serves you well." She drew a deep breath, ready to extinguish the candles.

"Make a wish first!"

She stopped immediately. "Of course." She edged back and closed her eyes. The only thing she could think of was to wish that she'd always remember this moment, and the warm light shining in Mr. Gallagher's eyes, later…when the way got lonelier.

Then she opened her eyes and blew out the candles. There seemed to be so many candles, but she didn't stop to count them. At that moment it didn't matter how old she was. She felt she was once again eighteen.

The maid removed the cake from in front of her and proceeded to cut it. Meanwhile the children clamored until she opened their gifts. She saw at once which ones were theirs. They were clumsily wrapped in brown paper with colorful string and ribbons.

Timmy leaned toward her. "That one's from me."

"Sit straight," his mother admonished.

Maddie took her time opening it, relishing the act. Inside

was a yo-yo, which she recognized as Timmy's own. She looked at him with a smile.

"That's my favorite one. You can have it now."

"Thank you, Timmy. It's very kind of you to part with your favorite yo-yo."

Harry grabbed a thin parcel "Mine next, mine next!"

"Goodness, Harry, where are your manners, reaching across the table like that!" Lady Haversham scolded.

"Thank you, Harry." Maddie smiled at the boy, taking the package from him.

Inside she found a folded paper. Spreading it flat, she saw a picture he'd painted with his watercolors.

"That's Ben Lawers from Loch Tay. And that's you falling down the hill."

Maddie looked more closely at the drawing. Sure enough, a sticklike figure was tumbling backward down a crudely drawn mountainside. She laughed. "Indeed it is. I'm glad I didn't fall quite so far." She looked across at Mr. Gallagher and met his smile. She handed the painting to him.

He looked at it, amusement lighting his blue eyes. "So it is. I agree with Miss Norton. It's a good thing she didn't fall quite such a distance. But you were very accurate. It certainly seemed as if she'd fallen that far the other day."

Lisbeth handed Maddie her parcel with a shy smile.

"Thank you, dear." She found one of the young girl's hair ribbons neatly rolled up in the small parcel. "It's beautiful," she said, fingering the blue satin ribbon.

"It will look very pretty against Miss Norton's hair," Mr. Gallagher told his niece.

Lisbeth looked pleased.

Maddie felt herself blush. A glance at the other two women at the table caused her to quickly put the ribbon back in its wrapping and gather the packages together.

"Miss Norton, you forgot your biggest present." Harry reached across the table and handed her the neatest looking package.

If she'd had any doubts whom it was from, Mr. Gallagher's next words dispelled them. "Many happy returns."

She lifted her gaze to meet his. "Thank you." His answering smile was so warm, she felt her heart squeeze with tenderness. How was she to manage without him?

"Aren't you going to open it, Miss Norton?" Timmy piped in.

Mr. Gallagher gave a slight nod. "Go ahead."

She wished she could take his gift up to her room and open it in private. Her fingers trembled as she untied the bow of the wide ribbon holding together the wrapping paper. She laid it on the table and parted the paper.

"Oh!" Inside lay a leather-bound book. She turned it toward its spine and read the golden letters: *The Poems and Songs of Robert Burns*. She opened the book and leafed through the gilt-edged pages, before looking toward Mr. Gallagher. "Thank you. It's beautiful."

"Just a small token to mark your day...as well as your holiday in the Highlands."

"Yes." How apt his gift. She would always remember her holiday in the Highlands.

"You'll find his poem 'The Birks of Aberfeldy' in there. It's said he was inspired by the burn that runs through the town."

"We must visit it, then," Vera said.

He turned his attention away from Maddie. "Yes, we could make an excursion there."

Maddie continued paging through the beautiful Moroccan bound edition, the voices around her fading as she read scraps of poetry. Already she was pondering what she could give Mr.

Gallagher on his birthday. She hadn't much to spend, and was mindful of what would be proper for a lady to give a gentleman that wasn't too personal. But she wanted him to have something to remember her by once he was far away in the desert….

After they'd eaten their cake, Lady Haversham rose from the table. "Miss Norton, please attend me in my room."

"Yes, my lady."

Feeling the hour of reckoning had come, Maddie gathered her gifts and followed her employer.

"I'll not say I'm happy with your conduct, Madeleine. You behaved with the utmost lack of decorum. Never forget your father is a respected curate—in a small parish, to be sure, but respected, nonetheless. If you're not thinking of yourself, at least think of him and his reputation among his flock.

"With this in view, I shall overlook your conduct this time. But, I warn you, I shall not be so merciful the next time. You must respect the office of your employment here."

Maddie bit her lip to keep from protesting. Her cheeks grew red. She could hardly believe the older woman would drag her father into the conversation. What had Maddie done? She couldn't fathom that a hike in the Scottish Highlands would be seen as such a wicked thing. "Yes, my lady," she finally managed in a quiet tone. "It won't happen again."

"I realize the fault is not entirely yours. I have spoken to my nephew and made him see that conventions here in England cannot be ignored, regardless of what type of civilization—or lack of it—he is accustomed to in the Middle East."

"Yes, my lady." She was still grappling with understanding what terrible crime she had committed, but now she felt doubly bad on Mr. Gallagher's behalf. He shouldn't have to endure his aunt's reprimand for offering Maddie an experience in the out-of-doors.

"Now, you may sit with me awhile and read to me from Dr. Hickey's sermons. I suggest you turn to the one on the 'wages of sin.' I believe it was found in the previous chapter."

"Yes, my lady." Maddie fetched the heavy tome and took a seat.

Three-quarters of an hour later, Maddie finally exited Lady Haversham's room, the stinging words of the sermon reverberating.

She made it back to her room, her mind slightly dazed. How had her life gotten so topsy-turvy in a few short weeks? She'd always prided herself on her decorum, her conduct at all times above reproach in the households where she'd worked.

She collapsed on the chair at the writing desk, bringing her palms up to her cheeks, which still felt warm at the reprimand. At least Lady Haversham had not dismissed her. Maddie tried to feel grateful, but at the moment all she wanted was to give her employer a few choice words and leave, never looking back.

The thought of never seeing Mr. Gallagher again stopped her. He'd been nothing but kindness itself. She closed her eyes and fisted her hands against her cheeks, trying to stem the emotions that flooded her at the thought of this gentleman, so different from any she had ever met.

A wave of despair assailed her whenever she thought of the future without him. *Lord, forgive me for getting distracted with such worldly thoughts. Help me keep focused on the ultimate goal.* She repeated the words of scripture that had always sustained her in the past.

Let us lay aside every weight, and the sin which doth so easily beset us, and let us run with patience the race that is set before us, looking unto Jesus the author and finisher of our faith; who for the joy that was set before him endured the cross...

She must remember her Lord's sacrifice to prevent herself from falling into self-pity. She opened her Bible that sat on the desk and retrieved her brother Todd's letter, which she had received the day after her fall. She unfolded the much-creased pages.

The letter was dated over a month ago and, except for the topmost note, was stained and smudged.

Dearest Maddie,

As you can see, I began the first part of this letter over two months ago. Much has happened since then. I have just returned to King's Town, where your last four letters awaited me. They were a most welcome sight, believe me, like a little bit of home right here in West Africa.

I was delayed upriver due to many things. Praise God, I was finally able to journey to the remote village of Oku Ban. Many had warned against going there, the tribes being known for cannibalism and aggressive warfare. But God is faithful. He protected me and the small group accompanying me.

His letter went on to describe all the things they had experienced during their time in that village, the drunkenness among the tribesmen, the fevers and the fighting between tribes.

Oh, Maddie, if you could have seen the illness and filth among those people, your heart would have wept. The supplies you sent on the last steamer were well used, believe me.

Never doubt, dear sister, that your sacrifice is seen and appreciated. I know you'd join me here in a moment if you could. The greatest breakthrough came when the chief accepted Jesus as his savior. Glory to God!

I was further delayed because I, too, fell ill with fever. It lasted some weeks, but praise God, He has brought me through to continue with my task here.

Don't forget we all run a race and until the Lord summons us home, we must do everything He calls us to do to finish our course....

Maddie looked up from the paper, the tears dampening her cheeks. Her brother's words had done her good. She must gird her loins, the way the Lord exhorted Job to do. There was too little time to sit around and feel sorry for oneself when so many souls were perishing.

She took out her handkerchief and wiped her eyes. Enough weeping for today. With God's grace she would continue in Lady Haversham's employment, under the woman's authority, knowing that through her obedience, a greater good would come about.

As to her feelings for Mr. Gallagher, she would have to entrust them to the Lord and depend upon Him to see her through any heartbreak.

Chapter Thirteen

Regret and relief warred within Reid when he left the Highlands. He didn't wish to cause his aunt any further distress or Miss Norton any more tension with her employer. He had no patience with the intrigues of women—and with his sister and aunt in league, he feared Miss Norton was at a distinct disadvantage.

Although he'd promised his aunt he'd find Miss Norton employment at the museum should she dismiss Maddie, Reid wasn't certain how well he could keep that promise. All the employees there were male and highly specialized in their field.

But more than these concerns was the deeper fear of being unable to contain his own growing feelings for Miss Norton. During the week of her convalescence it had been a daily struggle for Reid to treat her with simple courtesy and friendliness, when what he really wanted was to take her in his arms and hold her.

He would never forgive himself if he raised Miss Norton's expectations and then was unable to offer her anything more than friendship—and a temporary one at that—until he returned to Egypt.

He remembered her story of the suitor of her youth, already despising a man who would lead a young lady on and then not make her an offer of marriage. Worthless cad…

Yet, what more could Reid, himself, offer her? He could never permit himself happiness with another woman—not when he had been responsible for curtailing Octavia's life. Miss Norton's fall on Ben Lawers had been a rude awakening for him. He was not to be trusted with a woman's well-being. If he had proved such a terrible husband to Octavia in London, how could he possibly protect Maddie in a place like the desert?

His thoughts went round and round in this vein, coming up with no solution. One thing was certain. He would be unable to return to London and the working relationship he'd developed with Maddie. Ever since she'd spoken her name, he'd been unable to think of her as anything but "Maddie."

It would be impossible to have her at his side each day without… Well, he refused to let his thoughts go down that road.

He sighed. He'd just have to hire a new assistant. One of those earnest young chaps at the museum. Yes, that was the only solution. He'd been foolish to propose this arrangement to Maddie in the first place.

The day after they arrived back in London, his aunt made the decision easier for him when she called him into her parlor.

"Reid, I really cannot spare Miss Norton to work with you any longer. What strength I had has waned considerably, and I need her at my side."

Reid glanced at his aunt in surprise. "Did the trip to Scotland leave you worse off?"

"Yes and no." She fiddled with her jade necklace. "It certainly was a nice change, and I had a lovely time with both you and Vera. But the trip has exhausted me. You don't realize how I am getting on in years."

"I'm sorry. I know it was a long trip."

"You meant well in planning it for us. I'll always be grateful for it. But now I must take it easy. The heat in London leaves me feeling drained."

Reid looked away from her, knowing the news he was about to deliver wouldn't be welcome. He leaned forward and braced his elbows on his knees. "I've received word that the British have wrapped up their investigation and so I hope I'll soon be able to return to the Sinai."

"Oh, no…" Her head fell against the chair back. "I had so hoped you were home for good this time."

"I know." He tried to smile. "But you know my life is there."

She shook her head. "You and your uncle both yearned for adventure always." She sighed. "Ah well, at least I have your sister and her family."

"Yes." He coughed before continuing. "As I explained to you when I first undertook the task of Uncle George's artifacts, it's too much for one individual. My time back in England is limited."

Before he could continue, his aunt held up her hand. "I have given it considerable thought, and I've decided if you can bring in an assistant—someone who is quiet and will not disturb the household's routine—then I will not oppose it."

Reid smiled in relief. "I'm sure I can find someone to fit your requirements. In fact, I know just the chap. I'll have to talk to him and to the curator of the museum to see if his services could be spared for a few hours each day. It would help enormously." He didn't allow himself to think how much he'd miss Miss Norton's quiet, capable presence. Life had taught him that all good things came to an end, including his time with Maddie—Miss Norton. Soon, he'd be gone himself.

"Very well, I shall welcome him when he comes."

Reid rose. "Good then. I'll let you know as soon as I've arranged things."

"Your sister is planning a party for your birthday."

He frowned. "I'm not used to paying much attention to the date anymore."

"That may be so in Egypt, but here you're among family and we'd like to recognize this special day. After all, you're turning forty."

"You needn't remind me."

"There's no reason to feel down about it. Forty is a man's prime. You should be proud of your accomplishments. Not many men can boast of all you've done."

Wanting to end the subject, he moved toward the door. "Well, just let me know Vera's plans. I need to return to the museum." He hadn't seen Miss Norton since he'd walked in and wondered where she was. His aunt had said nothing, and Reid wasn't about to ask her.

As he was leaving the house, he spotted Miss Norton crossing the square, Lilah leading on her leash. He stopped and waited for her, telling himself it was just courtesy that made him want to greet her.

It had only been a day since their return, but he found himself taking in every inch of her appearance. Her cheeks were flushed in the heat of the noonday, and wispy strands of her hair that had escaped the thick roll at the nape of her neck framed her face. He had to clench his hands to keep from reaching out to touch one. "Good afternoon."

She gave him a smile, and he was struck afresh by her beautiful pink-tinged complexion. "Hello, Mr. Gallagher."

"Have you come from a ways?"

"I've just been walking Lilah, as well as coming from the apothecary's for your aunt." She indicated a small parcel.

He frowned. "It's quite a warm day for such a walk. Don't overdo it."

The color in her cheeks deepened. "I'm sure my head is all healed."

He cleared his throat. "I was talking to my aunt about…" He hesitated. How would she take the news? Disappointed or relieved? "About our working arrangement."

"Yes?" She looked at him, her clear tawny eyes watching him.

"My aunt has agreed to an assistant from outside, from the museum, that is."

"Oh." He couldn't read anything from her expression. Her gaze remained steady.

"I realize how much strain the work put on you, having to divide your time between my aunt's needs and mine. I hate to lose you as an able assistant, but I think this will relieve you somewhat."

"I see." He wished he could know what she really meant with the two words.

"I'm going to the museum now, to try to arrange something with a fellow I know there. He's quite knowledgeable on Egyptian antiquities…." Impatient with himself for fumbling for words, he touched his fingers to his hat. "Well, it's good seeing you back to normal again. Good day."

"Good day, Mr. Gallagher." She looked away from him and continued up the steps. He hurried to open the door for her and she passed through without looking at him.

He remained looking at the door after it had shut, feeling both irritated and annoyed without knowing why. Had he expected Miss Norton to weep at his announcement? He must be thankful she had taken the news so coolly. It proved her heart wasn't yet touched.

Not as his was beginning to be. After so long a slumber, it was proving a painful awakening.

Maddie removed her hat and hurried to deliver the medicine she'd gone to fetch for Lady Haversham. She stood while her employer inspected the bottle and asked her a host of questions.

Finally she was able to excuse herself. She escaped to her room, glad to have a few minutes to herself before she'd have to attend Lady Haversham again.

So, the bright spot of her days in London was to be snuffed out. Perhaps it was better this way.

Maddie went to her sewing basket and removed the needlepoint project she was working on. Better to keep her mind busy. She'd temporarily put aside the chair cushions to make this bookmark. She could only work on it while she was alone, but it was small so she was sure she'd have it done in time for Mr. Gallagher's birthday.

She held the marker away from her a moment. It was coming along nicely. She liked the colors she'd chosen, blue and maroon, suitably masculine, yet the bright gold letters kept it from being too somber. It was an appropriate gift, she decided. Not too familiar, useful, small, so he could easily carry it with him on his travels—and the message was her own way of making it personal and memorable….

Maddie wasn't able to wish Mr. Gallagher a happy birthday on the day because she didn't see him at all. His sister organized a party for him and Lady Haversham ordered her carriage to convey her, but didn't invite Maddie along, taking her maid instead.

After considering what to do with her small gift, Maddie decided to have it sent to Mr. Gallagher's lodgings. She penned a short note and wrapped up her gift and gave it to a footman with instructions to have it delivered to the Travellers Club.

She tried returning to the chair cushions, but found it hard to concentrate. Finally she put on her hat and went out, deciding a long walk was the best way to clear the cobwebs from her mind. A short interlude of her life was over, and she mustn't dwell on it overmuch.

Reid returned to the Travellers that evening after having spent the day at his sister's among a gaggle of friends and acquaintances of hers. He'd known many in his younger days, but shared little in common with them now. So much senseless chatter...

The tight collar chafed at his neck and his frock coat was stiff and uncomfortable.

The porter bowed to him in the quiet foyer of the club. "Good evening, Mr. Gallagher."

"Good evening, John."

"You received a telegram, sir. And here is your mail."

"Thank you." He took the envelopes handed to him, wondering what the wire was about. Was it his travel orders?

Before he could open it, a voice hailed him. He looked up to see Cyril striding across the lobby. "I say, old man, where have you been?"

"Scotland."

"Ah, yes, you told me you were heading up there." Cyril reached him and the two shook hands. "You look fit. The holiday must have agreed with you."

Reid nodded, releasing his friend's hand. "Yes, it was very pleasant."

"Get any fishing done?"

"Yes, quite a bit. I also got in some hiking." He remembered Maddie walking at his side, never tiring, never complaining.

"Have you tried the latest sport? I daresay you haven't had a chance to, being in the desert."

"Which sport are you referring to?"

"Why, cycling! You must have noticed everyone in London is pedaling around."

Reid thought about the number of bicycles he had seen since he'd been in London. "Yes, I suppose there are a few."

"A few? Thousands, I'd say. Since they came out with the pneumatic tires, it's a national pastime. Have you never been on one?"

Reid shook his head.

"You must. It's a great sport."

"I think I'm a little old for a new sport."

"Nonsense. My wife and I just learned this spring. We go all over the countryside when the weather is nice." He clapped Reid on the back. "Come on out, and I'll set you up. You'll be pedaling all over in London in no time." Without giving Reid a chance to refuse, he asked, "So, how much longer are you in London anyway?"

"Hopefully, not much longer. In fact—" Remembering the telegram he'd just received, he tapped it. "I believe this might be the good news I've been waiting for."

"You haven't opened it?"

"No, I was about to when you hailed me."

"Well, don't let me keep you. Go ahead."

Reid slit open the envelope and read the few words in a matter of seconds. He looked up to find his friend's gaze on him.

"Well, what is it? You look mighty puzzled for news you've been expecting."

He handed the paper across to his friend.

Cyril's bearded face split open in a grin. "By golly, you're to be awarded a knighthood by order of the Queen!" The next second he pumped Reid's hand. "Congratulations, old man! Splendid, I say." He shook his head. "Who would have thought picking about in old ruins would have been of more value to Her Majesty's kingdom than making filthy lucre in trade!"

"I can hardly believe it." Reid felt overwhelmed with the news. "I didn't expect…anything like this…."

"Oh, you'll get used to the honor. Well deserved, by what you've told me. Think how you've enriched the British Museum for future generations." He took up the telegram again. "It says here an official letter will follow with details for the ceremony. I hope you'll invite me to attend."

Reid was hardly listening. A knighthood. Like his Uncle George. He smiled. His uncle would have been proud.

Cyril stepped away from him. "Well, I'd better get to the train station. It's been wonderful seeing you again, old man. I'm serious about the invitation. Why not come out this weekend?"

Reid thought about it a moment. It might not be a bad thing to get away for a few days. He needed to gain some perspective on things. Being in Scotland in such close company with his family…and with Miss Norton—he admitted the latter only reluctantly—had thrown him off balance. It was not too late to rectify things. His uncle's artifacts could wait. If they'd waited this long, they could wait a few more days. With that uncharacteristic attitude, he nodded to his friend. "All right, if you're sure your wife won't mind a stranger in your midst."

"Of course not. She's a wonderful hostess." After giving him instructions for the railway, Cyril bid him good-night.

Reid headed up to his room. Only then did he remember the rest of his mail. He flipped through the small stack. The bottom one caught his eye because it was a bit thicker than the rest. That and the neat script on the outside, which looked very familiar.

He opened the flap. A folded sheet of notepaper slipped out, but he ignored that as he spied the richly colored object that came out with it. A bookmark, he saw immediately, its gold silken tassel identifying it.

It was beautifully worked, minute stitches filling in every space, the colors reminiscent of an Islamic mosaic—in hues of blues and purples. He narrowed his eyes at the letters in gothic script. "Wherever I wander, wherever I rove, / The hills of the Highlands for ever I love."

He recognized the words of Burns's poem and was immediately transported to that day on the mountains, before Maddie's accident.

He unfolded the paper that accompanied it.

Dear Mr. Gallagher, Just a small token for your birthday. I shall always be grateful for the wonderful holiday in the Highlands. May the Lord bless you. Yours truly, Madeleine Norton

Maddie's small, yet beautiful gift was just what he'd needed on this day marking his fortieth year. She'd understood. It touched him more than all the expensive gifts of shirts, ties, tiepins and waistcoats he'd received that afternoon. If he could have spent this day with anyone, she would have been the perfect companion, he realized, remembering his contentment during their fishing expeditions, her eager interest in all his conversations, her wide smile of pleasure. She would understand what he was feeling today.

He rubbed his thumb across the silken threads, feeling tears smarting his eyes. Hastily he wiped at the corners of his eyes, dismayed by his reaction.

He most certainly needed to get away for a while and get things in perspective. He would not, *would not,* be disloyal to his wife's memory. Her death would not have been in vain.

Maddie heard that Mr. Gallagher had gone away for the weekend. Hardly having adjusted to the fact that she only saw him briefly now when he came in to work in the library, she swallowed her disappointment that she wouldn't see him at all for a while.

She was surprised therefore when she received a note in the mail addressed to her. It was postmarked the day after his birthday. She unfolded the piece of paper.

Dear Miss Norton, I was touched by your beautiful gift. Please accept my sincerest thanks for your time and thoughtfulness. Sincerely, Reid Gallagher

Maddie tried not to feel disappointment at the stiff, formal words. They sounded so unlike the man she'd come to know on holiday in the rugged outdoors of Scotland. With a sigh, she folded the note back up and replaced it in the envelope, knowing she'd keep it even though there was nothing special she could glean from it, nothing to comfort her in future days. Had he no inkling of the love she'd poured into every stitch of the needlepoint? She'd tried to express through her own note what was in her heart without burdening him with the full force of her feelings for him.

Hearing Lady Haversham's bell, she tucked the envelope inside her Bible and headed to answer her employer's summons.

Reid returned from his weekend more glad to be back in London than he'd ever imagined possible.

He was pedaling his brand-new bicycle along the London street, on his way to his aunt's, wondering how soon he'd run into Miss Norton. He knew he'd gone away to try to get his feelings under control, but all he'd done while he'd been away was think of her.

He glanced down at the bicycle, the one reason he was glad he'd gone away. He was grateful now that Cyril had insisted he try out the sport. After a few false starts he'd gotten the hang of balancing on the two-wheeled contraption that had come a long way from its early days of one giant forewheel and two small rear ones, a tricycle a person needed assistance to mount.

After mastering the technique of riding, Reid had hardly been off it during the weekend. Cyril and his wife belonged to a cycling club and the two took excursions near their home every weekend. Reid had enjoyed their Sunday-afternoon tour all around the western suburbs of London. The bicycle made the miles go by in minutes.

He'd decided then and there to purchase his own bicycle and use it to get around London while he was there. When he returned to Egypt, he'd have it shipped to Cairo for when he was in the city.

Now he pedaled to his aunt's house, having arranged to meet the new assistant there at ten o'clock. As he turned the corner into Belgrave Square, he spotted Miss Norton heading from the opposite direction, Lilah tugging at her leash, and tried to suppress the joy that welled up in his chest at the sight of her.

Seeing Miss Norton walking behind the terrier, Reid felt his remaining discipline evaporate like raindrops in the sun. He also felt ashamed of the curt little thank-you note he'd sent her. What a coward he was.

He pedaled past his aunt's front door until he came to a stop before Miss Norton. Her hand flew to her cheek. "Mr. Gallagher!"

He grinned at her surprise, more glad than he could imagine at seeing her. "What do you think?"

She eyed the bicycle. "I didn't know you cycled."

"I didn't. I just learned this weekend."

"So fast? How is it possible?"

He got off the bike and pushed it alongside her. "It's really not difficult. I went to visit a friend and he prevailed upon me to give it a try. He wouldn't listen to any arguments that I was too old a dog to learn new tricks."

"Oh, no, you're not too old at all—" She stopped short at her words. "What a beautiful bicycle. Is it yours?"

He looked at her closely, trying to figure out why she'd interrupted herself. Did she mean it that she didn't consider him too old? "Yes," he said, trying to follow her change of topic, when his mind was reliving holding her in his arms during their dance together…helping her bring in the salmon…. He cleared his throat. "I just bought it. Would you like to give it a try?"

She stopped. "Me? Oh, goodness, no, I couldn't possibly—"

"Why not? I did."

"I couldn't learn."

"Of course you could. I thought it would be difficult but it's not. It would help you, having a bicycle, with all the errands you run for my aunt. Look how flushed you are in this heat. You could ride for twice the distance you walk now in a quarter of the time—"

She bit her lip.

"You'll see how easy it is to learn." Not giving her a chance to refuse, and not questioning his own motives, he hammered on, "I'll come by tomorrow morning and take you…let's see, what about the Green Park? There's plenty of room there and not many people will be out early."

They had reached the front door. "I don't know…I'm not in your aunt's best books right now. I don't know what she'd think."

"She won't fire you."

She frowned at him. "How do you know that?"

He grinned at her again. "I told her if she dismissed you, I'd hire you full-time at the museum."

Her tawny eyes grew large. "You said that?"

He nodded. "When she was being unreasonable about your fall at Ben Lawers."

"You stopped her from dismissing me?"

He felt his own face flush at her awed tone and regretted having repeated his rash promise.

"Oh, she just threatened to. I don't think she was serious."

"I don't know about that. She was rather angry at me."

"Anyway, cycling is very different from climbing Ben Lawers. Lots of ladies are doing it. I'll talk to her."

She bit her lip again. Before she could continue refusing, he reached over and opened the door for her. "It's settled. Meet me here at eight tomorrow morning."

She said nothing in reply but entered the house. He decided not to press her. He'd just have to wait and see if she showed up. She disappeared from sight, and he continued on to the back. He still wasn't sure what, if anything, he'd tell his aunt. There could be nothing wrong in teaching Miss Norton to cycle. He'd see about renting a bicycle before tomorrow.

Feeling curiously lighthearted as he hadn't since before the accident on Ben Lawers, Reid stowed his bicycle and headed for the library ready to confront the artifacts.

Chapter Fourteen

Maddie waited nervously on the front stoop the next morning. Lady Haversham hadn't said a word about the cycling last evening, so Maddie had no idea what Mr. Gallagher had told her.

She relived his words from yesterday. He'd have hired her if Lady Haversham had dismissed her! The same warmth welled up in her heart as it did every time she thought of his words.

She spied him cycling toward her, and watched in amazement to see him balancing another bicycle with his left hand. He'd brought her her own bicycle!

"Good morning," he said with a smile, coming to a stop in front of the house. She walked down to meet him. How on earth was she going to get on that high seat in her skirts? She'd worn her shortest and loosest skirt, yet…

"Good morning," she replied, eyeing the bicycle doubtfully.

He got off his own bicycle. "Here, take your bike and walk it along. We'll go to the Green Park on foot."

"All right." She went to the other bike and placed her hands on the handlebars as she saw him do. Together they left the square and headed for the large park, which was only a few blocks away.

"Beautiful morning, isn't it?" He turned to her with a smile when they'd gone a little ways.

"Yes." She felt lost in his blue gaze and was hardly aware of what kind of day it was.

When they passed through the tall wrought iron gates of the park, Mr. Gallagher scanned the area. "Let's head down this way where there's no one walking about."

They left a few nursemaids pushing prams and made their way to the empty path he indicated.

"All right, the first thing is to mount. I'll hold the bicycle so you won't fall. Once you begin to pedal, it'll stand by itself, you'll see."

She didn't like the idea of sitting up there on two thin wheels. She looked at the bicycle, then at Mr. Gallagher. "How can I maintain my balance?"

"Once the wheels are moving, the bicycle won't tip over. Just look straight ahead and pedal. Oh, and when you do want to stop, you push the pedals backward, and they brake."

She tried to keep it all straight in her head, envisioning herself falling on her face in worse shape than her fall off Ben Lawers.

He was eyeing her skirts again. "I do wish you'd get yourself a pair of bloomers. My friend's wife had a pair."

She smoothed down her skirt. "Maybe this isn't such a good idea."

"Well, I have seen ladies cycling in skirts. Come on, up you go."

Not wanting to appear a coward in front of him, she took a deep breath and asked for God's mercy. Once mounted, she gripped the handlebars until her knuckles hurt. Mr. Gallagher's larger hand covered her left one, his other holding the bike steady at the back of the seat. She felt herself teetering on the two large, narrow wheels.

"All right, I'm going to walk with you while you pedal. I won't let go until you've got the idea."

"A-all right."

They began to move and the pedals turned under her feet.

"Keep the steering wheel steady. That's it."

She tried to do as he said. She couldn't imagine being able to keep the bike upright if he should let go. He began jogging alongside her.

"You've got it," he said. The bicycle began to keep a straighter course. The path sloped downward slightly. Suddenly she was pedaling on her own. She wasn't sure quite when he had let go, but the bicycle was going by itself. The wind was blowing past her.

"That's right, just keep pedaling!" She heard his shout behind her.

Then she panicked and began to move the handlebars. The wheels wobbled. She gave a small scream as the bike tilted to one side. She put out her foot. Her skirts began to tangle with the pedal but finally she had her foot on solid ground and managed to keep the bike upright. Her heart was pounding with fear.

Mr. Gallagher ran up to her, a wide smile on his face. He clapped her on the back. "You did it!"

She was panting, more from the fear than her exertion. She looked at him in amazement, only then remembering how she had been riding for a while on her own. "I did, didn't I? Oh, my goodness, I can't believe it."

"Let's try it again."

Her heart sank. "I don't know…" She gazed at the level

path before her. "There's no slope here. That's probably all that kept me upright."

"Then let's go back there. This time, don't move the handlebars so. Just keep a steady course when you reach the bottom."

"What if I want to stop? I almost fell off this time."

"You'll learn to ease to a stop then put one foot down the way you did." As he spoke, he led her back to where she'd started.

Her fear grew that he'd make her do it on her own this time. "Will you take hold of the bicycle again, please?"

"Of course. I won't let go until I see you've got your balance."

Once again, she mounted the bike and waited for him to grip it firmly. This time she concentrated on keeping the handlebars steady. She prayed for the Lord's direction. She was praying so hard she didn't even notice when Mr. Gallagher removed his hold. Before she knew it she reached the end of the slope and kept going.

Steady, Maddie, keep the wheel straight, she told herself. To her amazement, the bike didn't fall over but kept going. Once again, when she started to think about it, her balance faltered but this time she kept her head and was able to bring the bike to a less abrupt standstill.

Mr. Gallagher ran up to her again. "Well done, Miss Norton."

She beamed at him, breathing heavily. "I can hardly believe it. It's a wonderful feeling, like sailing through the air."

He smiled at her. "Precisely. I wasn't convinced, either, until I tried it. Come on, let's fetch my bicycle and we can try it again."

They spent the next hour practicing. Every time she got

back up on the bicycle, she felt a little more confident of not falling off. By the end of an hour, they were able to circle the park. Her only moments of fear came when they had to pass a pedestrian or nursemaid with a pram. Maddie usually came to a full stop and let the person pass before daring to get back on the path.

When they left, Mr. Gallagher persuaded her to bicycle back. She was afraid of the horse-and-buggy traffic so they walked their bikes across the busiest street near the park, and remounted them on the quieter side streets.

They put their bicycles away in the mews behind the back garden. "We'll do it again tomorrow morning," he told her.

"Is the second bicycle yours?"

"I rented it for you. You can use it this week and then we'll see about getting you your own."

"Oh, Mr. Gallagher, I couldn't possibly purchase one."

He rubbed a spot of dry mud off the front bar of one of the bicycles. "You wouldn't have to. I'm thinking of purchasing another to leave here in England and taking this one with me when I go back to Cairo. You could keep mine for me until I return."

The thought of his leaving took away any pleasure his words would otherwise have given her of entrusting his bicycle to her keeping. "I see."

"You wouldn't mind looking after it, would you?" His blue eyes searched hers.

"No, of course not."

They walked through the garden together. At the back door, she turned to him, her fingers threaded together. "Well, I'd better go see about walking Lilah before she makes a mess in the house."

"And I'd better see if my new assistant has arrived." He

cleared his throat, looking away from her. "Listen, I meant to tell you how much your gift meant to me."

"Oh—" She flushed, remembering her puny gift. "That was nothing, just a small token—"

"No, it wasn't nothing. It was a beautiful piece of workmanship."

She warmed at the praise. "Nothing like an artifact."

He was looking at her so intently. "No, the same. Both are works of art. It was a very appropriate line of verse you chose, as well."

"I've enjoyed the poems very much. That one seemed… fitting."

"Very. It was just the antidote I needed for the vague melancholy that hit me as the day wore on."

Maddie couldn't look away from his steady gaze. Had he experienced the same kinds of thoughts she had on her birthday? It didn't seem possible. His life was too full. "I'm glad you liked it then. It wasn't much—"

"It was a great deal."

"I imagined you surrounded by a crowd of acquaintances on your birthday."

"I was and yet I felt quite alone. When I got back to my rooms, your gift was just the lift I needed. It took me back to Scotland."

Her stomach fluttered, and she averted her eyes from his steady blue gaze. "I'm glad I could be part of your day in some small way then," she whispered.

"So am I."

Without daring to look at him to read what was in his eyes, Maddie opened the door to the corridor behind her. "Well, I— I'd better run along."

"Yes." He didn't move and she could feel his gaze still resting on her.

She finally forced herself to take a step away from him. They heard Lilah's bark somewhere on the ground floor. "Oh, dear, Lilah's getting restless. Thank you for the cycling lesson, Mr. Gallagher." With a quick curtsy, she turned and hurried down the corridor.

"Miss Norton—"

She whirled around at the sound of his voice. "Yes?"

He held up his hand. "Until tomorrow."

A few idyllic mornings followed. Mr. Gallagher was always on time and the two spent the next hour cycling first along the quieter routes of Hyde Park, and then down to Chelsea. One morning they pedaled all the way to the embankment where they rested a while gazing out over the Thames and across to Battersea Park.

It was only by chance, while attending to Lady Haversham in the parlor, that Maddie heard of the great honor about to be bestowed upon Mr. Gallagher. "I've told him he must have all new stationery ordered. Sir Reid Gallagher, what a fine ring it has," Mrs. Walker said to her aunt.

Sir Reid Gallagher. So, he was to be knighted.

Mr. Gallagher's sister continued with a sound of disbelief. "He said it wasn't necessary. What was he to do with fine stationery in the desert? Can you believe that?"

Lady Haversham shook her head. "I don't know how he comes upon such outlandish ideas. Well, the ceremony is in a few nights. I wish I could be there, but alas, it would be too much for me."

"Yes, I know. But Theo and I shall be in attendance. Oh, I've ordered the most beautiful gown, an emerald satin embroidered in glacé silk. It features the new puffed sleeves. I had it copied from *La Mode Illustrée*...."

Maddie listened intently but nothing more was said about

Mr. Gallagher. She sat in awe of his impending knighthood. He hadn't said a word to her about it. But of course, why should he tell her anything of his personal affairs?

Her heart warmed, though, at the thought of the honor. If anyone deserved such recognition from the Crown, it was Mr. Gallagher. How she wished she could be there to see him knighted by the Queen.

Should she say something to him about it? Offer him her congratulations? Perhaps when they went cycling tomorrow morning. But the fact that he hadn't told her meant he didn't want her to know. Perhaps he was just being modest. From all she'd gotten to know of him, she understood how little outward distinctions meant to him.

She decided not to say anything unless he gave her any indication of the upcoming ceremony.

The next two days it rained and Maddie didn't see Mr. Gallagher at all. She knew he came by to work in the library with his new assistant, but she was kept so busy by Lady Haversham that she had no opportunity to see him at all.

Reid made an impatient sound as he nicked himself a second time with his razor. What was wrong with him this afternoon?

He dabbed at the blood with a washcloth, then paused at the knock on his door.

"Come in."

Cyril's head appeared around the doorway. "Just popped in to see how you're getting on before the big event." His friend sauntered in, dressed in black tailcoat, his thick hair plastered down with macassar oil. "Goodness, man, aren't you ready?"

Reid turned back to the mirror over the basin, dressed in

shirtsleeves. "Almost, if I don't leave my face a road map of cuts."

"Why don't you have a valet?"

"I travel light," he answered shortly, concentrating once more on his razor. Finally, with a last swipe to his jaw, he rinsed the remaining soap off his face and toweled it dry.

Cyril lifted a book off his nightstand and flipped through it. Reid struggled to attach the starched white wing collar to his shirt. His fingers felt twice their normal size on the small buttons.

"Pretty bookmark," remarked Cyril. "Quite lovely, in fact. Picked it up while you were in Scotland?"

"Er—no." He looked at himself in the mirror and took each end of the tie in his hands. "It was a gift."

Cyril raised an eyebrow. "Very nice. Have to ask my wife to fashion me something like this." He noticed Reid's task. "Good gracious, man, you're making a hash of that tie. Here, let me."

His friend took the white ribbon from his fingers. "My wife always does mine." In a few deft movements, he managed a presentable bow. Patting down the points of Reid's turndown collar, he stepped back. "There, that should do it. You really need to get yourself a valet, or at least a wife." With a chuckle he retrieved Reid's coat on a chair and helped him on with it. "Ready? You don't want to be late for the Queen. The way it's raining, the streets are jammed."

Reid tugged at the shirtsleeves under the coat sleeves. Why was he feeling so on edge? Could a knighthood bring him to this state of nerves? He wasn't the kind of person to let things get to him, much less ceremonial nonsense.

Or was it because he hadn't been able to talk to Maddie in so many days? She didn't even know what he'd be going through this evening. What would she think of it? Would it matter to her at all? Would she think this was just a worldly vanity?

Cyril clapped him on the back. "Relax, old fellow. It's not as if you're going to the gallows."

He smiled at his friend's attempt at humor. "It certainly feels like it at the moment." He paused. "Listen, I promised my aunt I'd stop in before I left for the ceremony. She's not up to attending, herself."

"Capital idea. I haven't seen Lady Haversham in an age."

Reid hesitated. He'd really been hoping to catch a glimpse of Maddie at his aunt's, and he felt awkward enough as it was. It seemed his aunt kept Maddie hidden away these days. "Why don't you—uh—meet me at the palace? You'll see Vera and Theo there."

"If you'd prefer. We'll wait for you there then. Don't be long. Remember the traffic."

"Yes, I'll be only a few minutes behind you."

The two left Reid's room. At the entrance to the club, they parted. Reid hailed a hansom, thinking of the coming few hours. What he really needed was to see and talk to Maddie. He tapped a finger against his knee, wondering how to manage that if she wasn't sitting with his aunt. And if she was, how to see her alone? He needed to—what? Talk to her? He glanced out the rain-streaked carriage window, trying to analyze the longing he'd felt since the last time they'd gone cycling together. He'd be happy with just a few moments in her quiet presence. That would rectify everything.

Maddie opened the door to the parlor to fetch her needle-work.

She stopped short at the sight of Mr. Gallagher. She hadn't seen him in three days, but it seemed longer. She certainly hadn't expected to see him tonight. She knew it was the day of his knighthood.

He turned at the sound of the door and her breath caught. Never had she seen him so distinguished looking, not even the night of the dance in Scotland. He wore an elegant black tailcoat and trousers, a gleaming white shirtfront and low-cut, black silk waistcoat and bow tie. His blond hair was combed meticulously, making it shimmer. "Miss Norton."

Her hand went to her chest, as if to quiet its heartbeat. "I'm sorry…I didn't know anyone was in here. Have you come to see Lady Haversham?"

"Uh—yes."

She moistened her lips, unable to tear her gaze away from him. She should excuse herself. He was here to see Lady Haversham. This was his big night. "I…I'll leave you then."

"No." He cleared his throat. "That is, won't you stay a moment?"

She hesitated, knowing Lady Haversham wouldn't be pleased to find her alone with her nephew. Maddie hadn't missed the fact that Lady Haversham excluded Maddie from any occasion on which Mr. Gallagher visited his aunt.

Finally, she took a few more steps into the room, deciding she would at least offer Mr. Gallagher her best wishes. "I haven't had a chance to congratulate you."

He quirked an eyebrow. "You've heard?"

She nodded with a tentative smile.

"The ceremony is this evening at Buckingham Palace."

"It's quite an honor."

He made a gesture. "Yes. I don't know as I deserve it, but the Crown seems to think I've done them a service with my work in antiquities."

"Oh, yes!" she added.

When he said nothing, she said, "Your aunt must be very proud of you."

"Yes…" He gave a slight smile. "I'm sorry my Uncle George isn't around to give me some advice. He received a knighthood, as well."

"I'm sure he'd have been very proud." She moved farther into the room. "Is the ceremony…very long?"

"I don't know. It depends on how many are being honored, I suppose. My aunt won't be attending, so I thought I'd stop by and see her before going on to Buckingham."

"Of course, how thoughtful of you. I know she'll be gratified to see you dressed so elegantly—" She stopped, feeling herself begin to redden.

He made a motion of dismissal about his appearance. "She rarely has that privilege…those things are important to her…" He ended, his gaze shifting away from her. "Have you ever met the Queen?"

"No. I saw her during the Jubilee a few years ago, but it was from quite far off. She was riding by in an open carriage."

He turned away from her and began fiddling with a pile of sheet music on the top of the piano.

"Have you ever met her?" she said after a moment.

"No…I never have…" He tapped the piano top, still looking away from Maddie. He seemed distracted, and she wondered if she should leave.

Instead, she approached the instrument. "Are you nervous? About the knighthood, I mean?"

"Yes…I suppose…a bit." He coughed. "It's a silly thing really." He fidgeted some more with the sheet music, realigning it into a neat pile.

Maddie took a few steps closer to him, trying to decide what she could say to ease his mind.

He swung around and he seemed surprised to see her standing so close. "Oh—"

"I'm sorry—" They both began to speak at once and just as quickly fell silent.

Suddenly the atmosphere between them was charged. Maddie couldn't move although courtesy dictated she take a step back if she stood this close to a person. He, too, seemed unable to move. Before she could command herself to breathe again, he reached out and touched a loose strand of her hair by her temple.

Her lips parted as she stared at him. He seemed fascinated by the lock. His gaze shifted to her lips. Maddie found her own glance going to his lips and she wondered what his thick mustache felt like. Was it soft or bristly?

Before she could stop the absurd direction of her thoughts, he was leaning toward her.

His lips touched hers. A kiss as soft as a breath…

She felt the earth crumbling beneath her like grains of sand loosening until nothing was left but a tiny pinnacle directly under her toes. Then that, too, was gone and she would have fallen if his hands hadn't come up to hold her.

He pressed his lips more firmly to hers, the soft hairs of his mustache brushing her skin. She sighed, lifting her arms to his waist, her fingertips touching the soft wool of his jacket. The strength of his back seemed to emanate through the material, as her arms encircled him.

His kiss deepened and she was lost in the touch and scent of him. Sandalwood…the softness of his lips…the rough-smooth feel of his shaved skin…the thickness of his mustache.

The next instant empty air met her as he took a step back. She would have lost her balance if she hadn't reached out and found the solid piano beside her.

He half turned from her, his hand covering his mouth and

jaw. "I beg your pardon. I—please forgive me for taking such liberties—"

Maddie was too stunned by what had just happened to take in his words.

He turned his back fully to her. "I'm sorry…I don't know what I was thinking—" He seemed to be collecting himself.

Her head swung around at the sound of the door. "Ah, there you are, Reid. Why didn't you tell me you'd arrived? How elegant you look." Lady Haversham frowned at Maddie. "I didn't know you were here, Madeleine." Her eyes went from Maddie to Mr. Gallagher. "Is there something you need?"

Maddie pressed her lips together, her heart feeling as if it had been yanked from her and now was trying to find a way to retreat back into herself away from harm. "I w-was ju-just on my way out." She glanced at Mr. Gallagher but he hadn't looked at her once since breaking their embrace. She didn't know how she managed to reach the door. Her fingers gripped the knob as if it was her only hold on reality. At last she was able to close the door behind her, softly but firmly. She brought her fingers up to her mouth. Had she just dreamed his kiss? It had been over so quickly she wondered if she'd just conjured it up from some deep-seated desire. The lingering scent of his cologne was her only evidence that it had been no dream.

Oh, Lord, what happened? Was it wrong of him to kiss me? Was it wrong of me to kiss him back? She clutched her chest, feeling a pain so deep at his rejection of their kiss. What was she to do now? How could she ever face him again, having revealed her own feelings so fully when he'd so obviously repudiated their kiss?

What had he done? Reid got through his interview with his aunt somehow, thankful she'd probably attribute his lack of coherency to his nerves before the ceremony.

He hurried from her house and remounted the awaiting cab, cursing himself once more. What had he done? Had he gone mad? Kissing Miss Norton! He no longer dared call her Maddie. That kind of liberty meant only one of two things: either he had no respect for her or the complete opposite— he meant to ask for her hand in marriage. The former was certainly not true, and the latter…was impossible.

He rubbed his jaw in frustration, wishing he could undo the last quarter of an hour, at the same time craving another moment in Miss Norton's company. He remembered being mesmerized by the look of her rosy, half-parted lips, feeling all restraints in him snap at the sound of her soft intake of breath.

What was worse was her look of shock when he abruptly drew away from her, the sheen of tears in her eyes the more he'd heaped a pile of inept apologies on her. He could murder himself for having taken advantage of her sympathetic nature. She probably thought him the most insensitive, worthless scoundrel and she'd be right in her estimation.

She deserved at least a decent explanation from him. Could he bring himself to do that? Not having had to bare his heart before anyone for so long, he didn't know if he was capable of it.

The investiture ceremony, which should have been a high point in his career, went by in an indistinct haze as his mind kept reliving what had occurred in his aunt's parlor just previously. Reid knelt before the old Queen and scarcely felt the blade of the sword as she touched him lightly on each shoulder. He went through the motions, barely aware of the usher leading him away into the courtyard where a photographer took pictures of him and his family. He automatically shook hands with all those who congratulated him. Afterward, they all went to his sister's where a crowd of well-wishers gathered.

At last it was over, and he was able to return to his room. He lay on his bed, in his shirtsleeves and trousers, his head pillowed under his arms, thinking only of Maddie. How was it possible to care for another woman the way he'd cared for Octavia so many years ago?

He turned on his side, away from Octavia's photograph, but even so, her soft features reproached his back. The re-criminations became unbearable until he could no longer stand them but was forced to get up and walk to the French windows that led to a narrow balcony. He stood, leaning his head in his hands against the stone railing, condemnation weighing against him like an avalanche.

When Mr. Gallagher had left, Maddie found herself summoned once more, this time to Lady Haversham's sitting room.

The older lady was standing, her walking stick planted into the carpet beside her. "What have you to say for yourself, Miss Norton?" The woman's pale blue eyes glittered at her in outrage.

"I'm not sure what you mean, my lady."

Lady Haversham stamped the stick into the carpet. "Don't be impertinent with me, pretending no knowledge of what I saw in the parlor."

"Saw in the parlor?" Maddie repeated in a faint voice. Could she have seen? Maddie was certain she hadn't heard the sound of a door until after Mr. Gallagher had moved away from her.

"You were obviously waiting to have a private interview with my nephew." She narrowed her eyes at Maddie. "Don't think I haven't seen what you've been up to. Insinuating yourself into his company. A lonely widower." She gave a dry bark of a laugh. "You thought he was easy prey, didn't you?"

"No, my lady, of course not—"

Lady Haversham took a few steps toward her, brandishing her walking stick at her. "I'll not have it, do you hear me? You think you can finagle my fortune for yourself by bamboozling my nephew with your wiles. Parading around in a pair of trousers, pretending to fall in the Highlands so you could stay out all night with him—"

Maddie fell back. "How could you think such a thing?"

The old lady narrowed her eyes at her. "I've been watching you. With your quiet ways, pretending to be such an innocent. I should never have brought you into my house, you brazen hussy—"

Lady Haversham began to tremble. Suddenly the cane fell from her hands. "My salts—"

"Yes, my lady." Maddie rushed to her side and helped her into her wing chair then fumbled for her smelling salts.

Lady Haversham looked deathly pale beneath her rouged cheeks. She revived slightly with the ammoniac. "I'm warning you, Madeleine, if you don't desist with your designs on my nephew, you shall regret it." Her eyes bulged. Maddie, fearful for her health, only nodded.

"Shall I ring for your physician?"

"I'll cut him out of my will! I shall name Vera my sole beneficiary. Do you hear me?" Her shaky voice rose with each threat.

"Yes, my lady." Maddie's alarm grew at the woman's pallor.

"I swear it. I shall summon my solicitor immediately."

"Yes, my lady. Let me call Dr. Aldwin." She rose and hurried away to summon the doctor and Lady Haversham's maid.

What had she done? Had she caused Lady Haversham irreparable harm? Maddie paced outside Mrs. Haversham's room while the doctor examined her.

Lord, don't take her in this condition. I pray for your mercy for her. Show her the truth, that she needn't fear anything from me, that I'm not after her wealth, that I haven't done anything underhanded with her great-nephew. Maddie wrung her hands, anguished at the rage she'd seen in the old lady's eyes. *Don't let her depart with unforgiveness in her heart. Have mercy on her soul…*

She swung around when she heard the doorknob turn. "How is she, Doctor?"

Dr. Aldwin shifted his bag to his other hand as he closed the door softly behind him. "She'll be all right, I expect, by tomorrow. I gave her a sedative. She gets a little too excited about things no matter how much I tell her to take it easy."

She breathed a sigh of relief, her hands clasped in front of her. "She was very upset with me, I'm afraid."

The old doctor patted her arm. "I wouldn't worry too much about it. Just keep out of her way until tomorrow. Bessie is in there and can attend to her tonight."

After the doctor had left, Maddie felt too restless to go to her room. She was tempted to take her—Mr. Gallagher's, she corrected—bicycle out, but was afraid to leave the house in case there was another emergency with Lady Haversham. She finally settled in the parlor with her Bible. But that room held no peace. All she could think of was what had occurred there earlier.

Could Mr. Gallagher really feel something for her? Once again, Maddie touched her lips, reliving the feel and scent of him so close to her. How she longed to be held by him again.

He'd pulled back so quickly. What had passed through his mind? Was it because of his wife? Remembering his words about her and his tenderness toward her, Maddie realized it must indeed be his love for his deceased wife that had stopped Mr. Gallagher. She hated the thought that she was causing him pain.

She hugged herself now, feeling bereft without Mr. Gallagher's warm smile and kind words. If she'd thought she'd miss him before, what would it be like now that she'd tasted his kiss and had an inkling of what he might be feeling for her?

Reid knew he had to see Maddie again and explain why he couldn't—why *they* couldn't—

Early the next morning, he stood at his aunt's front door and rang the bell, his palms sweaty. The maid who let him in told him that his aunt was still abed and that Miss Norton had gone out with Lilah earlier and as far as she knew wasn't back yet.

"Thank you. I'll just wait in the front parlor."

He stood in the bay window, watching the street through the filmy lace curtain, his stomach clenched in knots. He'd hardly slept. This morning he'd looked a long time at his dear Octavia's portrait. Was it to engrave her in his mind before facing Maddie?

He finally spied Miss Norton turning down the street, the dog trotting along in front of her on its short legs. Reid's heart twisted at the sight of Miss Norton's fresh features, her pert hat scarcely hiding the beautiful shade of her hair. He watched her approach the house and when he heard the front door opening, he went to the entrance of the parlor.

She was crouched beside the dog, undoing its leash. "There now, Lilah, hold still while I take this off you—" She looked up at the sound of the door.

"Good morning, Miss Norton."

She rose slowly, letting the dog scamper away, its nails clicking on the uncarpeted portions of the floor. "Good morning, Mr. Gallagher." She looked as serious as he felt.

"May I—" He coughed then began again, "May I speak to you?"

She glanced down the corridor toward the interior of the house. "I'm…not sure. Lady Haversham was unwell last evening."

What was the matter with Aunt Millicent now? "Just for a moment. I'll go see my aunt directly we're through."

She bit her lip then with a slight bow of her head assented.

He held the door open as she walked past him into the parlor. He closed the door quietly behind him.

"I…" How could he begin? Where could he begin? "I wanted to apologize for my conduct yesterday."

Her gaze slid away from his. "There's no need, Mr. Gallagher."

He took a step closer to her, and he noticed she took a step back. Was she as reluctant as he to rekindle the…attraction he was feeling for her? Part of him was relieved. Perhaps this would make it easier for what he had to say. "There's every need. I want you to know I'm not in the habit of forcing myself upon ladies—"

"Please, Mr. Gallagher! There's no need. You needn't say anything more." She half turned away from him as if the whole topic were distasteful to her.

The last thing he wanted was to upset her further. "I'll make this as brief as possible, Miss Norton. Just hear me out, please."

She bowed her head and he had to strain to hear her words. "Very well."

He cleared his throat. "As I said, I'm not in the habit of forcing my attentions upon a lady—any lady. I can only blame my behavior on having been in the rough company of men too long. I—" he stopped, feeling exceedingly awkward "—I've grown very fond of you." His face grew warm. "I would never have kissed you otherwise. It's just that—" he ran a hand through his hair "—that I'm not ready to enter into…into…that kind of…of union with another woman… not after my…wife…" His voice cracked on the last words.

"I'm sorry, Mr. Gallagher." Her soft voice came to him after a few seconds. "I don't wish to cause you any pain. I know you cared—continue to care—for your late wife. I would do nothing to come between you and…your memory of her."

"Thank you, Madd—Miss Norton," he amended, checking himself in time.

They were silent for another moment before her voice came to him hesitatingly. "You've mourned your dear wife a long time."

"I'll never mourn her long enough!"

They stared at each other, and in her shocked gaze, he realized he owed her the truth. He took a deep breath and forced himself to continue. "Since it was I who caused her death." In the stillness that followed, he could scarcely believe what he'd admitted. Miss Norton looked even more stunned. He gave a weary smile. "You find that hard to believe? It's true."

She took a step toward him. "Of course you didn't do any such thing. Many people feel a sense of guilt when a loved one passes away."

Reid collapsed into the nearest chair, feeling utterly old and exhausted. "Octavia died of the influenza…complicated by a…miscarriage.

"Oh no!" Her voice was full of sympathy.

He forced himself to continue. "Nobody knew she was with child but myself…and her physician." The words, even now, ten years later, were so hard to utter, as if saying them brought back every scream of agony when the baby came too soon. And the bleeding…so much blood. Nothing he could do could stanch it. "She might have survived the influenza if she hadn't been so weakened by the early months of pregnancy."

Now that he'd begun, he felt compelled to finish, speaking of things he'd never voiced aloud. "She was always afraid of having children. Her mother had died in childbirth, so it was understandable. It was I who wanted to start a family."

Miss Norton drew up a chair close to him. "Please, Mr. Gallagher, you needn't tell me. I understand."

He leaned forward, no longer seeing Maddie, but Octavia in those last agonizing hours. He gripped his hands together, bracing himself to go on. "At first I was patient. As I told you, we traveled a good deal. But…as the years went by, I yearned for children to make our union complete. I began to pressure my wife more. It wasn't natural *not* to have children. As she neared her thirtieth birthday, it was as if I panicked a bit, thinking that soon she'd be too old to have children. I became more insistent. I'd spoken to our physician, and he'd confirmed my fears that it became more and more dangerous for a woman to have children—particularly her first—the older she became."

He bowed his head, finding it harder to go on. "Eventually I wore down her resistance. She would face childbirth out of love for me. And I would get what I wanted because I'd known how to use someone's love to get my way. I sometimes wonder whether love really exists or is it all an excuse to manipulate a person to one's will?"

"Oh, no, Mr. Gallagher, love does exist! You must believe that." Her expression radiated only kindness. "God loves us and He's given us the capacity to love, even when it means sacrifice."

He nodded. "Octavia certainly sacrificed out of her love for me."

"But you mustn't ever believe you didn't love her. Your desire for a family was no evil. You didn't set out to make your wife feel guilty. Your desire was natural."

He looked away from the compassion in her eyes. He didn't deserve her understanding.

"She got terribly sick—morning sickness they call it—she could hardly keep anything down. But still, she'd bravely insist on accompanying me whenever I lectured. It was after one of these lectures, that she…collapsed."

He passed a hand over his eyes, reliving those days. "I called our physician at once, and he diagnosed the influenza. There were several cases that winter. She must have contracted it at one of the crowded lecture halls. The physician would have been optimistic, with Octavia's youth, but he said her weakened condition…because of the morning sickness…"

He forced himself to continue. "After some days, she started bleeding…. I tried to stop it…." His hands kneaded the cloth at his knees, his head bowed low. He wanted to stop talking about it, thinking about it, but he couldn't. It was as if he were unburdening a great weight he'd carried so long by himself. "There was nothing the doctor could do, he said. I tried to save her but I couldn't. She slipped away from me. She was so cold, so pale. I tried to warm her, but I couldn't do anything." His voice had grown hoarse. He looked across at Maddie, hardly noticing the tears filling her eyes. He wished he could weep, but no tears came. He'd cried all the tears he had in him a decade ago and in the years following.

Maybe the harsh desert air had dried up everything inside him.

Miss Norton reached over and covered his hands with hers. "Don't distress yourself, Mr. Gallagher. You mustn't speak anymore of it. It wasn't your fault, please believe that."

But she was wrong. It *had* been his fault. And nothing he could ever do would change the fact. If he hadn't worn down her resistance…he'd used every argument, every logical reasoning, every cajolement… His very reason had overcome her illogical fears…except they hadn't been so illogical. They'd been very real fears.

His selfish desire for a family had been his young wife's death sentence. He didn't deserve to be happy again.

Chapter Fifteen

When Maddie saw that nothing she said would comfort Mr. Gallagher, and that her presence only seemed to cause him more anguish, she finally left, her heart breaking at the revelation.

She went up to her room, climbing the stairs slowly, wishing with all her heart she could help Mr. Gallagher accept the forgiveness he sought. She could only pray for him and…leave his aunt's side.

She'd resolved on that course the night before and would hand in her resignation as soon as Lady Haversham awoke. In the meantime, Maddie could write her letter and begin packing.

She sat at her desk and bowed her head, asking for the Lord's wisdom. Then she took up her pen and a sheet of note-paper.

Dear Lady Haversham,

It is with a heavy heart I tender my resignation as your companion. Please understand it is with no admission of guilt at your charges that I feel it best we terminate the conditions of my employment, but rather to ease your mind. I'm sorry if you misinterpreted my actions or behavior in relation to your great-nephew. My conduct with Mr. Gallagher has been above reproach. I have never sought his attentions, nor has he forced his upon me, in any way.

She paused at this last sentence. Searching her heart, she knew it was truthful in essence. Mr. Gallagher's words and conduct this morning showed clearly that he did not wish to pursue anything with her. And he certainly had not forced himself upon her. She had been a willing recipient to her own folly and grief.

She continued.

That said, I would rather leave your household than be the source of any anxiety for you. I wish you and your family all God's blessings and happiness. Please forgive me for any upset I may have inadvertently caused you.

Yours sincerely, Madeleine Norton

She folded the paper, placed it in an envelope and sealed it. Then she wrote Lady Haversham's name on it. Maddie would either give it to her in person or have her maid deliver it for her.

Feeling a weight lifted from her shoulders, although a heavier one weighed on her heart at the thought of never seeing Mr. Gallagher's dear face again, or of not being able to assuage his secret grief, she rose and went to dig out her portmanteau.

After being told his aunt was still sleeping, Reid spent a miserable morning working among the artifacts in the library.

No longer were the lifeless relics of the ancient past enough to make him forget everything else. His enthusiasm now was merely to keep up appearances before the young man working attentively by his side.

In the afternoon Reid spent a while at his aunt's bedside. She looked pale and haggard and complained of a general malaise.

"My dear Reid, this is why you must reconsider your decision to go back to Egypt. I feel myself getting weaker every day. I don't know how much longer I'm good for on this earth."

He held her hand. "Don't talk such rubbish. I'm sure you'll outlast me."

"Oh dear no. You must be here to oversee my affairs. You and Vera are my heirs, you know."

He shifted on his chair, unable to give her the reassurance she sought. In an effort to lighten her mood, he said, "Uncle George's collection is coming along very well. I'm working with my new assistant to write everything up in a catalog that I can present to the college."

She gave him a wan smile. "I knew you'd know what to do with all his treasures. Your Uncle George would have been so proud of you with your knighthood." She patted his hand and closed her eyes.

"I don't want to tire you. Would you like me to call Miss Norton for you?" Part of him longed to see Miss Norton again. What was the point after telling her he wanted nothing to do with her? He would only hurt her more.

"No, not that woman. I want Bessie."

He rose, troubled by his aunt's reaction to Maddie's name. "All right, I'll fetch her."

On his way out, he looked around for Miss Norton, but didn't see her anywhere. It was for the best, he reasoned, placing his hat on his head before walking out. He left by the back to get his bicycle from the mews. Once on the walkway in the garden, he couldn't help one last glance at the upper-story windows, wondering if she was behind one of them.

When he got to the shed, he felt a pang at the sight of the second bicycle, remembering the rides he'd enjoyed with Miss Norton. Were they never to be repeated? Obviously not. She'd take no pleasure in a man's company who had treated her so shabbily.

When Maddie heard that Lady Haversham was still feeling under the weather, she decided not to aggravate the elderly woman with her presence. The letter could wait one more day.

After packing most of her things, Maddie left the house. On the spur of the moment, she decided to take her bicycle out. Mr. Gallagher's bicycle was not there. She wondered whether he still wanted her to take care of this second one when he left England. Clearly not, if she wouldn't be in his aunt's employ.

She pedaled the bicycle away from the square, not sure where she would go, only knowing she wanted to be away from Belgrave Square. If only she could flee somewhere far, far away. The bicycle ride was the next best thing. She ended up going through Hyde Park all the way to Kensington Gardens. By the time she returned to the house, it was late afternoon, and she felt somewhat better. After she'd put the bike away, she entered the quiet house and took the back stairs up. As she came onto the landing, she heard a male voice. Thinking it might be Mr. Gallagher, she stopped short, unwilling to upset him further with her presence.

But it wasn't Mr. Gallagher. She recognized the voice as that of Lady Haversham's solicitor. Mattie's heart thumped in fear. Had she made good on her threat so soon? She could hardly believe Lady Haversham would cut her only nephew out of her will. Oh, why hadn't Maddie given her the letter earlier? Would it do any good now? It *must.*

She'd ask the maid to deliver it to Lady Haversham as soon as possible. Maybe it wasn't too late to help Mr. Gallagher.

Reid arrived at his aunt's early the next morning. He wanted the time alone in the library to collect his thoughts before having to face his assistant.

Collect his thoughts…or catch a glimpse of Miss Norton? He'd thought his confession the day before—things he'd spoken of to no one in a decade—would somehow eradicate his feelings for Miss Norton. Surely, she would want nothing to do with him now. Why then did he still long to see her?

He parked his bicycle alongside Miss Norton's, remembering the miserable night he'd spent. How had he made such a mess of things so quickly? If only he hadn't kissed her like that—

He went immediately to the library. But once there, he found it hard to settle down to work. He stood every few moments and walked around, stopping at a window and glancing out, or picking up an artifact, realizing after a few seconds he wasn't studying it at all, but picturing Maddie's face.

Finally, he stepped out of the library. All was quiet. Where could Miss Norton be? Would she already have left to walk Lilah? Was she even up yet? Breakfasting? He decided to check the breakfast room. No one was there but a maid, picking up dishes from the sideboard. He stepped back at the sight of her, but she'd already turned around.

"Good morning, sir. I was just clearing things. Would you

like some breakfast? I can bring you a fresh plate of ham and eggs."

"No, thank you."

"A pot of tea, then? Or coffee?"

"No, thank you. I'll ring for something later from the library."

"Very good, sir." She curtsied then left the room with a tray.

After hesitating a few more seconds, he exited the room, as well. Where else could he look? He walked toward the main staircase with no clear plan in mind. Just as he looked up, debating whether to go up or not, Miss Norton appeared around the curve of the staircase.

She stopped short. For a second, he thought she'd retreat. But she said, "Mr. Gallagher."

"Good morning, Miss Norton." How he wanted to bound up the stairs and grab her up in his arms.

"Do you need anything?" Her quiet voice was all business. They might never have been sitting together in the parlor a day ago, he breaking down.

He cleared his throat. "No."

"Lady Haversham is still abed, I believe. I—I haven't seen her myself." This was the first sign she gave of nervousness.

He realized he couldn't be honest with her. The only reason he was standing at the bottom of the stairs was to catch a sight of her. Now, all he could do was feast his eyes, knowing that's all he would do.

They both turned at the sound of running feet on the stairs above Miss Norton.

"Oh, miss," Lady Haversham's personal maid came to a panting halt. "Oh, miss, please, come quickly. It's her ladyship. I don't know what's wrong with her. She can't move!"

Reid didn't wait to hear more. He took the stairs two at a

time, Miss Norton already ahead of him. Together they entered his aunt's room.

His aunt was lying on her bed, her nightcap still on. Reid bent over her. "What's wrong, Aunt Millicent?"

She gasped, struggling to get each word out. "I…I don't… know. Can't seem…to move…"

Reid noticed then how stiffly she lay. Miss Norton had reached her other side and laid a hand on her forehead. "I'll have Dr. Aldwin fetched. I'm sure he'll put you to rights."

Reid took hold of his aunt's hand but it lay inert in his. He tried not to think the dire word *apoplexy.*

By the time the doctor left he had confirmed the dreaded suspicion. Indeed, Lady Haversham had suffered a stroke. Maddie didn't leave her bedside, but tried all she could to make her comfortable.

A few hours later, Mrs. Walker arrived. After a whispered consultation with Mr. Gallagher in the corridor, she hurried to her aunt's bedside.

"Dearest Auntie," she said, taking the woman's hand in both of hers. "I came as soon as I heard. You poor dear."

Lady Haversham tried to utter something but only unintelligible sounds came out. Her condition had worsened over the last few hours. What little mobility she had had earlier in the morning was gone, and she was completely paralyzed.

Maddie rose and excused herself though no one took notice of her. When she entered the hallway, she was surprised to see Mr. Gallagher still there.

"I was hoping I'd see you," he began at once. "I wanted to let you know I'm going by the doctor's now to inquire about hiring some nursing help."

"Oh." She hadn't considered that, thinking she'd assume that duty. Then she remembered she was no longer employed by Lady Haversham. But perhaps no one else was aware of the fact? It didn't matter. She knew she couldn't leave her employer until…well, not in this state. "Very well, Mr. Gallagher," she finally replied.

"Good then. If you don't mind looking after her until we can get some full-time help, I would greatly appreciate it."

"Of course I wouldn't mind. Anything I can do—"

He brought his hand up to her shoulder and squeezed it before quickly dropping it away. "Thank you. I knew I could count on you." His blue eyes looked keenly into hers for a few seconds, and she wished she could reach out to offer him comfort, but he turned and entered his aunt's bedroom before she could say anything more.

In the days that followed, Maddie could hardly think of anything but Lady Haversham. Watching the poor woman struggle to speak, Maddie's heart went out to her. The only sounds which came out of her mouth were gurgles, and Maddie tried to soothe her, seeing that the woman's efforts only aggravated and exhausted her.

If only there was a way to communicate. She tried getting Lady Haversham to clasp her hand, but it lay inert. Finally Maddie thought of something. "My lady, can you blink your eyes?"

After a second, Lady Haversham's eyelids moved slowly but surely.

Maddie pressed her hand. "That's excellent. If you blink once, let that be for 'yes,' and if you blink twice, let that mean 'no.' Do you think you can manage that?" She watched the woman's eyes intently.

Lady Haversham blinked once.

"Wonderful. Now, let me try to figure out what you'd like. Are you thirsty?"

One blink. "Would you like a sip of water?"

Another blink. "Very good." Maddie placed a bolster behind her head and with difficulty managed to prop her up enough for her to take a few sips from a glass. "There, that's better, isn't it?"

She noticed Lady Haversham's agitation when she began to sputter something.

"What is it? Did I hurt you?"

Two blinks. "Do you want to lie back?" Two blinks. Maddie pursed her lips, trying to think what else she might want. "Are you too warm?" Two blinks. "Are you cold?" Two blinks.

Maddie straightened the covers and sat back down on the chair beside the bed. "Would you like me to read you some Scriptures?"

The pale blue eyes stared right at her, as if imploring her. One blink.

"Very good. Let me get my Bible." It was beside her on the nightstand. "Would you like to hear something from the Psalms?"

One blink. Maddie leafed through them until coming to the twenty-third one. "'The Lord is my shepherd, I shall not want…'"

When she'd finished, she asked, "Would you like me to read some more?" One blink.

Maddie found another. "'God is our refuge and strength, a very present help in trouble…'" Then she flipped further. She began reading Psalm 112. She got to the tenth verse, "'The wicked shall see it, and be grieved; he shall gnash with his teeth, and melt away: the desire of the wicked shall perish.'"

Lady Haversham began to whimper again. "What is it, my lady? Shall I stop reading?" Two blinks. More whimpering.

Maddie pressed her lips together. Perhaps that last verse had been too harsh. She flipped over to a more soothing psalm. "'Oh give thanks unto the Lord; for he is good: because his mercy endureth forever…'"

But Lady Haversham's agitation continued. "Lady Haversham, I don't understand. I know you want to say something, but I'm afraid I remain in ignorance. You must be patient with me. Would you like me to send for your maid?"

Two blinks. "For Mrs. Walker?" Two blinks. She swallowed. "For Mr. Gallagher?" Two blinks. "Do you wish to tell me something?" One blink. "All right. Is it about the Scriptures?"

One blink. "Did you like that last psalm?" Lady Haversham didn't react. "Was it the one before that? Let's see…" Maddie turned the pages back. "Psalm 112. 'Praise ye the Lord. Blessed is the man that feareth the Lord.'" A hesitation then one blink.

"Would you like me to read it again?" One blink. "Very well, I shall read it again." When she reached the tenth verse, once again, Lady Haversham made noises in her throat. Maddie reread the verse slowly. "'The wicked shall see it, and be grieved…the desire of the wicked shall perish.'" She looked up to Lady Haversham. "Is that the verse that particularly interested you?" One blink. Maddie reread the verse to herself, puzzling over it. She looked back at Lady Haversham who was eyeing her, as if waiting for her to draw some conclusion.

"Is there someone who has harmed you, Lady Haversham?" Then it dawned on her. "Do you think it is I who wished you harm?"

Two rapid blinks. Maddie breathed a sigh of relief. "I'm glad, my lady. Did you receive the note I wrote you?" One blink. "I wrote the truth. I truly didn't mean to come between you and your nephew in any way. In fact, I would be gone from here by now, if you hadn't…hadn't fallen ill."

Lady Haversham began to moan. "What is it, my lady? Are you in pain?" One blink. Then two.

"Shall I move you a bit?" Maddie half rose from her chair but Lady Haversham began to whimper again. Maddie sat back down and reread the verse slowly. When she next looked up, she saw in alarm that the old lady's eyes had watered and two tears were running down her wrinkled cheeks.

"Oh, dear, you mustn't be upset." She got a handkerchief and dabbed at the tears. "Why don't I let you rest a little? I'll read to you some more later."

Lady Haversham closed her eyes and Maddie rose with some relief.

The following days were similar. Both Lady Haversham's niece and Mr. Gallagher spent some time sitting with her, but the bulk of the time was shared between the nurses Mr. Gallagher had hired and Maddie. Each time Maddie attended Lady Haversham, the woman wanted her to read from the Scriptures. Each time Maddie read something dealing with wickedness, sin or forgiveness, Lady Haversham became overwrought. Maddie began to understand that Lady Haversham had something weighing on her heart.

Maddie reassured her by reading texts from the gospels about the forgiveness offered through Jesus Christ. But Lady Haversham's obvious frustration only increased, and Maddie could see it wore her down.

Mr. Gallagher came into the sickroom every day. The first time, Maddie immediately stood, ready to leave at once, but he motioned her to remain where she was. He took a seat on the opposite side of Lady Haversham's bed.

He held one of the old lady's hands in his and smiled at

her. "Good morning, Aunt Millie, how are you doing today?" He then proceeded to tell her about the work in the library.

He didn't stay long. When Maddie left the room, Mr. Gallagher was waiting for her. "Miss Norton—"

She stopped in the corridor, her heart pounding anew each time she was near him. No matter how hard she tried, she couldn't forget the feel of his lips against hers. Her glance strayed to his mustache, remembering the feel of it. Quickly, she looked back at his eyes, and found them searching hers.

"I just wanted to thank you again for being so patient with Aunt Millicent."

"You don't have to thank me, Mr. Gallagher."

"She seems to want you near her."

"Perhaps it's because we've developed a simple method of communicating." She explained the way of having Lady Haversham respond by blinking.

"That's ingenious. I must put it into practice and explain it to Vera." He sighed. "It must be so frustrating for her not being able to speak or move."

She nodded. "I believe something weighs on her heart." She hesitated, but seeing Mr. Gallagher waiting, she continued. "Perhaps if you summoned her minister, he might be able to pray with her, perhaps offer her the solace she needs."

"Of course. I should have thought of it myself." He shook his head. "It's times like these that we realize how unimportant everything else we've put our energies to is, and there's only one thing of lasting value." He looked at her gravely. "You seem to have known that all along."

"Please don't credit me with anything out of the ordinary." She gave a slight smile. "I was raised by a curate, remember."

He nodded, and she sensed the short interview was over. "I shall contact Reverend Steele straightaway."

"Yes, thank you." With a quick bow of her head, she

entered the room, glad they'd managed to achieve something of their former friendship, yet sensing still an invisible and insurmountable barrier.

When Reverend Steele had visited Lady Haversham, the vicar told Maddie and Mr. Gallagher, "I agree with Miss Norton that Lady Haversham is not at peace, but I'm afraid I couldn't get anything more specific than that." He patted Maddie's hand. "I suggest you continue sitting with her and the Lord will illuminate you concerning this."

"Yes, sir." She only hoped he was right. She'd been praying steadily for Lady Haversham, but had felt no breakthrough.

The days passed slowly. The house was even more quiet than usual. Mrs. Walker's children were not permitted to visit. Only Lilah was allowed by the lady's side. The little dog seemed to understand her mistress's condition and spent most of her time curled up at the foot of Lady Haversham's bed.

All Maddie could do was pray for Lady Haversham. She knew the prognosis was virtually hopeless, so she asked the Lord that if Lady Haversham were not to recover that He would give her peace and take her unto Himself. As she was meditating over one of the Scriptures that seemed to cause Lady Haversham agitation, it occurred to Maddie that perhaps Lady Haversham wished to ask for God's forgiveness. Perhaps she regretted her fury toward Maddie that last evening before her stroke. Lady Haversham only seemed to exhibit her distress in Maddie's presence.

Seated at Lady Haversham's bedside the next day, her Bible on her lap, Maddie began, "My lady, pardon me if I'm being impertinent, but do you wish to ask God's forgiveness for your own sins?"

Lady Haversham looked at her intently and blinked once. Maddie swallowed and braced herself to continue.

"Very well. Remember the Lord says in His word that if

we ask forgiveness He is faithful and just to forgive us our sins. You may just pray along with me in your heart." She bowed her head. "Dear Heavenly Father, I come before you asking for forgiveness for my sins. I ask for the cleansing blood of Jesus Christ to wash away all my iniquity. I accept His atoning work on my behalf."

She paused and watched Lady Haversham. The elderly lady had closed her eyes and was mumbling, but they weren't sounds of agitation but rather as if she was praying along. Satisfied that Lady Haversham had been able to pray, Maddie continued. "Now, would you like to ask someone in particular for his forgiveness?" Immediately the lady's eyes opened and she blinked. "One of your family members?"

Two blinks. "One of the servants?" Two blinks. "One of your friends?" Two blinks. "An acquaintance?" Two blinks. Having eliminated all the more obvious, Maddie finally dared asked, "Would you like to ask my forgiveness for anything?"

Immediately the lady blinked once. Maddie's heart began to pound, surprised that she'd been correct, and humbled to realize the Lord was working in Lady Haversham's heart. She took one of the lady's limp hands in her own. "Please know that there is nothing to forgive. I don't feel you have wronged me in any way."

Lady Haversham began to whimper and Maddie squeezed her hand. "Let me continue, my lady. I do forgive you, for whatever you wish. If there's any way you feel you have wronged me, know that I *do* forgive you. I love you with the love of our Savior, Jesus Christ, and hold nothing in my heart against you. Please believe me."

The lady's eyes filled with tears. Maddie tried to soothe her, and when at last the lady appeared at peace, Maddie gave her a sleeping draft that the doctor had left prepared.

After that time, Maddie noticed Lady Haversham grew

quieter as the days wore on. All she seemed interested in was hearing the Scriptures read.

Finally one morning, the maid summoned Maddie to tell her Lady Haversham had passed away in her sleep.

Maddie could only breathe a prayer of thanks that her ladyship's suffering had ended. She wondered how Mr. Gallagher and Mrs. Walker would receive the news.

They soon arrived and Maddie could tell little from Mr. Gallagher's closed expression. Mrs. Walker immediately began to cry. Maddie left Mr. Gallagher to comfort his sister.

She went to her room and knelt by her bed. Although sad for the sake of the lady's relatives, Maddie felt a deeper, inner joy knowing Lady Haversham had been at peace with her Maker. She gave the Lord thanks for having used her to communicate the Savior's love to her employer. All the petty offenses disappeared in the greater work the Lord had wrought in Lady Haversham's life.

With a sigh, Maddie rose. She should repack the belongings she'd unpacked during Lady Haversham's illness. She decided to remain until everything had been arranged for Lady Haversham's funeral and then she would tell Mr. Gallagher she was leaving. Perhaps she could ask him for a character reference. She would have to obtain a new position and didn't know how long that might take. In the meantime, she'd need her last wages to get a room somewhere.

Maddie paced her room, trying not to think too far ahead. She must trust in the Lord to see her through to a new assignment.

She made every effort not to think of Mr. Gallagher and what he would say when she told him she was leaving. He'd seemed so kind and gentle since his aunt's stroke. Would he miss Maddie at all? Would he wish her to stay? But what reason could there be for her to stay?

She had been, after all, only an employee of his aunt's. At the demise of her former employer, she had been expected to leave right away.

Mrs. Walker certainly wouldn't welcome her any longer than necessary. The woman had never treated Maddie with more than bare civility.

Maddie sighed as she closed up her portmanteau. Once she knew where she was going, she would leave her forwarding address.

If Mr. Gallagher needed her for anything, then he would know where to find her. She tried not to let a spurt of hope rise from that decision. Let the Lord's will be done, she repeated to herself, as she'd trained herself to do all her adult life.

Between funeral preparations and wrapping up the work on the artifacts, Reid hardly had a moment to consider the future. All he knew was that with the passing of his aunt, an era had passed.

For so long, whenever he'd returned to England, she had been his main family contact. Even though Vera was his only sibling, Reid had felt himself growing further and further apart from her each time he'd come back. He resolved to rectify that, if only for the sake of his nephews and niece. He'd become reacquainted with them over the short holiday in Scotland, and he'd be sorry to lose that once he returned to Egypt.

Egypt. He knew he could return as soon as he and Vera decided what would be done with Aunt Millie's estate. The reading of the will was the next day, but he expected no surprise there. He and Vera were his aunt's only heirs. It would just be a matter of hearing about all her charities, helping the servants with references, deciding if the house was to be shut up or sold.

He had no strong opinion either way and would leave it up to Vera. She was sure to have something to say.

The only issue of any importance was the one he shied away from, but it remained like a big nebulous cloud in the center of his thoughts.

Maddie Norton.

How could he bear to leave her behind when it came time to sail for Cairo?

And how could he suggest a future with her when he would never expose her to the dangers and rigors of such a harsh place as Egypt? If he couldn't protect his own wife in her native England, what could he do overseas with someone who, by her own admission, had been weak and frail as a girl?

He sighed, coming to no conclusion, preferring to shove the issue to the back of his mind as he did each time he glimpsed Maddie's face in his comings and goings to and from his aunt's residence.

Chapter Sixteen

Maddie attended Lady Haversham's funeral and remained afterward to help serve the many people who came to the house.

The next day, the solicitor called everyone to assemble in the parlor for the reading of the will. Maddie sat in the rear with the servants. She would have preferred not to attend. She was too new an employee to receive anything, unlike the rest of the servants, but the solicitor had insisted all household employees be present.

As the lawyer's voice droned on, Maddie's attention wandered. She glanced at the back of Mr. Gallagher's head from time to time. He sat with his sister and brother-in-law near the front. She'd hardly exchanged any conversation with him since his aunt's death, and those few words had only concerned his aunt.

The lawyer finally began with the bequests. He mentioned the gift of the artifacts to the University College with the stipulation of her great-nephew as overseer. A few other charities received generous gifts.

Maddie breathed a prayer of thanksgiving when she heard

of Mr. Gallagher's trusteeship. It must mean that Lady Haversham had not made good her threat to disinherit her great-nephew, after all.

As expected, a long list of legacies followed to each and every servant in Lady Haversham's employ. Lady Haversham had not overlooked even the lowliest scullery maid, who received five pounds. Maddie glanced over to the young girl, whose smile showed her appreciation. Suddenly Maddie started up, hearing her own name.

"…to my paid companion, Madeleine Norton, who has only been in my employ since April last, I leave nothing. For she has proven herself a conniving, deceitful woman and if I die prematurely, it is likely due in great part to her."

Gasps and murmurs broke out. Maddie felt the room spin around her. She grasped the edge of her chair to steady herself. What was happening? Was this some terrible nightmare?

She suddenly found Mr. Gallagher at her side. "Don't pay attention to those words. They were clearly the words of a senile old woman."

Maddie struggled to rise, and his strong hands helped her.

Mrs. Walker appeared at her brother's side. "Make her leave this house immediately!" Her eyes narrowed at Maddie. "How dare you cause my aunt such pain? Because of you, sh…sh…she's gone—" Her voice broke at the last words. Her husband came up to her and put his arm around her, gently leading her away from Maddie.

Again, Maddie tried to pull herself away from Mr. Gallagher, but he held her firmly. "Don't listen to her, Miss Norton. Vera's just overcome with her grief. She doesn't mean what she's saying."

There was no recrimination in his eyes or tone. Maddie's lips trembled in gratitude, and she was afraid she would break down in front of him, in front of everyone in the crowded parlor.

Mr. Gallagher's attention was diverted to the lawyer as the elderly man approached them. "What kind of nonsense is this in my aunt's will? How could you permit such vile language in a legal document?"

The lawyer responded in a quiet tone and Mr. Gallagher in a louder one. Maddie realized how everyone in the room was staring at her. She would have fallen down in shame if Mr. Gallagher's hand had not held her. But she knew she mustn't make things more difficult for him. She managed to slip from his grasp while he was disputing with the solicitor.

"Wait, Maddie—"

But she only shook her head and fled the parlor. When she reached the solitude of her room, the thoughts came. How could Lady Haversham have done such a horrible thing to her? Did she hate her that much? Maddie's tears flowed freely now, as she blindly began to collect her last belongings. At all costs, she must be gone from this house before anything else happened. She should have left when Lady Haversham first charged her unfairly with deceitful behavior.

But would her ladyship have died forgiven of her sins if Maddie had not been there? The question brought her up short and she dropped the shawl she held in her hands. *Forgive me, Lord.* Had the Lord kept her deliberately, because He knew Lady Haversham would not have died in peace if she had continued angry at Maddie, no matter how unjustly?

Was Maddie's call to serve the Lord only valid when it was convenient for her to serve Him? Was her commitment to help in her brothers' missionary work only paying the Lord lip service? Maddie felt more shame as the questions rose in her mind. She'd always prided herself on her unwavering commitment to the work overseas, not minding whatever deprivation she must suffer if it meant she could send more material help to the field.

But was she able to suffer shame on her Lord's behalf? It was much more difficult to be reviled by those around her than to live without luxuries. She remembered the stares of everyone downstairs. They'd looked at her as if she'd murdered Lady Haversham.

Yet, if she hadn't remained by the lady's side— Maddie thought about Lady Haversham's agitation during those days before her death. She had known what awaited Maddie.

Maddie sank down onto the bed, staggered by the realization. Lady Haversham had known no peace until she had obtained Maddie's forgiveness. Maddie bit her lip as something else occurred to her. It had been easy to forgive her then when it had seemed only a blanket forgiveness for little slights. But now, could she forgive a woman who was gone but who had left Maddie an awful legacy of shame to live with?

A knock interrupted her thoughts. Likely the housekeeper demanding she leave the premises immediately. Maddie rose slowly, hating to have to face accusing eyes.

Mr. Gallagher stood there. She covered her mouth. What must he think of her?

"Please don't—" He held his hand out as if afraid she'd close the door on him. "May I speak with you for a moment?"

She tried to compose herself. "Let me assure you, Mr. Gallagher, I'll be gone within a few minutes—"

"No! I haven't come to ask you to leave. Please stay as long as you need." He cleared his throat. "First of all, let me apologize for that unforgivable statement in my aunt's will. I don't know what she must have been thinking. The lawyer tells me she only recently rewrote her will, making no changes, except to insert that terrible statement. He assures me she had a legal right to do so, but it means nothing."

She shook her head, still unable to compose herself.

"Please, Maddie, hear me out—"

He'd called her by her first name for the second time. Her hand gripped the doorknob, her heart warmed by the fact that he hadn't condemned her.

"May I…come in?" At her nod, he entered the room, his eyes never leaving her face. Once more, he cleared his throat. "I—that is, you must marry me. You must see that."

She stared at him, too stunned by his words. That was the last thing she'd expected to hear. *He wanted to marry her.* He ran a hand through his hair, leaving it in disarray. How she ached to smooth it down for him. "You see the necessity of it. My sister is threatening legal action."

No… she realized, his meaning becoming clear. Her heart plummeted from the leap it had taken. He felt he *had* to marry her.

"I appreciate your concern, Mr. Gallagher." She was amazed at how calm her voice came out. "But you needn't feel you must marry me."

"Vera is alleging you somehow brought about my aunt's death."

She'd thought it couldn't get any worse. "How can that be?"

"I know it's nonsense, but she will twist the words in the will around and have a magistrate investigate. It could get messy. If you're my wife, she wouldn't dare bring any legal charges against you."

"Oh, Mr. Gallagher, I didn't do anything to your aunt, please believe me. Please tell your sister that."

"I know that. I saw how you soothed her in the end. She would have known no peace if you hadn't been at her side, demonstrating a devotion she didn't deserve. I've told Vera all these things and will continue to do so. But she's distraught. There's no telling what she'll do in this state."

He took a step toward her.

"So you see the necessity. If Vera knows you are to be my wife, she won't make a public scandal, no matter what she may think in private."

Maddie shook her head, unable to get any words out. Did he really think she would marry him just to save herself?

"You must consider this rationally. It's the only thing that will stop my sister."

"Please don't mention marriage anymore."

His brows drew together as if in irritation. Before he could wear her down with further arguments, she drew herself up. "I'm not afraid of what Mrs. Walker might do. I know I didn't do anything to harm your aunt. My conscience is clear on that score."

"I know it is, but you don't understand the damage this might do to your reputation."

"Not with those who matter to me."

His blue eyes looked into hers offering her his full conviction in her honesty. "I know. But with all those who don't know you—it can affect your chances for future employment…."

She knew his words were accurate, and she had no idea what she would do in that event. But she wouldn't marry without his love, and he had said no word of his affections. "I appreciate your kindness to me, Mr. Gallagher, but you needn't marry me out of fear for my future."

"Miss Norton, I must insist you look at this more sensibly. You don't know my sister when she gets a notion into her head."

"I appreciate your warning."

He let out a frustrated breath. "You mustn't be so stubborn, Miss Norton. You don't want to end up in the street, with no prospects for employment—"

"I'm not a charity case, Mr. Gallagher."

He drew back. She hadn't meant to speak so sharply, but if she didn't stop him, she was afraid he'd weaken her resolve. And her principles were all she had left.

This time it was he who took a step back. "I never suggested you were, Miss Norton. Please forgive me if my proposal was unwelcome to you." His stiff tone broke Maddie's resistance even further, but she knew she mustn't give in to the tempting idea of accepting his well-intentioned proposal.

"There is nothing to forgive. You only wished to protect me." She stood quietly by the door until, with no further word, he left the room.

Reid stalked away from his aunt's house, too angry to sit in a cab. Women could be the most infuriating creatures on the face of the earth, beginning with his late aunt, continuing with his sister and ending with Miss Norton. Her behavior topped them all.

How had things come to this pass? He could not understand what had possessed his aunt to insert such a ludicrous statement into her last will and testament. Probably some fit of pique over something as minor as Maddie not having treated Lilah with all the care Aunt Millicent expected. She'd probably gotten over it by the next day and hadn't gotten around to changing things. She might not even have thought about it anymore. Or the stroke had prevented her from making any other changes. Reid thought back over his conversation with the solicitor. He had been called in the day before Aunt Millicent's stroke.

Reid's pace slowed, trying to remember what might have set his aunt off at that time. He stopped in the middle of the pavement, remembering his kiss with Miss Norton. Could Aunt Millicent have witnessed it? She had walked in on them—not in the very act, but soon enough after that Reid was hardly aware of what he was saying. Could Aunt Millicent have suspected something?

It hardly seemed possible, but his aunt was an inquisitive woman—and very protective of her relatives. Who could tell what had gotten into her head. She'd probably mentioned it to Vera, and between the two of them, who knew what they'd cooked up. He'd have to confront Vera with it. His mind recoiled at the thought of having to reveal any of his own feelings to his sister.

He came back full circle to the original reason for his exasperation, still flabbergasted at Miss Norton's reaction to his proposal of marriage.

Instead of gratefully accepting his offer, she'd refused him! He recommenced his rapid stride. Of all the high-handed, proud reactions. Against his better judgment, he'd been willing to betray Octavia's memory, to expose Miss Norton to countless dangers and risks overseas, in order to save her reputation…only to be told she wasn't a charity case!

Women! The sooner he was back in Egypt the better. But he couldn't leave Miss Norton to the mercy of the courts. He'd have to strangle some sense into Vera if it was the last thing he did.

He wasn't put to so drastic a measure. The next day, before Vera could call the local magistrate, Aunt Millicent's personal maid discovered a letter Miss Norton had written to her before the stroke.

Reid reread the letter of resignation, which the maid

handed him, then passed it to his sister. "I think this proves for once and for all Aunt Millicent's judgment was clouded by an unfounded prejudice against Miss Norton."

"This letter proves nothing at all, unless to show Miss Norton did have some designs on you."

He turned from his sister in disgust. "For goodness' sake, will you face the facts? Aunt Millicent began fabricating a supposed attraction between Miss Norton and me. The fact is the two of us were working closely together. I admire and respect Miss Norton highly, but that doesn't mean I was going to run off with her!"

Vera came up to him and gazed into his eyes. "Are you sure, Reid? It's been a long time since…Octavia passed away. I know it must be lonely for you. You're in a vulnerable position if a woman comes along and pretends a kindness and sympathy that might perhaps not be sincere—"

He gave a bark of laughter. "Like Cecily, for instance."

"She's someone from our own class, your equal in every way. She doesn't have to pretend something she doesn't feel."

His jaw hardened. "Miss Norton is as much a lady as you, Vera."

"That may be, but her position in society is nothing to be compared to ours. Really, Reid, Miss Norton is a paid companion. Her folks are as poor as church mice from what I understand."

"That's enough. Her good name has already been libeled by our aunt. I won't have her further ill-treated by our family."

"I'll do anything to protect you, Reid."

He exhaled in frustration. "Can't you see the poor woman was already willing to give up her job for my sake? What more do you want of her?"

"I want to be certain she didn't do anything to upset Aunt Millicent to precipitate her collapse."

"Listen, Vera. For your information, I proposed marriage to Miss Norton the day I heard Aunt Millicent's cruel insinuations read to everyone under this roof." At his sister's shocked expression he continued, his tone deliberately quiet. "*She* turned me down."

Vera's mouth dropped open.

"Yes, you heard me. So much for your accusation of self-interest. So, I'll say this only once, Vera. Desist with your ridiculous threat to call in a magistrate to investigate Miss Norton's behavior toward our aunt, or I'll do everything in my power to force my suit with Miss Norton."

Vera's mouth snapped shut and she turned away as if in a daze. "Oh, Reid, I had no idea you'd go so far. I'm sorry." She turned stricken eyes back to him. "Did you…care very much for her?"

He looked away from her. "It doesn't matter what my feelings were. I wasn't going to stand back and see her treated so unjustly."

"I see. I misjudged Miss Norton then. She is an honorable woman."

Reid left her then. He hadn't seen Miss Norton since the day before. All he knew now was he wanted to see Maddie, to offer her his help in any way she might need. He realized his anger at her refusal had been his own wounded pride, but he still worried about her situation. If she refused to marry him, there must still be some way to get her to accept his help, perhaps with finding a new position.

He stopped a young footman. "Could you please tell Miss Norton I'd like to see her?"

"I'm sorry, sir. She's gone." At the look in Reid's eyes, he added, "Didn't you know, sir?"

"No. Gone where?"

"Don't rightly know, sir. She left with all her bags—or bag, I should say. Would you like me to find out?"

"Yes, please do." He paced the entry hall as he awaited a reply. After a few minutes, Mrs. Reeves, the housekeeper appeared.

"Good afternoon, Mr. Gallagher."

He nodded. "When did Miss Norton leave precisely?"

She pursed her lips, thinking. "Why just after the reading of the will." She looked down as if embarrassed.

He hesitated, hating to have to ask, but needing to know. "How was she?"

"She didn't let on much about her feelings, if that's what you mean, sir, but I could see she felt she could no longer lodge here." She cleared her throat softly behind her hand. "I must say I understood her position."

"Yes, quite. Can you please tell me where she has moved to?"

She pursed her lips. "I couldn't tell you, sir."

He suppressed his impatience. "What do you mean?"

"I mean I don't know, sir." She hesitated. "I'm not sure if she herself knew precisely where she was going to and she left no forwarding address."

If the floor had shifted beneath him a few minutes ago, now he felt a fear growing in him as great as when he'd seen his wife begin to bleed. He tried one more avenue, knowing instinctively the futility of the inquiry. "Perhaps someone else in the house would know? Or perhaps she has been in touch with another servant since she left?"

"I can look into it, sir."

"Yes, please do. I'll wait in the library."

"Very well, sir. Would you like me to bring you some tea?"

"No, thank you. Just fetch me the moment you know something."

It wasn't long before his suspicions were confirmed. Maddie had told no one where she was going. He then proceeded to ask if anyone knew her family's address. No one knew.

His panic mounted as the day waned. He racked his brain, trying to remember if she'd ever told him anything that would help him find her now.

He finally notified Vera of what had happened. All she could add was that she believed Maddie's parents hailed from Wiltshire. He ransacked his aunt's desk, searching for any correspondence from Maddie, but all he found were receipts of the salary payments his aunt had made to her, a paltry sum paid quarterly. That presented a new worry. Had Maddie been paid her last earnings? If so, had she already sent everything to her parents and missionaries as she was accustomed to? Where would she go? How was she going to live? Finding nothing else useful, Reid finally enlisted the housekeeper's help, as well as that of Aunt Millicent's personal maid, to search his aunt's bedroom and sitting room.

At last he found a letter from an acquaintance of his aunt's, recommending Maddie for the position of companion. Attached to it was a letter from Maddie herself. A pang stabbed him when he recognized her neat script. At the heading was a London street address. He clutched the letter, half crumpling it in his fist, the first tide of relief washing over him. Could Maddie have gone back to this location?

He left the house and hailed a cab, praying the whole way. The address turned out to be a modest boardinghouse in a respectable middle-class neighborhood near Paddington.

But once he rang the bell and spoke to the landlady, he obtained no new information. The lady vaguely remembered Maddie, a quiet woman who had only stayed a few days with her. No, she had left no forwarding address.

Reid's shoulders slumped. He turned away, viewing the setting sun over the buildings, thinking only of what Maddie was doing, alone in London, with little money, no references. Where would she go? What would she do? He dearly hoped she would seek refuge with her parents. But would she? She *must.* It would be the logical thing while she was seeking new employment. But how successful would she be, without his aunt's reference?

Maddie blotted the short note and reread it one last time.

Dearest Mother and Father,

This is to let you know I am safe and well. I have left the residence of Lady Haversham following her demise. The poor lady had a stroke, which left her immobile. I can only thank the Lord that He granted me His grace to minister to her in her last days. She died in peace, having found mercy in her Savior.

I am presently seeking new employment. I have enclosed no return address. Please don't be concerned over this fact. I do not wish to be contacted by anyone from my last place of employment. It is possible you would be requested to provide some information on my whereabouts by someone from Mrs. Haversham's family.

Maddie bit the edge of her pen, wondering if she was being presumptuous that Mr. Gallagher would try to find her. In any case, she couldn't run the risk. She continued reading.

I don't want you to be in a position where you would be forced to conceal something that it is not in your nature to conceal. Please be assured I have done nothing wrong or of which I am ashamed. Only know I endured a painful experience at the end of my term with Lady Haversham and would prefer to put it behind me.

As soon as I find new work and a more permanent living situation, I will send you my address as well as some money. I trust it will be soon. Please don't worry. The Lord is watching out for me and I am not in want of anything.

Your loving daughter, Maddie

With a sigh and final glance over the letter, she folded it up and placed it in an envelope. She would post it tomorrow when she went out again in search of employment.

She slumped over the scarred, uneven table at which she sat. Her search had been unfruitful in the week since she'd left Lady Haversham's residence. All the reputable employment agencies she'd contacted frowned upon the fact that she could provide no references from her last place of employment. Because her last two positions had been found through informal arrangements of someone recommending her for the position, Maddie had no record with any of these agencies. She'd also scanned the newspapers every day for positions, but nothing suitable had appeared. She had no experience as a nursemaid or nanny, and knew that those, too, required impeccable references. She had tried applying for seamstress positions at a few places, but unsuccessfully.

She didn't know how much longer her scant savings would last. She bit her lip, knowing she mustn't dwell on the issue, reminding herself of the words in James:

The trying of your faith worketh patience. But let patience have her perfect work, that ye may be perfect and entire, wanting nothing.

She sighed again and rose to prepare for bed, not looking too closely at her surroundings. They were ruder than anything she'd ever faced, even as a child in their humble dwelling in Jerusalem. She'd found the least expensive room she could find, but it came at the cost of dirt and squalor. Street noises continued far into the night and began again early in the morning. Thankfully, her third floor room was high enough that she didn't fear sleeping with her tiny window open. Otherwise she'd suffocate in the heat and stale odor of the narrow room, which barely had space enough for a bed, a chair and table. Only a few nails on the back of the door were available to hang clothes, but she'd left most of her belongings in her portmanteau, the only clean place in the room. She wished she'd brought her own sheets. The stained and musty-smelling ones on the lumpy mattress were distasteful.

When she'd finished her few preparations, she climbed into bed. These moments were the only ones in the day she permitted her mind to dwell on things that had no future.

She knew she'd done the right thing in leaving Lady Haversham's household when she had. Mr. Gallagher's gallant proposal proved he was much too honorable a gentleman not to leap to her defense against the awful accusations in Mrs. Haversham's will and his sister's threat to bring legal action against Maddie.

Maddie had never been so touched in her life as when Mr. Gallagher had told her they must marry. No matter that the request hadn't been attended by all the romantic avowals of love a woman longs to hear. Maddie knew how much more special this man's proposal was in light of his still-strong feelings for his wife, as well as Maddie's own inferior social situation to his. She'd never thought about his financial position before. He certainly seemed to be respectably off in his own right, but now, with his aunt's inheritance, he must indeed be a wealthy man. As well as a knight, she reminded herself. What need had he to look Maddie's way, except out of pity? But Maddie valued the pity that had prompted his proposal. How different Mr. Gallagher's conduct from that of her former beau. He'd been a handsome, charming young gentleman. At least she'd thought him a gentleman, but now with the experience of time, she realized what a shallow, self-centered young man he was to have led her on and dropped her the way he had.

Mr. Gallagher had proven a true gentleman from the moment he'd met her. Maddie turned on her side, resting on her arm. Knowing him now the way she did, she had the strong suspicion he'd continue wearing down her resistance, insisting she marry him in some noble effort to save her from the magistrates. She smiled in the growing gloom of her room, touched by his gallantry.

She'd left because deep down she didn't know how long she'd be able to resist him if he kept on trying to offer her his protection. What a shallow woman she'd prove to be if she married a man only to provide herself with material security.

No, she would never do that to him. She loved him too much to ruin his life…the way she had ruined her parents'.

She turned onto her back and looked up at the cracked, stained ceiling. This was the moment she permitted herself to dream. As she lay in the sweltering heat, she could ignore the shouts from down below in the street, she could forget the dingy sheets she lay between and whatever critters inhabited the mattress under her and dream about what it would have been like to be married to Reid Gallagher and live in far-off Egypt…. Only in the darkness did she permit herself to weave a hundred dreams of that life, where she would be busy with the Lord's commission and Reid would be uncovering the secrets of the past....

Chapter Seventeen

Reid couldn't concentrate on anything. In the fortnight since Maddie had left, he'd hired a private detective and spent just about every waking hour scouring the streets of London himself. But Maddie was nowhere to be found. In the city of over three million, it was as if she was one particle of sand in the vast desert.

The only progress the detective had made was in locating Maddie's parents. Reid took the train out to the village they lived in in the west of England. They were a very nice elderly couple and treated Reid with warmth. They had only heard once from their daughter, they told him, but they had no idea of her whereabouts. Her letter had been postmarked London, but she might have moved elsewhere if she'd found a situation as she intended.

Reid had found a lot of common ground with them. Maddie's father was a scholar on Biblical archaeology, and the two spoke about Reid's work, as well as Mr. Norton's time in Jerusalem.

"Your daughter proved an able assistant to me in cataloging an extensive collection of my late uncle's," he said, in order to explain his association with Maddie.

Mr. Norton smiled. "She has always had an interest in the Middle East. It's a pity she was never able to return."

"She told me it was due to her frequent ill health as a young girl that you were forced to return."

"It is true she was frequently ill," Mrs. Norton said, "but it wasn't the only reason we decided to return to England."

"That's right," Mr. Norton added. "You see, it was about that same time that this curacy fell open and I was asked to take it. The church here had fallen upon hard times and was on the verge of closing its doors. It's a poor community." He turned to his wife and patted her hand. "We spent some time in prayer about it, but the Lord confirmed it to both of us—" he tapped his chest "—in here, where it counts, that it was His will that we return from the mission field and make this community our mission field. We haven't ever regretted the decision. The church is thriving and, not too long ago, the Lord sent me a young assistant who is showing much promise to take over when I start slowing down." He smiled a gentle smile, which reminded Reid of Maddie.

Reid spent as much time with them as he dared to spare, learning of Maddie's young life. He thanked her parents for their time, and Mr. Norton accompanied him back to the small train station. The two men shook hands when Reid's train pulled in.

Mr. Norton released Reid's hand. "I hope you find her."

Reid nodded, unsmiling. "I do, too."

He returned that night to his room at the Travellers Club. A fitting place for him, a traveler, except the name no longer appealed to him. He no longer wanted to be a mere nomad, passing through a city with no roots anywhere. He longed for a home and wife and children.

When he entered his quiet room, the street sounds muffled by its thick walls and drapes, everything in order, it only augmented the hole he felt in his heart. He took off his jacket and loosened his tie before going to sit on his bed.

He took up his wife's portrait and stared at it a long time. Octavia's face smiled lifelessly back at him. How long he'd acted as if she were still alive. Of course, his love for her had never died, but she would always be what she was now, a lifeless image in a portrait…not a living, breathing, warm woman. As he'd done with everything in his life, he was living in the past.

He sighed heavily. "I'm sorry. I'm sorry, but I can't live without her. I need to find her. Please forgive me." He bowed his head. "I never meant to cause you harm, to betray your memory with another woman. I'm so sorry, but I need her. Please forgive me…"

After a moment, he continued, "please forgive me, Lord." The portrait fell to his lap. "Let me find Maddie, please. Show me where she is. Oh, God, protect her, wherever she is. I'm so sorry I hurt her." What a blunder he'd made of his proposal. No wonder she'd gone away. He'd be lucky if she ever wanted to see him again.

He'd already endured untold agonies imagining the worst possible scenarios of her alone in London. He realized he'd rather chance the risk of losing her at his side than never see her again.

He continued praying for Maddie, as if her unerring faith had infused his own heart in his hour of need. What a fool he'd been! Why hadn't he ever told her he loved her?

Early the next morning, a footman handed Reid a note just as he was leaving his room. It was from the private detective.

Good news. Come to my office as soon as you receive this.

    Sam Abbot.

His hopes soared. Had the detective found her?

Barely fifteen minutes later, Reid walked into the man's office.

Abbot stood at once from his desk, his checked jacket and trousers calling attention in the somber office. "Mr. Gallagher, we've hit the jackpot." He held out a crumpled piece of paper to Reid.

Reid's hand shook as he read it. It listed a street.

"She has a room there."

Reid eyed him. "You're certain?" They'd followed false leads before.

The man gave him a satisfied look. "As certain as my granny's name is Jane. It took me a while, but I scoured every neighborhood, every boardinghouse. I knew if she hadn't left London, I'd find her. All it takes is persistence. One by one, I tracked them down."

"Thank you, Mr. Abbot. I'll go there at once. If she's there, I'll come by your office and settle with you this afternoon, including the bonus I promised you if you located her within a month."

"She'll be there, all right, or my name's not Sam Abbot."

Reid checked the address again, thanked the detective and went for a cab.

Maddie left the rooming house to begin her weary trek through the city once again. She gave the warped door a second yank to get it to close properly then turned toward the pavement.

"Maddie."

She froze.

Was she dreaming? There, a few feet from her, stood Mr. Gallagher, as devastatingly handsome as the first time she'd seen him, his blue eyes piercing into hers.

Her first impulse was to run to him. Then she remembered. He only pitied her. She must flee before she broke down in front of him. Where could she go? She began pushing through the crowd, away from him. She didn't feel strong enough to resist his noble intentions.

"Maddie, wait!" She quickened her step, but too many people stood in front of her. In a moment she felt a strong hand clasp her shoulder and she was forced to face him.

Her heart constricted at the sight of his dear face. His eyes looked tired, the lines around his mouth deepened. "Maddie, why did you run away from me?" His quiet tone sounded hurt.

"Please, Mr. Gallagher, you shouldn't have come—"

"Why are you afraid of me, Maddie?"

She shook her head and tried to speak but couldn't. She raised a hand to her mouth to hide its trembling and finally turned away.

"Why didn't you come to me?"

She looked down at her feet, too ashamed to look him in the eye. Why did he have to see her like this?

"We have to talk. Is there somewhere we can go?"

She wanted to weep at the concern in his tone. "Please," she whispered.

"Maddie, trust me."

She raised her eyes to him and felt her resolve slipping. She'd tried so hard to give him up. But there he stood, so solid and sure. How could she ever say no to him? She took a deep breath. She'd hear him out. She owed him that much, but she must remain strong. She *must.* "All right." She led him back to the boardinghouse, hating the thought of taking him there, but knowing of nowhere else.

The door stuck as usual. Before she could give it an additional shove, Mr. Gallagher put his greater strength to it and held it open for her. She slipped past him and led him into a dingy side parlor.

Murky sunshine only highlighted the years of grime on the upholstery and carpet. She didn't offer him a seat nor did he take one. He removed his hat and held it in his hands. "I saw your parents."

Her gaze flew up to his. "You did? When?" The next second, she asked, "Did they tell you where I was?" No, how could they? They didn't know.

He shook his head. "They said they didn't know."

"No…they didn't."

He cleared his throat. "You needn't have run away. We found the letter you wrote to my aunt just before her stroke. It convinced my sister you had no ulterior motives. She's sorry she misjudged your character."

Maddie's back straightened. "I didn't run away out of guilt or fear—" She stopped, afraid she'd give away the real reason.

"I know you didn't."

She remained silent, feeling the fear grow in her.

"Your parents send their love. They're concerned about you."

"You didn't tell them anything—"

"What could I tell them? You disappeared. I merely said you were my assistant, as well as my aunt's companion."

She stared at him, wondering what her parents had thought of him.

"I think your parents understood the real reason I was there looking for you."

"The real reason?" She waited, hardly breathing.

His gaze remained steady. "That I love you."

Her lower lip began to tremble again and she bit down on it. "Don't, Mr. Gallagher. Pl-please don't say anything more. You don't owe me anything."

"I owe you a great deal. You gave me back hope and life and such a deep sense of happiness. You helped restore my faith and feel young again."

Her eyes filled with tears so she could no longer see him in front of her. "You mustn't speak like that." Overcome, she sniffled, turning away from him. "I'm not worthy—"

He approached her and took her wrist in his hand, forcing her back though she held her face away from him. "Why? What are you afraid you'd do to me?" As he spoke, he rubbed the inside of her wrist with his thumb. "What are you afraid of if you married me? Other than making me the happiest man on earth?"

"I'm not g-good enough f-for you. Look what your aunt said about m-me."

"My aunt was a selfish old woman—"

"You mustn't speak ill of her—" She could hardly think for the feel of his thumb pad against her skin.

"Marry me, Maddie, and come back with me to Egypt. You've always wanted to go back to the Middle East. Come with me." His soft voice wore down her control. How could she fight him reasonably when he stood so near, his touch and low tone hypnotizing her?

"I'd only ruin it for you the way I did for my parents," she whispered, knowing she must persuade him any way she could.

"Your parents told me they didn't come back because of you."

Maddie stared up at him.

"They said the Lord led them to the curacy your father now

holds. They said they prayed long and hard about it and felt it was the Lord's will for them to return to that village in England."

Maddie pondered his words. She knew her father had been content in the village where they'd lived upon their return. Why would her father say such a thing to a stranger unless it were true?

Mr. Gallagher offered her his handkerchief, a large white square of finest cotton. She took it and wiped her nose and eyes.

Before she knew what he was doing, he leaned toward her, until his face was almost touching hers. "Marry me, Maddie…and don't make me go through the agony you put me through in the last fortnight." As he spoke, his lips skimmed her temple and cheek, his mustache brushing her skin.

"Agony?"

He nodded, his cheek grazing hers. "I've searched high and low for you. I couldn't rest until I saw your face and held you in my arms."

"How did you…find me?"

"I hired a detective."

She drew back from him, unable to believe what she was hearing. Did he care that much about her? She tried again, though her voice sounded wavering to her ears. "I'd hold you back—"

"How could you when you give my work meaning? These last couple of months with you have made me realize how little it all means if I have no one to share it with. You've reminded me there's something greater than my little, self-protected world. You've given me hope." He fell silent and touched his lips to her cheek, raining soft kisses along her jaw, not stopping until he'd reached the corner of her lips.

Before she lost all reason, she asked the hardest question of all "What…about your wife?"

He drew away a fraction and she was sure this was the end of his proposal. But he held her gently by the shoulders. "I loved Octavia very much, but you've shown me it was time to let her go. She's gone and I think I've finally laid her to rest." His blue eyes searched hers. "Can you forgive an old fool for not realizing until you left me how much I love you?"

"You loved your wife."

"And now I love you. You showed me my heart hadn't died with Octavia. Maddie, marry me because I can't live without you—" He stopped in midsentence. "Oh, I can, literally. I can survive, as you well know, just as you can without me. But I'll only be existing the way I've done since Octavia died. I know we have eternity, but I don't want to miss the chance to enjoy your company in the here and now as long as the Lord gives us."

He touched her cheek with his fingertip and stroked it softly. "Marry me, Maddie. Don't let me turn into one of those fussy old bachelors who snaps at his servants and can't remember where he put his reading glasses and when they point them out at his side, he'll never admit it's his failing memory that's at fault." As he saw the humor begin to lighten her eyes, he pressed on, "Don't let that terrible fate befall me. I need you, Maddie. I'm desperately in love with you and can't imagine not seeing your beautiful face beside mine each morning."

Her cheeks heated, no doubt turning a bright shade of pink. He continued his caresses with his fingertips.

"Why didn't you tell me any of this the first time you proposed to me?"

"Perhaps I didn't want to admit it, even to myself."

She appeared to consider his words. Seconds passed, in

which she seemed to be weighing his words, determining their authenticity, and Reid was reminded of himself when he studied an artifact. Was it genuine or a cleverly masked fake? And now his own words were being weighed in the balance. He could feel the thud of his heart, pounding loudly in fear.

She glanced at his left hand still resting on her shoulder. His ring finger was bare, the paler skin where his wedding band had sat so many years making its absence all the more evident.

She stared back at Reid. He nodded, telling her with his eyes that he had finally relinquished this most tangible sign of his first marriage.

Seconds passed. She moistened her lips. "Perhaps I should rethink my refusal. I wouldn't want to subject you to such a miserable fate."

He hardly understood the first part of her words, but by the end, he discerned the humor warming her tawny eyes.

He pulled her to him and her hand came up to his chest. "What are you doing?"

"Exacting my revenge." He lowered his face down to hers.

"For what?"

"For putting me through an agonizing fortnight."

"Oh." His lips touched hers and he was relieved she made no more move to stop him.

He scowled at her rosy face. "Is that all you have to say?"

"Was it so very bad?" She touched his cheek.

"It was in direct proportion to the pleasure I shall exact from you now," he murmured between light kisses to her mouth.

"I see. Will it be so very bad for me?"

"Let's just say Aunt Millicent would find it most inappropriate—" he touched her lips again "—indeed."

"It sounds dreadful," she breathed against him as her arms

came up to wrap themselves around his neck. Then she was unable to speak anymore.

He kissed her long and deeply, his senses reveling in the taste and touch and scent of her.

After a few minutes, she broke away from him. "I'm sorry that I caused you any pain. I thought loving you meant I had to give you up."

He lifted her chin with his fingertip. "Never run from me again. You almost killed me with worry."

"I'm so sorry."

"You should have come to me."

She smiled. "I will the next time."

"There'd better not be a next time," he growled.

She laughed softly.

He drew a deep breath, separating himself from her only far enough to say what he meant to say. "Now that you are sufficiently penitent, permit me to rephrase the question I put to you so inelegantly after that dreadful reading of my aunt's will."

Her eyes clouded at this reminder and she would have looked away if he'd permitted it, but he cradled her face between his hands. He cleared his throat. "Maddie, will you marry me? I love you with all my heart and soul and breath."

The warmth that began in her beautiful eyes spread to her mouth as she smiled. "I will indeed, for I think I have loved you since the first day I met you at Lady Haversham's."

"I'm sorry it took me so much longer."

"Oh, Reid, you'll never know how grateful I was that day you offered me your protection." She hugged him fast. "You are the most wonderful man!"

He laughed in response. "Just keep thinking that for the rest of your life."

"That won't be difficult."

"I like hearing my name on your lips, by the way."

"Reid," she repeated softly, her color heightened. "How I love you and thank God for bringing you into my life."

"As do I." His smile met hers as he leaned in until she was a blur and he closed his eyes and kissed her again.

Epilogue

Cairo, Egypt 1900

Reid felt the deep sense of satisfaction that coming home always gave him. He led the donkey by the reins as he approached the large whitewashed palazzo he called home. The words on the brass plate by the door, The Good Shepherd Orphanage, announced the dual function of the building.

The Cairo sun was low in the sky, washing the front of the building in its golden light. The air resounded with the muezzin's call to prayer. A servant boy exited the building. Spotting Reid, his face broke out in a smile.

"Sir Gallagher!" Quickly he came and took the reins from Reid and led the donkey toward the stable in the back. Reid entered through the heavy front doors. He came to a tiled courtyard filled with orange trees. A fountain tinkled in the middle. Children's voices could be heard from there and above in the galleries.

He smiled as he saw Maddie among the group of children.

She was blindfolded, her arms stretched outward. The children screamed in laughter, jumping around her, just out of reach.

Over the years, she'd gained a lot of confidence around children. When he'd first brought Maddie to the Middle East, she'd proved a willing and able partner, not only donning men's trousers once again when she'd worked alongside him on archaeological digs in the field, but also the roomier, more comfortable Arab and Turkish garb.

Cairo under the British was a city of many races and religions. He and Maddie had purchased a large house in the Coptic quarter of the city. With the birth of their first child, she had blossomed into the mother she was meant to be. Reid had remained in Cairo then, helping to establish a museum to house the antiquities. Soon after, he and Maddie had received their first foundling, a homeless boy. Over the years, other children were left with them.

Now, ten years since they'd married, he and Maddie had three children of their own, and twenty additional children who called this place home.

"Papa Reid!" a child's voice cried out, spying him. He motioned the boy with a finger to his lips to be silent. The boy understood at once. With a conspiratorial smile, he accompanied Reid as he approached Maddie.

The crowd of children fell silent at his signal, their faces alight with anticipation.

Reid positioned himself close enough to Maddie to let her catch him. Her hands landed on his front, and she stopped immediately. "Reid?"

The next moment she whipped off her scarf and broke into a joyous smile. Before he could do more than return her smile, he was bombarded by several children's bodies flinging themselves around his legs and waist. "Papa Reid! Papa

Reid!" He looked over the children's heads at the elegant woman in front of him.

Maddie had changed little in their ten years together. Still as slim as when he'd met her, her tawny hair was hardly touched by gray, but best of all, she had the warmest smile in the world.

Slowly, the children parted as he took a step toward her. Her arms wrapped around his neck as he took her in a bear hug.

She looked up at him, giving him the smile he'd dreamed of in the desert. "Welcome home, dearest."

"Hello, Maddie. I've missed you."

His own firstborn son came running up. "Papa!"

"Alex!" He gave the blond-haired eight-year-old a tight hug. Then he turned to his five-year-old daughter, Pippa, who was pulling at his arm. Last of all, their Egyptian nurse brought their youngest, two-year-old Troy, for him to hold. He raised him high in the air amidst his giggles.

"Papa." The toddler's chubby hands came up to play with Reid's hair.

Reid put the child on his shoulders as he gave his attention back to his wife.

Together, the group walked toward the house, Reid and Maddie arm in arm. His darling Pippa, her hair as tawny as her mother's, her eyes as blue as his, clung to his free hand and chattered all the way. His oldest son walked alongside his mother. Reid gave him a special wink, promising they'd have that "man-to-man" time alone later.

Reid squeezed Maddie's shoulder. She met his look. These days, as director of the orphanage, she ran a staff of people and never turned a child away. Best of all, her life reflected the gospel she preached—feeding the hungry, clothing the naked, visiting the prisoner.

He was proud of his wife and never ceased thanking God for giving him this opportunity to love again. Maddie had taught him over the years to open his heart and not to be afraid to give of himself. With each child they welcomed, they risked their hearts. With the Lord's love sustaining them, they never refused the call to love.

* * * * *

Dear Reader,

My family and I had decided to move back to the Netherlands after an absence of eight years. It was with much trepidation that we brought our preadolescent and adolescent children here—it's a tricky time of life at the best of times, but to ask them to face new friends and a new school situation in a different culture and language???

Three weeks after arriving, we found a house to rent. It was after our first night here, sleeping on a mattress on the floor, that I woke up with a story idea. I grabbed pen and notebook and jotted down the beginning of a scene. Over the next few days, my imagination took hold and the general outline for *Hearts in the Highlands* unfolded.

I took it as God's blessing on our move overseas.

I hope you enjoy this old-fashioned love story as much as I enjoyed writing it.

Be blessed in the reading,

QUESTIONS FOR DISCUSSION

1. What attracts Maddie to Reid initially? What are some of the things they have in common?

2. What has helped Maddie accept her lot in life—the narrow, confined life of a paid companion to a hypochondriacal, rich old lady?

3. When Reid enters Maddie's life, how does the vivid picture of life on the archaeological field in Egypt awaken old dreams in Maddie?

4. How is Maddie's life's work in some sense more rewarding—or more permanent—than Reid's?

5. Since his wife died, Reid has kept himself from the love and companionship of another woman by isolating himself in the desert among the company of men. Despite his resolve not to notice Maddie as a woman, what are some of the things about her that begin to reawaken him?

6. The Highlands of Scotland play a pivotal role in the story, breaking down Reid's reserve around Maddie. How does her acceptance of the outdoors, and the male activities he indulges in, further draw Reid?

7. When she has her accident, how does Maddie's behavior during her ordeal further attract Reid?

8. How does her accident serve to push him away?

9. After the fishing episode, Reid deliberately goes about planning how to get closer to Maddie. Sometimes when one is dead set against doing something, another part of them deliberately sets out to do it. How does an intelligent, rational person succeed in so fooling himself in his motives?

10. When they return to London, Reid chooses to avoid confronting his growing feelings for Maddie by running away for the weekend. What is the result of this when he sees her again?

11. Both Maddie and Reid face a new decade at his/her birthday. How do they each feel about turning older? Have you ever had trouble dealing with a milestone birthday? How did you deal with it?

12. How do the letters Maddie receives from her missionary brothers help her continue with her own endeavors?

13. Why is Maddie's presence beside Lady Haversham at the end so important?

14. How does the story illustrate the theme that sometimes the greatest work for the Kingdom of God is the least recognized?

Don't miss
THE BOUNTY HUNTER'S BRIDE
by Victoria Bylin

You'll be moved by this powerful romance
about a rugged bounty hunter and the courageous
mail-order bride who heals his aching heart.

Available May 2008 from
Love Inspired Historical.

Colorado, June 1882

"You know the story of Cain and Abel?"

"I do."

"Patrick was Abel. I'm Cain."

Daniela Baxter gaped at the man in the doorway. Unshaven and bleary-eyed, he looked enough like Patrick to be his brother. She and Patrick were engaged to be married. She'd expected her fiancé to greet her with a smile. Instead, she'd been assaulted by this stranger's sneering question about Cain and Abel.

Dani knew better than to judge by appearances, but the stranger had declared himself to be Cain, the brother who'd surrendered to sin. Even so, God hadn't left Cain. Cain had abandoned God.

"Patrick's dead."

Dani blinked. "I must be at the wrong house."

The man studied her. "Who are you?"

"Daniela Baxter. I'm his fiancée."

His gaze stayed hard, but his voice softened like hot caramel. "I'm sorry, miss. Patrick died five days ago."

Gasping, Dani clutched her reticule. It held her only picture of the man she loved. She yearned to be a mother, both to his girls and the babies to come.

"I'm Beau Morgan. Patrick's brother."

Patrick had mentioned his brother just once. *He's not a man I'd trust with my girls. I made a will before Beau went crazy. As soon as we're married, I'll change it. I want you to adopt the girls.*

Beau stood with his arms crossed and his feet spread wide. If he'd been wearing boots, Dani might have been intimidated. Instead, she saw a hole in his sock. She suspected his life was in the same sorry shape and prayed he'd leave Patrick's daughters in her care.

"Patrick asked me to adopt the girls," she said.

Mr. Morgan raised one brow. "And would he want you to have the farm, too?"

"I suppose." She needed a way to support the girls.

"Miss Baxter, you're either naive or a con artist."

Dani gaped. "How dare you!"

"No, how dare *you*. You waltz in here and announce you want my nieces and the farm. I have an obligation to my nieces and I intend to meet it. A train leaves in the morning. I want you on it."

"Absolutely not. I promised Patrick—"

"I know what you promised." His voice turned gentle. "I also know what it's like to be grief stricken. It leaves you numb, but only for a while. Once the shock passes, you wake up screaming. It'll eat you alive if you let it."

Peering into his eyes, she saw a kinship borne of suffering. Who had Beau Morgan mourned?

If he felt the connection, it didn't show. "But I'm prepared to offer a compromise. I'll move to the barn while we sort things out. You get room and board in exchange for keeping house."

She wanted to say yes, but she had to protect her reputation as well as the children. "I'd prefer the hotel if the girls can stay with me."

"I can't allow it. You're too naive."

Dani bristled. "I've just traveled a thousand miles—"

"And I've traveled ten thousand." He raised his chin. "Have you ever seen a pack of wolves?"

She'd heard howling near her father's farm, but the wolves had stayed out of sight. "No."

"I have," he said. "The kind with two legs."

"Castle Rock seems safe to me."

His eyes glittered. "It was before I got here."

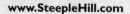
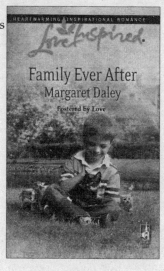

REQUEST YOUR FREE BOOKS!

2 FREE INSPIRATIONAL NOVELS
PLUS 2
FREE
MYSTERY GIFTS

Love Inspired
HISTORICAL
INSPIRATIONAL HISTORICAL ROMANCE

YES! Please send me 2 FREE Love Inspired® Historical novels and my 2 FREE mystery gifts (gifts are worth about $10). After receiving them, if I don't wish to receive any more books, I can return the shipping statement marked "cancel". If I don't cancel, I will receive 4 brand-new novels every other month and be billed just $4.24 per book in the U.S. or $4.74 per book in Canada, plus 25¢ shipping and handling per book and applicable taxes, if any*. That's a savings of over 20% off the cover price! I understand that accepting the 2 free books and gifts places me under no obligation to buy anything. I can always return a shipment and cancel at any time. Even if I never buy another book, the two free books and gifts are mine to keep forever. 102 IDN ERYA 302 IDN ERYM

Name	(PLEASE PRINT)

Address	Apt. #

City	State/Prov.	Zip/Postal Code

Signature (if under 18, a parent or guardian must sign)

Mail to Steeple Hill Reader Service:
IN U.S.A.: P.O. Box 1867, Buffalo, NY 14240-1867
IN CANADA: P.O. Box 609, Fort Erie, Ontario L2A 5X3

Not valid to current subscribers of Love Inspired Historical books.

Want to try two free books from another series?
Call 1-800-873-8635 or visit www.morefreebooks.com

* Terms and prices subject to change without notice. N.Y. residents add applicable sales tax. Canadian residents will be charged applicable provincial taxes and GST. This offer is limited to one order per household. All orders subject to approval. Credit or debit balances in a customer's account(s) may be offset by any other outstanding balance owed by or to the customer. Please allow 4 to 6 weeks for delivery. Offer available while quantities last.

Your Privacy: Steeple Hill Books is committed to protecting your privacy. Our Privacy Policy is available online at www.SteepleHill.com or upon request from the Reader Service. From time to time we make our lists of customers available to reputable third parties who may have a product or service of interest to you. If you would prefer we not share your name and address, please check here. ☐

LIH08

Love Inspired
HISTORICAL

TITLES AVAILABLE NEXT MONTH

Don't miss these two stories in May

THE ROAD TO LOVE by Linda Ford
During the depths of the Depression, widow Kate Bradshaw
was struggling to raise her children and hold on to her farm.
Then Hatcher Jones came by. His kindness warmed her
heart, and she longed to make the troubled drifter see that
his wandering had brought him home at last.

THE BOUNTY HUNTER'S BRIDE by Victoria Bylin
Mail-order bride Dani Baxter was left to raise three little
girls when her intended suddenly died. She was determined
to keep his small family together. But her deceased fiancé's
brother Beau Morgan wasn't about to let her go it alone.
Together they could make this family whole again.